BRUSSELS NOIR

EDITED BY MICHEL DUFRANNE

Translated by Katie Shireen Assef

Published by Akashic Books
©2016 Akashic Books

Series concept by Tim McLoughlin and Johnny Temple
Brussels map by Sohrab Habibion

ISBN: 978-1-61775-398-5
Library of Congress Control Number: 2015954024

First printing

Akashic Books
Twitter: @AkashicBooks
Facebook: AkashicBooks
E-mail: info@akashicbooks.com
Website: www.akashicbooks.com

ALSO IN THE AKASHIC NOIR SERIES

ORANGE COUNTY NOIR, edited by GARY PHILLIPS
PARIS NOIR (FRANCE), edited by AURÉLIEN MASSON
PHILADELPHIA NOIR, edited by CARLIN ROMANO
PHOENIX NOIR, edited by PATRICK MILLIKIN
PITTSBURGH NOIR, edited by KATHLEEN GEORGE
PORTLAND NOIR, edited by KEVIN SAMPSELL
PRISON NOIR, edited by JOYCE CAROL OATES
PROVIDENCE NOIR, edited by ANN HOOD
QUEENS NOIR, edited by ROBERT KNIGHTLY
RICHMOND NOIR, edited by ANDREW BLOSSOM, BRIAN CASTLEBERRY & TOM DE HAVEN
RIO NOIR (BRAZIL), edited by TONY BELLOTTO
ROME NOIR (ITALY), edited by CHIARA STANGALINO & MAXIM JAKUBOWSKI
SAN DIEGO NOIR, edited by MARYELIZABETH HART
SAN FRANCISCO NOIR, edited by PETER MARAVELIS
SAN FRANCISCO NOIR 2: THE CLASSICS, edited by PETER MARAVELIS
SEATTLE NOIR, edited by CURT COLBERT
SINGAPORE NOIR, edited by CHERYL LU-LIEN TAN
STATEN ISLAND NOIR, edited by PATRICIA SMITH
ST. LOUIS NOIR, edited by SCOTT PHILLIPS
STOCKHOLM NOIR (SWEDEN), edited by NATHAN LARSON & CARL-MICHAEL EDENBORG
ST. PETERSBURG NOIR (RUSSIA), edited by NATALIA SMIRNOVA & JULIA GOUMEN
TEHRAN NOIR (IRAN), edited by SALAR ABDOH
TEL AVIV NOIR (ISRAEL), edited by ETGAR KERET & ASSAF GAVRON
TORONTO NOIR (CANADA), edited by JANINE ARMIN & NATHANIEL G. MOORE
TRINIDAD NOIR (TRINIDAD & TOBAGO), edited by LISA ALLEN-AGOSTINI & JEANNE MASON
TWIN CITIES NOIR, edited by JULIE SCHAPER & STEVEN HORWITZ
USA NOIR, edited by JOHNNY TEMPLE
VENICE NOIR (ITALY), edited by MAXIM JAKUBOWSKI
WALL STREET NOIR, edited by PETER SPIEGELMAN
ZAGREB NOIR (CROATIA), edited by IVAN SRŠEN

FORTHCOMING

ACCRA NOIR (GHANA), edited by MERI NANA-AMA DANQUAH
ADDIS ABABA NOIR (ETHIOPIA), edited by MAAZA MENGISTE
ATLANTA NOIR, edited by TAYARI JONES
BAGHDAD NOIR (IRAQ), edited by SAMUEL SHIMON
BOGOTÁ NOIR (COLOMBIA), edited by ANDREA MONTEJO
BUENOS AIRES NOIR (ARGENTINA), edited by ERNESTO MALLO
JERUSALEM NOIR, edited by DROR MISHANI
LAGOS NOIR (NIGERIA), edited by CHRIS ABANI
MARRAKECH NOIR (MOROCCO), edited by YASSIN ADNAN
MONTANA NOIR, edited by JAMES GRADY & KEIR GRAFF
MONTREAL NOIR (CANADA), edited by JOHN McFETRIDGE & JACQUES FILIPPI
NEW HAVEN NOIR, edited by AMY BLOOM
OAKLAND NOIR, edited by JERRY THOMPSON & EDDIE MULLER
PRAGUE NOIR (CZECH REPUBLIC), edited by PAVEL MANDYS
SAN JUAN NOIR (PUERTO RICO), edited by MAYRA SANTOS-FEBRES
SÃO PAULO NOIR (BRAZIL), edited by TONY BELLOTTO
TRINIDAD NOIR: THE CLASSICS (TRINIDAD & TOBAGO), edited by EARL LOVELACE & ROBERT ANTONI

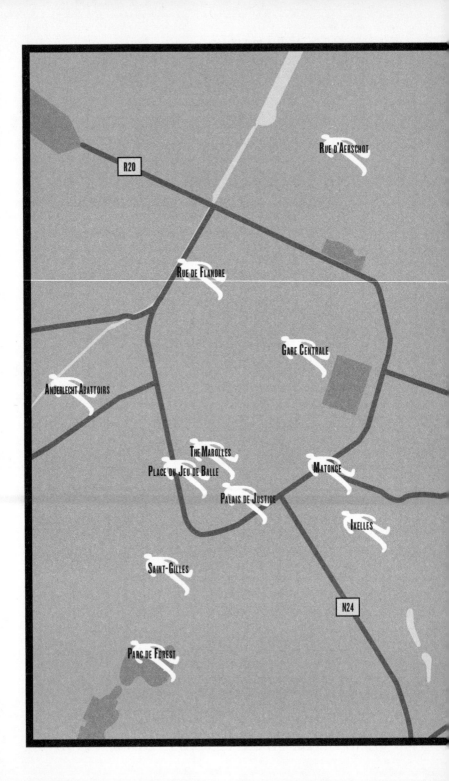

RUE D'AERSCHOT

R20

RUE DE FLANDRE

GARE CENTRALE

ANDERLECHT ABATTOIRS

THE MAROLLES

PLACE DU JEU DE BALLE

MATONGE

PALAIS DE JUSTICE

IXELLES

SAINT-GILLES

N24

PARC DE FOREST

BRUSSELS

R21

BEGRAAFPLAATS
VAN BRUSSEL

JOSAPHATPARK

REYERS

WOLUWE-SAINT-LAMBERT

PARC DU CINQUANTENAIRE

N3

N4

PARC DE WOLUWE

VRIJE UNIVERSITEIT
BRUSSEL

TABLE OF CONTENTS

PART III: ROOM TO MANEUVER

INTRODUCTION
BENEATH A LOW, GRAY SKY

Genesis 11:1–9 tells us that God, angered to see the Tower of Babel rising to the heavens, decided to confound the universal language and scatter it over the surface of the earth; the text fails to mention that a piece of this tower must have landed in the center of the marshland north of Gaul, where, according to Julius Caesar, the people are the bravest (and the most barbarous) in the land, and given birth to . . . Brussels!

Brussels the cosmopolitan, multilingual capital. Brussels, whose geography and demographics are reminiscent of a small rural town. Brussels, a city that tourists can walk across in a few hours, but that groans under the weight of its complexity and multiple identities. Brussels of a thousand faces, a city in the heart of Europe where communities live side by side in (almost constant) peace and harmony, without ever seeking to get to know one another. Brussels, at the center of all Belgian disputes . . . Brussels, the specter of Europe constantly raised by Europhobes . . . Brussels . . .

It's impossible to write about my city without first drawing a portrait of the bureaucracy at the origin of all its misfortune— and all of its richness. Brussels (or *Brussel* in Dutch . . . here we go!) is a small village of just over a million inhabitants, situated an hour and twenty-five minutes from Paris and two hours from London, Amsterdam, or Cologne. The capital of the federal state known as the Kingdom of Belgium, it is enclaved within the region—relatively autonomous, Flemish-speaking—of Flanders, of which it is also the capital (despite the fact that few of its inhabitants actually speak Flemish). But, to keep anyone from kicking up a fuss, it's also the capital of the French-speaking community of Belgium, represented by an entity called the Fédération Wallonie-Bruxelles. And if this isn't already hard enough to keep straight, Brussels also insists on being a region in itself, with its own elected government, which geographically covers the city of Brussels: a city made up of nineteen municipalities (*arrondissements*, for those who speak Parisian), the largest of which is named . . . Brussels. Are you lost yet? This is the moment to recall that, down to its very institutions, Belgium is a land of surrealism, of pragmatism, and of a certain irony—for want of knowing any better—and that all of this is part of the fabric of everyday life. I will spare you the symbolic titles of my city (the "capital" of Europe, of NATO, etc.)—and its history, which is also the history of the Spanish, Austrian, French, Dutch, in that order and disorder.

Fortunately, Brussels, my city, is more than the sum of its administrative roles; it is also known the world over for *bruxellisation*, its tendency to destroy the urban fabric in the name of modernity, to the detriment of its residents; for its *façadism*, the practice of conserving only the facade of buildings and destroying the rest; for its urban tunnels and metro stations that overflow with commuters at rush hour, but are deserted the rest of the time . . . for its waffles, its chocolate, and its beer (phew)!

A less than flattering portrait of my city? Perhaps . . . but have I not already mentioned Belgian pragmatism and irony? I should probably have also warned you about the excessive modesty of *ces gens-là** of the flat country.

---

* *The title of a song by the late Belgian singer Jacques Brel.*

But is Brussels a noir city? The first response that comes to mind is the most *bruxellois*: "Well, no, maybe!" (a turn of phrase that translates, in the rest of the Francophone world, as, *Yes, of course!*); but reflection gives way to anxiety. From the Grand Place, preserved by the illustrious Freemasons of Belgium, to the legacy of Expo '58; from the Brabant murders to the Heysel Stadium disaster, not to mention its judiciary history, Brussels is overflowing with stories and mysteries to feed any writer's imagination. But does the city really spark the creativity of its own children? To ask the question is to plow full force into the wall of the Belgian inferiority complex, for if no one is a prophet in his or her own country, the Belgian is even less so. Belgian writers of every era have generally sought recognition in Paris, which has often served them well, considering the careers of Stanislas-André Steeman, Roger d'Arjac, Edmond Romazières, René Charles Oppitz, Paul Kinnet, and Jean Ray, to cite just a few authors who preceded the benchmark, the now inimitable (as Hergé is to the comic book genre) Georges Simenon. Faithful to this tradition, Belgian "genre" writers have blended, without fanfare, into the editorial landscape of their neighbors while preserving the sensibility—acquired beneath their low, gray sky so dear to Brel—unmistakable to any discerning reader.

Whether foreigners in Brussels, or *bruxellois* expatriates, Belgians from either region or community of Belgium; whether Francophone, Dutch, or Hispanic, the thirteen (we're not superstitious in my city) contemporary authors found in this anthology are *bruxellois* at heart and have found the words— often sharp, always affectionate—to describe their love for the city that gives rhythm to their days. Whether practitioners of detective fiction, thrillers, fantasy; whether comic book authors or, even worse, journalists, they will take you for a ride that is sure to be dark, funny, bloody, harrowing, whimsical . . . in short, Belgian!

For our grand tour, please be seated, ladies and gentlemen readers, in Tram 33 . . . and no, there's no rain in the forecast today, just a leaden sky; for that matter, considering the time-tables of the STIB, it's probably better to go on foot than to take public transport. We'll explore the city center, that pentagonal surface defined by urban highways and a canal, home to the real old Brussels, the historic core. We'll take a dainty stroll through an edifice that achieves the feat of being more vast and monolithic in style than St. Peter's Basilica: the Palais de Justice. From there, it's easy to glide down to the Marolles; then let your feet carry you from *kabberdouch* to *stamcafé,* as you wander in an ethereal, even surrealist mode through the heart of the city, and finally come full circle. Having whetted our appetites, we'll play leapfrog along the boulevards to make our way to the inner ring road and tiptoe across the razor's edge of the city, where blood, alcohol, and debauchery know how to coexist . . . or not. And if the life of the abattoir hasn't sated you, you'll have plenty of room to maneuver as you stray from the center and discover the oh-so-serene neighborhoods of the greater ring, home to our venerable European institutions above all suspicion.

One last piece of advice before setting you loose in the streets of my city—always keep in mind this little tune of local folklore, which will remind you that you're indeed in Brussels and nowhere else:

> J'suis bruxellois, voilà pourquoi / Bruxellois am I, and here is why
> En vill' je suis chez moi / I'm at home 'neath this sky
> J'aim' de flâner sur le boul'vard / And on my city's boulevards
> Au milieu des richards . . . / Where all the rich folk are

Mais bien plus qu'eux je suis heureux / But much more gay am
I than they
Car je m'content' de peu / At the end of the day
J'arrang' ma vie selon mes sous, / I'm content with what I've got,
Je ne suis pas jaloux . . . / A jealous fellow I'm not . . .

—Jan de Baets, "L'Heureux Bruxellois"

Happy reading!

Michel Dufranne
Brussels, Belgium
March 2016

PART I

THE RAZOR'S EDGE

THE PARAKEET

by Barbara Abel

Saint-Gilles

I f I remember well, it was my husband who had the idea. Jean isn't usually bursting with initiatives, at least as far as family projects are concerned, but that morning, when he spoke to us about renting out the room upstairs, I was immediately intrigued by the proposal. In the twenty years since we bought the house—we've only just finished paying it off—this room has gone by many names: rec room, guest room, workshop, storeroom, and so on, while never quite living up to any of them. Virgile, our son, for whatever reason, never staked claim on the space, which is not, however, without charm. He sleeps on the first floor; even after he was old enough to climb the steep staircase leading to the attic, he preferred to keep his room rather than move into one that would have attracted any other child his age.

Virgile is eighteen now. He is finishing high school at the prestigious Robert Catteau School.

My name is Emma Parmentier and I have no paid profession, even if my schedule is just as busy as that of any woman who sacrifices her life to a career. We live on the upper end of the Saint-Gilles municipality: a pleasant neighborhood of single-family homes side by side with apartment houses, no more than three or four units per building; close-knit, convivial dwellings with kindly neighbors.

We are happy. At least, we were. A simple family. A fairy tale.

I don't understand how all of this could have happened. I have always placed our family at the forefront of my concerns, devoting to my son and husband as much time as energy, attention as good intentions, not to mention my unfailing love for them, a love that never calls into question this commitment that I, as a wife and mother, consider natural. As I've said, my days are very full: when I'm not busy keeping the house in order, which already takes up three-quarters of my time, I manage the bookkeeping for Dr. Dutoit, a general practitioner whose office is situated near the town hall, in exchange for a symbolic wage and free consultations. This is what I like most about the place where we live: we value social relations, and solidarity is not an empty word. Our neighborhood has, for that matter, improved a great deal since we first moved in.

Despite the apparent calm of the surroundings, organized gangs were once rampant in the area, wrecking cars when they didn't steal them, vandalizing the facades of houses, snatching purses from women walking home alone at night. The gangs would meet at place Louis Morichar, a vast space converted into a public square, bordered by splendid houses in eclectic and art nouveau styles. Back then, old public urinals still stood in the middle of the square, a sordid sight, covered in obscene graffiti, where delinquents gathered to take drugs and share the fruits of their larceny. The place became, several years ago, the scene of a disgraceful crime: during an altercation between two young people, one brutally stabbed the other and left him there without the slightest chance of survival. This happened on a Sunday afternoon. In broad daylight! I have never understood the root cause of such violence. The attacker and his family lived a few blocks away from us. I remember it perfectly because we had just settled to the neighborhood, and the incident had upset me to the point where I considered moving again.

The affair caused a great commotion in the neighborhood. A committee was put in place, and we demanded a firm stance on the part of the local authorities. It was inconceivable to us that we should continue to live near these people. A neighborhood is shaped every day by the will of its residents. They are the ones who lend it a rhythm, a dynamic, a character, an atmosphere. It is they who imbue it with kindness or brutality, with joy or tragedy. With peacefulness or intimidation. We are responsible for the place where we live. It is our daily landscape. And if we leave our mark on it, it influences us in turn.

After the tragedy of place Morichar, it became vital for us—I mean, for all the residents of our neighborhood—that the family of the young murderer leave the area. We put pressure on them to do so, first by mail and then by more explicit means. Some of our neighbors even went so far as to empty a few garbage bins in front of their door. I am not saying that the method was decent, but it was, at least, efficient.

Fortunately, things have changed since then: place Morichar has been completely renovated, and now children can play there without fear of being attacked.

There was a time when we had planned to have more children, but life decided otherwise. It must be said that my recovery from Virgile's birth was rather difficult, and a new ordeal of that sort was not advisable for me. And then, as I told my husband, we were so content, just the three of us, that regrets never had the chance to encroach on our daily life. Jean shared my opinion, beyond the shadow of a doubt.

And so, about eight months ago, my husband proposed to convert the upstairs room into a student's loft, so that we could house a young foreigner eager to spend a few months in Belgium. By "foreigner," I understood he meant an English or American boy. We liked the idea of providing Virgile with an English-speaking companion. And of putting this space, whose vacancy had for some time weighed subconsciously on us, to good use. Virgile, for his part, did not seem opposed to the idea.

It was the beginning of the month of June. Time was running out if we wanted to be ready by September. We contacted an organization that took care of this sort of arrangement, and sent in the application to be recognized as a host family. Despite the short time frame, after having filled out all the necessary forms, we quickly received a positive response. I suspect they did not have enough applicants to host the numerous hopefuls. Furthermore, our conditions were not very strict: we asked only for a boy, more or less the same age as our son, whose mother tongue was English.

By mid-July, we had received a letter containing the identity of the young man who would be spending a few months with us. His name was Michael Hampton and he was from Brighton, England. He had just turned nineteen and wanted to take a training course in graphic design at one of our universities, while improving his scant knowledge of French, and fifteen days later the organization confirmed the date and time of Mike's arrival.

We spent the month of August converting the upstairs room. It was a charming space that, once renovated and furnished, resembled exactly the kind of intimate loft every student dreams of living in one day. We repainted the walls white, replaced the carpet, and set up a handsome single bed with posts of light wood, an oak desk that had belonged to my father-in-law, and a wardrobe varnished to a beautiful sheen.

Mike arrived on Thursday, the third of September, at

three forty-five in the afternoon. The three of us were waiting for him at the Brussels-Midi station, a bit nervous, admittedly, since we had no idea what sort of person we would be dealing with. My husband stayed at my side, holding up the cardboard sign on which we had written Michael Hampton's name in thick black marker. Virgile stood in the background, silent and taciturn as usual. The Eurostar swept into the station and quickly unloaded its passengers. Jean raised the sign above our heads so that Mike could easily identify us. The minutes that followed were nerve-racking and exciting all at once.

He looked older than I'd imagined. At first glance, I would have guessed he was at least twenty-five. Virgile, only a few months his junior, seemed so much younger. I can't say that Mike made a poor impression on me; he was probably just as apprehensive as we were. His graceless features contrasted with the intense blue of his eyes, and at first I thought the poor boy was afflicted with crossed eyes. He walked hesitantly toward us, as if giving himself one last chance to turn around and call everything off. But he must have liked the look of us, since he ended up planting himself in front of Jean and holding out his hand with a bewildered smile. The introductions were made politely, perhaps not quite as warmly as I would have liked.

Everything went wonderfully for the first few weeks. Mike seemed pleased with his new room and he quickly adjusted to the family schedule. We eat at precisely seven o'clock every evening; Tuesday and Thursday are cleaning days, and on Wednesday we do laundry. If I take care of the housework in all the common areas, namely the living room, the dining room, the kitchen, and the bathroom, I expect everyone to devote a portion of his time to keeping his own room in order. We do our grocery shopping at the nearest Carrefour on Friday night, for the full week, as a family—I'm very strict on this point. On Saturday, finally, we tend the garden.

On Monday, September 14, Mike began his graphic design classes, and from that point on, he was rarely home before dinnertime. The evenings are calm at our house, and that seemed to suit him. At least at first. At the dinner table, we chatted about everything and nothing—Belgium, England—and I made an effort to correct his grammatical errors as often as possible. I was disappointed, however, that between him and Virgile, an open camaraderie was slow to take hold. The boys remained mutually on their guard, slyly observing each other's reactions, exchanging only vague *good mornings* and *good nights* with a cold courtesy.

Meanwhile, between Mike and my husband, a certain complicity set in as early as the first evening. Jean has a basic understanding of English, which allowed him to chat with an ease that Virgile and I did not have. Each night, as usual, Virgile would go upstairs to his room as soon as the meal was finished, which I deplored. As for me, after clearing the table and drinking a cup of tea with Mike and Jean, I would leave them to talk together—I might even say "between men," so naturally did the rapport seem to have formed.

At first, this curious friendship did not give me pause. Jean seemed happy to have found in Mike an interesting interlocutor, despite their generational difference. I understood that this relationship was precisely the one I had hoped to see develop between Virgile and Mike—and even more, dare I admit, between Virgile and his father—but what would be the point of questioning it? Men are ambiguous and complicated beings, and I long ago gave up trying to understand them. Lying in bed, I could hear them laughing and chatting freely about I don't know what.

Virgile has never been much of an extrovert. It's not in his nature. He doesn't often go out with children his age and, aside from a few classmates he only rarely mentions, I have never known him to have real friends. He has always been a withdrawn boy. From childhood, he showed little interest in the company of his fellow students, and whenever a few of them did come to play at our house, I constantly had to intervene to keep them from tormenting my son. Over the years, he has grown increasingly solitary. It must be said that from very early on, he showed an unusual maturity for his age. The other children seemed so babyish in comparison. I did what I could to protect him from the surrounding idiocy, and helped him see the richness of his difference in a positive light. I was constantly trying to warn him against the perversity—jealousy, mainly—of many of his schoolmates. It's a sad fact that the flaws of human nature manifest themselves early in life, even in young children. I was quick to teach Virgile that sometimes it's better to be alone than in bad company.

I had thought I could count on Jean's support in helping our son become friendly with Mike, or at least in giving the two of them a chance to get to know one another. But instead, my husband monopolized every conversation at the dinner table, and once Virgile withdrew to his room, Jean never asked him to join them to finish out the evening. Mike's arrival had given me hope that Virgile, through contact with him, might open up a bit more to the outside world.

It's important to know that Saint-Gilles is divided in two. La Barrière serves as a symbolic border, a roundabout with constant traffic from which arterial roads extend like tentacles: avenue du Parc on one side, rue de l'Hôtel des Monnaies on the other. The upper end of the municipality offers calm, well-tended streets arranged in a regular grid pattern, where functionaries, students, and retirees walk peacefully alongside one another. As for the lower end, it's another story entirely. The course of those streets, like the ambiance surrounding them, is brutally winding, incoherent, nearly treacherous. A jumble of architectural styles, few if any single-family homes, only buildings overflowing with a chaotic population. And the prize at the end of this labyrinth of urban shadows: the Parvis. I have never understood the enthusiasm this place inspires in my fellow citizens. I can't deny a certain charm; I sometimes go there on Thursday to stock up on natural products, both at the outdoor market held on that particular day, and at Manuka, the organic grocery I wish was located closer to my home. It is, in fact, the only business in the neighborhood that finds favor with me, as well as with my palate. As for the rest, the cafés, bistros, and bars are havens for Saint-Gilles's most erratic residents. Artists, the unemployed, and immigrants all brush shoulders in the noise and confusion. The church that stands there long ago lost its aura; its role has been diminished to that of a cheap ornament. Worst of all is the Clos Sainte-Thérèse, a daytime homeless shelter that attracts individuals as filthy as they are malicious. An infected wound. An abscess. It's impossible to walk by without being harassed by the scum of society, their arms extended to ask for a coin, yet showing no signs of deformity; arms they might instead use, it seems to me, to earn an honest living. An unbearable sight, this degeneration, one I always took care to protect Virgile from when he was young, even if it meant making a detour by way of the rue du Fort to avoid the Parvis. Until now, I have always been able to keep misery at a distance from our household.

Michael Hampton undermined all my efforts. He destroyed the most powerful armor that exists: ignorance.

* * *

Once the early days of this growing complicity had passed, I began to feel uncomfortable supporting such a close relationship between a man long past fifty and the boy that was Mike. What was this about, anyway? And how could Jean act so childishly in front of our son? It seemed to me the roles had been reversed. I tried to share my opinions with my husband, but he hardly listened to me, claiming he had never prevented Virgile from keeping company with them once dinner was over.

Virgile and his father's relationship is complicated. They love each other, of course, but Jean has difficulty expressing his emotions in general, and showing his son the tenderness he feels for him in particular. As for Virgile, he waits for recognition from his father with a vigilance that sometimes borders on obsession. They are alike, in the end: both equally reserved, too often allowing their pride to stand in the way of their relationship.

One night, I woke up after just an hour or two of sleep. I could no longer hear any sounds coming from the ground floor, though Jean's place beside me in bed was empty. So were the living and dining rooms. I am not the sort of woman to wait up all night for her husband to come home from the bistro. In fact, on that night, the idea that Jean had gone out for a drink with Mike did not even occur to me. I went into Virgile's room; he was sleeping peacefully. I shook him awake. I wanted to talk with him, to ask him what he thought of Mike. Why didn't they speak more to one another? Was he disturbed by this presence at the heart of our family? Did he feel we'd rejected him by taking an interest in this young Englishman?

Virgile looked at me as if seeing me for the first time, then rolled over in his bed, mumbling, "Leave me alone, Mom."

When Mike and Jean finally came home—at eleven

o'clock—they reeked of beer. I tried to tell my husband that this chumming around with Mike was unacceptable. What would people think of him? Going out at night to God knows what infamous dive, with a young man his son's age! Not to mention that he was cruelly interfering in a possible friendship between Virgile and this boy. Had we not brought Mike here to give our son the companion he had so sorely missed as a child?

This was our first fight regarding Mike. Jean insisted that it was normal for a man to relax after a long day at work, and that the Brasserie de l'Union was by no means an infamous dive. He did not see, he said, why I was making this into a federal affair.

The Brasserie de l'Union! One of the Parvis bistros, the first you see coming from our house when heading along rue de l'Hôtel des Monnaies. The "place aux pigeons," as many call it, in reference to the legions of birds that children and dogs chase for amusement there. So my husband had gone to compromise himself in this seedy, rundown bar, with its walls yellowed by cigarette smoke—to give you a sense of the decrepitude of the place—with its more than questionable decorative motifs, its deplorable service, its indigent clientele.

"Stop looking so disgusted, Emma! You'd think I just vomited on you."

I pointed out to Jean that the terms *relax* and *Brasserie de l'Union* were mutually exclusive, and that as for his last remark, it did, in effect, rather accurately sum up what I was physically feeling.

Jean looked at me with eyes full of pity. "My poor Emma . . ." Then he went off on an absurd liberal rant, arguing that the Parvis and the surrounding establishments had nothing licentious about them; that, to the contrary, life abounded there in all of its richness and passion, that social diversity was good for our municipality, and that my narrow, repressed petite-bourgeoise attitude was very slowly beginning to break his balls.

"Did Mike put these ideas in your head?" I asked, stunned by his words.

"Leave Mike out of this."

"You're drunk, my dear. You don't have any idea what you're saying."

"Actually, Emma, I've never been so clear-headed."

It was on this night that I became fully aware of the threat Mike represented to the unity of our household. Jean was not in his right mind, that much was obvious.

This discussion marked the beginning of a rupture. I no longer recognized my husband; he seemed truly bewitched, enchanted by the siren song of a decadent youth. The nocturnal jaunts continued, without any regard for our household rules, or even the most basic level of respect. I deplored Jean's attitude, and told him so without mincing words; I said that Mike was a harmful influence on our family, that the worm was in the fruit and it was incumbent upon us, as responsible adults and parents in charge of our child's education, to extract it. Neither my objections nor our repeated arguments had any effect on his point of view, and even less on his behavior.

It didn't stop there. On the evening they finally asked Virgile to join them, I thought the earth was trembling beneath my feet. Clearly it was their intent to provoke me. I hoped my son would decline the invitation. To my great dismay, Virgile, at first surprised, soon nodded his head, visibly delighted. I tried to oppose it, to make Jean listen to reason. I begged him not to lead our child into that sordid neighborhood where shiftlessness and vice, crouching in every corner of the street, lurk in wait.

When the door closed behind them, I understood that a war had been declared.

I slept very little that night, my thoughts racing. I feared this sort of outing would become a habit, and the following week, my fears were confirmed. After the third occasion, it was time to take action, and quickly.

And so the next morning, once alone in the house, I got ready to go out. I chose my clothing with care and precision: elegant without being ostentatious, classic without being austere. I left home at eight thirty. I turned onto rue de la Victoire, hoping the street's name would prove prophetic to me. I followed it to the crossroads at rue de l'Hôtel des Monnaies, passing, on the way, a group of schoolchildren led by their teachers toward the Victor Boin swimming pool or some other cultural destination. Then I cut across the square, heading to the Parvis. As usual, hordes of pigeons cooed while pecking at the bread that neighborhood retirees enjoyed tossing their way. I've never understood what elderly people see in these foul birds, these nests of microbes, these flying rats. Among their ranks were a few wild parakeets that pilfered the bread, seizing the crust between their claws at the exact moment when a pigeon made an instinctive, almost mechanical movement to plant its beak there. Then the parakeet would swoop off and land on a tree branch to feed with complete impunity. The dispossessed pigeon would continue its search without even the least show of indignity at this theft.

Behold, the supremacy of skill over instinct! What a stupid thing a pigeon is.

I arrived at the Parvis. Still gorged on its excesses of the night before, it seemed half-asleep even with the market held there—a few fruit and vegetable stalls, a stand selling various accessories for one euro apiece, and a shoe merchant—spread out between the Brasserie de l'Union and the Café du Louvre. Although it was the middle of November and somewhat cold out, a few smokers sipped their coffees on the narrow terraces of the bistros.

As I neared my destination, I slowed my step, overcome by sensations of fear and disgust. In front of the Clos Sainte-Thérèse was a line of homeless or otherwise needy people, already twenty or so of them, waiting for the doors to open so they could receive what they were no longer able to procure for themselves. I studied their expressions, their postures . . . How was I going to do this? At that moment, I became completely disoriented. Though I had spent most of the night formulating my plan in the greatest detail, I suddenly had no idea how to proceed. In the snug warmth of my bed, things had seemed so simple. Now, confronted with the harshness of reality, I nearly abandoned everything.

I gave myself time to stop at the bank, a few meters away, where I withdrew two hundred euros in notes of fifty and put them away in my purse. I then summoned my courage and walked back toward the group of vagrants. I would never have imagined that one day I would be forced to speak to this sort of creature, and my resentment toward Jean intensified.

I could tell the choice was going to be difficult and, after a few interminable moments of doubt, resigned myself to proceeding by elimination. I thought again of the parakeets stealing the pigeons' bread before they could get to it, and the obvious strategy came to me: among this flock of pigeons, I would have to find a parakeet.

After five minutes, I had set my sights on one. He stood a bit apart from the group, his features marked by the hardships of life, a cagey look about him. Well past fifty, he gave off a combination of hostility and resignation which, I hoped, would serve my cause. He wore a light-green anorak that recalled the parakeets' colorful feathers. I took that as a sign. Swallowing my disgust, I approached him, and once I'd offered him a hearty breakfast as well as remunerative work, he followed me without needing to be persuaded, just as I had foreseen.

We sat down at a café, La Maison du Peuple, a supposedly trendy establishment that, in the daytime, attracts neighborhood bourgeois bohemians and pseudo-artists, while in the evening it becomes the favored spot of students, divorced parents on their week off from the children, and forty-somethings in full-swing midlife crises. I waited for someone to take our order before explaining to my parakeet what I required of him, but despite the horde of waiters bustling about behind the bar, no one came over to ask what we wanted. The situation was becoming embarrassing. I hailed one of the waiters, who informed me in an annoyed tone that it was up to me to order at the counter. I did not remark on the absurdity of the procedure; there were more pressing matters to deal with.

Once we'd been served, I took out a photograph of Jean and Virgile from my purse and placed it on the table, right in front of my parakeet.

"These two men come regularly to the Brasserie de l'Union, just a few meters from here. You know the Brasserie de l'Union?"

The man nodded his head while continuing to wolf down the pastries I had ordered for him. He was as voracious as he was untalkative.

"They come with a third man whose photo I don't have, but he's not the one I'm interested in," I continued. "What

I'd like you to do is to simulate an attack on these two, on the younger one in particular. That's right, *simulate*. I want you to frighten them. Really frighten them. But under no circumstances do I wish for them to be hurt. You understand? I'm asking you to stage the scene, not play it out. This is how I see it: when they leave the Union around eleven o'clock, they'll walk back toward the upper end of Saint Gilles, passing by the place aux Pigeo . . . rue de l'Hôtel des Monnaies. That's where you come in. Grab at them, provoke them, tell them to give you their money, whatever you want. If they refuse to comply, as I suspect they will, make your tone more threatening. Scare them as much as possible. Don't touch a single hair on their heads, but threaten them with violence if they so much as set foot in the Parvis again . . ."

Chewing with an unusual deliberateness, the man stared at me indifferently. He was clearly nonplussed by my request. Attempting to keep my calm, I reached back into my purse and took out the money I had just withdrawn, then placed it on top of the photo.

"This is for you. You'll receive it as soon as you've done what I ask."

I expected a more enthusiastic reaction this time. He said nothing.

"Well?" I asked, trying to hide my perplexity.

He took his time swallowing the last bite of his croissant before responding in a hoarse voice: "No."

"Excuse me?"

"I'm not interested. I don't know what you're scheming, but the whole thing sounds like a pain in the ass. Find yourself another pigeon." Then he took his cup of coffee, emptied it into his throat, and stood up. "Thanks for the breakfast."

Before I had time to gather my wits, he was gone.

I won't bother describing the intensity of my confusion and disappointment. Don't anyone try to tell me these people are looking for work! Good-for-nothings, bums, deadbeats. Nothing more.

I wasn't going to let this discourage me, however. Abandoning my own drink, I too left the café and walked back toward the Clos Sainte-Thérèse. In the meantime, the shelter had opened its doors and the line of derelicts was now crammed inside. Entering this miserable place was too much for me to stomach; I had to wait outside. I watched the comings and goings for a good fifteen minutes before laying eyes on a second candidate. He was younger than his predecessor, seemed less damaged by life and more inclined to provide the service I would ask of him: his unrelenting gaze and crude swagger provoked in me, at first glance, an instinctive fear. A fear I had to overcome.

Unlike the other one, he accepted my offer right away. We planned to meet at the same place the morning after the encounter, as long as things went exactly as I wished. I returned home in a state of extreme nervousness.

Lord knows that under no circumstances did I wish harm on my son, nor even on my husband. My intentions were pure: rather than wait for the threat to strike blindly, not knowing where or when; rather than give in to violence without a means of defense, and suffer its consequences, I wanted to control it. To keep it on a leash. In taking these steps, I did nothing but fulfill my role as a mother: to protect my child from life's dangers and the ferocity of the outside world. To make him aware of the peril that surrounds him when he ventures into certain neighborhoods at an ungodly hour. To help him overcome the temptation to adopt an idle and decadent lifestyle. To sharpen his critical faculties and teach him to follow no one, not even his father, without reflecting on the possible consequences.

I never wanted it to happen this way. In my heart and mind, I believed I was acting in my son's best interest. I had, it seemed to me, considered all the potential risks; I had analyzed and made sure to eliminate them. Is it my fault if things took a bad turn? If I couldn't predict the unpredictable? Can we ever force destiny without paying a price?

That night, at home alone, was hell for me. Around eleven o'clock, I began keeping watch by the window for the drunkards' return, ready to offer my son all the comfort he needed to move past the incident which I hoped, all the same, was upsetting enough to make him afraid of repeating it. The minutes went by with a dreadful slowness, and the silence grated on my nerves. I was startled by the slightest noise coming from the street; my heart raced at a glimpse of the rare passerby outside my window.

At midnight, still nothing. What was happening? Why were they taking so long? Had my parakeet kept his side of the agreement and refrained from all physical violence? I began to seriously doubt it. Exhausted, tormented, I paced in circles like a lion in a cage. The anxiety turned my stomach; my throat was raw, my heart in agony.

At half past midnight, no longer able to stand it, I tried to reach Jean on his cell phone. I had promised myself I would do nothing out of the ordinary, but the pressure was too strong. The ring sounded over and over, with a terrible indifference, until it went to voice mail. I thought I was going crazy. I hung up immediately, afraid I wouldn't be able to hide the anxiety in my voice. What would I have said, in any case? There is nothing worse than ignorance in such situations, when imagination gets the better of reason. I was unable to stop myself from imagining the worst.

The coup de grâce came around two thirty in the morning. I was at wit's end; I had called Jean's phone multiple times, disregarding all the rules I had set for myself. I could no longer think clearly, had even considered going to the Parvis to put an end to this terrible waiting. Only the fear of exposing myself to the dangers of the night kept me at home.

I immediately registered Virgile's absence. When Jean and Mike stepped through the doorway, my nerves snapped. I rushed toward them, assailing them with cries and questions: what had happened to my son, where was he, in what state? Jean looked distraught, he stared at me without seeing me, as if indifferent to my cries, to my tears and interrogations. Mike quickly moved to stand between us, and tried desperately to calm me down, to hold my attention, while rattling off a string of sentences, of which I understood not a word. Maddened by this endless logorrhea, this obstacle standing between me and my son's fate, I violently pushed him aside, threw myself on my husband, and began beating his chest with my fists.

"Tell me my son isn't dead!" I screamed, abandoning myself to a fit of rage.

"Dead?" mumbled Jean, looking at me as if I'd gone insane. "He's . . . he's not the one who's dead."

I didn't understand. Not right away. I asked where Virgile was. Jean stood still in front of me, motionless, as if staring into a void; his gaze seemed so vacant, you'd have thought he was blind. So I slapped him across the face. A one-way ticket to reality.

The shock ran through him for a moment; his eyes twitched repeatedly before focusing on us again, finally showing a glimmer of discernment. That was when he broke into sobs. And then he told me.

Everything had gone as I'd planned. At first. After leaving the Union around eleven o'clock, they took a shortcut up rue de l'Hôtel des Monnaies. That's where they were cornered by my parakeet. First came the insults, spewed in their faces like gobs of spit. Jean told them not to react, and they obeyed. Exasperated, the man moved on to threats: he planted himself in front of them, blocking their way, then, taking out his switchblade, ordered them to hand over their wallets. This time, they had no choice but to react. Jean stood in front of Virgile and tried to reason with the vagrant. It was a waste of time, he said; the man seemed under the influence, of alcohol certainly, but probably other, more illicit substances too. When Jean refused to give in to his threats, my parakeet became even more aggressive. He began to twirl his blade under Mike's nose, then Jean's. Virgile, still in the background, seemed paralyzed by the scene. The tension was growing by the second: Mike urged the man to calm down, Jean tried to get him to listen to reason. A crowd quickly gathered, a handful of curious people watching the fight unfold, some of whom also tried to diffuse the situation. That was when . . .

Virgile, without anyone understanding what had unleashed such fury, suddenly let out a scream and leapt at his attacker, reversing the roles. Already somewhat dazed in his intoxicated state, the man was completely disarmed. Virgile knocked him to the ground, and the switchblade fell from his hand and rolled onto the cobblestone. My son grabbed it, and before Jean had the time to react, he had thrown himself on the man.

It is difficult for me to describe the scene. Jean's account of it was disjointed, the words struggled to escape his throat; he was still petrified, in shock, and his terror stood in the way of all attempt at coherence. As they'd changed from onlookers to witnesses, the people had begun to scream, horrified by the violence of the assault. Several of them immediately called the police. According to my husband, it was as if Virgile had lost his mind—he continued beating the unfortunate wretch who had stopped fighting back, burying him under an avalanche of blows. Then the blade pierced flesh and suddenly blood was spurting everywhere, and no one was able to put a stop to this murderous frenzy . . .

Our lives stopped there, at the moment when that poor soul escaped from his wounded body.

I don't understand. We were happy. A simple family. A fairy tale.

The press relayed the incident as soon as the following morning. In the miscellaneous-news column.

Virgile has been incarcerated for two months in the Prison de Forest, awaiting his trial. Mr. Morago, his lawyer, is fairly pessimistic regarding his release. According to him, my son faces fifteen years in prison. Minimum.

Once the period of disbelief had passed, we began the struggle to regain our footing in a world that had become permanently hostile to us. These days, keeping our heads high is a battle fought as daily as it is in vain. Two weeks after that night, Michael Hampton moved out: he now lives in an apartment with two other students, in the municipality of Ixelles.

This morning, while leaving my house to buy a few groceries, I saw that two garbage bins had been emptied in front of our door.

DAEDALUS

by Katia Lanero Zamora

Matongé

A train hurtles past a row of dilapidated buildings. The muffled rhythm of the cars passing over the rails wakes Lea from her dream. Her body still aching from the day before, she clutches her bedsheets as if trying to hold on to the night. But the alarm clock doesn't lie. Its hands point cruelly at 5:55.

Lea would rather smother herself with her pillow than step out into the biting cold. Lucas isn't sleeping either; he silently counts the mechanical *tick-tock*. When the alarm goes off, she presses the button to stop the metallic shrieking. Lucas rolls over to face her.

"Lea . . ."

She turns her back to him, sits up at the edge of the bed. "Lucas, please, not this morning."

He sits up too, pulling the sheets tight around him to try to keep warm. "Lea, I'm begging you, don't go. Nothing is forcing you . . ."

She grabs the alarm clock with both hands, resets it, and places it back on her nightstand. Then she drags herself out of bed, shivering. "You know perfectly well that I have no choice."

She stumbles into the bathroom. It's so cold that her breath forms clouds around her mouth. At six o'clock sharp, the light turns on; in the bathroom, the heater starts up and the news comes blaring out of the radio. It's the end of the blackout.

"Regional Europe must make economic efforts."

Her watch reads: twelve hours until the next blackout.

"You're listening to la Première. It's six o'clock."

Lea turns the shower tap all the way hot to warm up the bathroom. She leans over the sink, washes her face with cold water, and looks at her reflection in the mirror. There are deep circles under her eyes. Her body is drained from the stress of running against the clock.

Traffic news: *"A few delays on the Walloon highways. Congestion on the E40, already backed up to Leuven. Cars are at a standstill at Tervuren, and a one-to-two-hour delay is expected for those coming to the European capital by car this morning."*

A small number of privileged commuters own cars; it takes them two to three hours to reach Brussels. Lea hopes that one day they'll earn enough, she and Lucas, to allow themselves this luxury. In the meantime, they'll have to make do with public transport. Staring at her reflection, she tells herself: *It could be worse. If others can manage, you can too, Lea.*

She takes a quick, scalding shower.

More violent clashes have broken out between police and the insurgents of the Free Quarter of Matongé, home to Brussels's large Congolese community. All night long they've been chanting, *"Udhalimu"*—"injustice" in Lingala.

"The tension continues to rise today among protestors who've set up their headquarters in the Hôtel le Berger, itself a symbol of the struggle against the Europeanization of Brussels, caught in a stranglehold between the European quarter and the wealthy avenue Louise. It's been nearly one hundred days since the barricades were raised and the activists rallied behind the popular leader Amani Muntamba to protest the expansion of the union's administrative departments."

Lea steps out of the shower, dries herself vigorously, turns off the radio. The hearing that will determine whether Matongé must yield to Europe is set for today. Everyone at the office is on edge, the Deciders are constantly changing their minds, their reasoning is impossible to follow, and she can't sleep from worry. She puts on her linen pants, tank top, and cotton shirt, ties her hair back in a ponytail, and applies a dash of eyeliner and a touch of mascara, even though the Security Council highly discourages commuters from wearing makeup. She clings to this last ritual of femininity, insists on performing it every morning, as she did before. Before everything changed.

She comes face-to-face with Lucas in the hallway. He hurries after her and stops her at the top of the stairway.

"Please, Lea, don't go back there!"

"I'm sick of fighting with you every morning."

6:15. Eleven hours and forty-five minutes until the next blackout. She rushes down the stairs, grabs her backpack in the entryway, and stuffs it with protein bars, a flask of potable water, and her pair of woolen shoes.

"You're sitting on a powder keg, Lea, next to a bunch of kids playing Pickup-sticks with matches!"

"I have two more dossiers to work on, just two dossiers, then I'll have my telecommuting license."

"And if it's two dossiers too many? Quit, damnit, you can find a job *here!*"

"I'm not going to quit just because you tell me to every morning. We can't get by on two Walloon salaries, and you know it."

Lucas looks away, angry. Lea softens and takes his hands.

"I'll stay until I'm on the waiting list to be transferred to a regional office." That was the plan.

"To hell with the money. It's gotten too dangerous."

Lea reaches into the front pocket of her backpack and takes out her Mark III 9mm, which she'd bought on the black market from Fabrique Nationale, the arms manufacturer, when she started working in Brussels, and tucks it in the back of her pants. "I know how to defend myself."

Lucas smiles faintly. "I know." He sighs before kissing her lips.

She laces up her combat boots and throws on a wool sweater. After checking to make sure she has some matches left, she puts on her worn jacket, pulls the zipper up to her chin. She kisses Lucas again. "See you tonight, maybe."

She leaves the house, pulling on her fingerless gloves, and heads out into the darkened street. A yellowish light seeps from old utility poles. A train passes, making the security barriers between the buildings tremble. Sparks fly as sheet metal grazes iron. Lights come on in apartment windows. The blackout is over, the day has begun.

The streetlamps buzz, flickering weak light onto the cobblestone. 6:20. Eleven hours and forty minutes until the next blackout. Lea hurries toward the bus stop where passengers wait for the 1, which will take them to the Gare de Liège-Guillemins.

When you're a commuter, you know when you leave home. But you don't know when you'll return.

At the end of the street, the bus's headlights pierce the fog. First step: swipe her AboScan card over the ticket machine. The commuters board in single file, scan their cards one by one under the weary gaze of a visibly exhausted bus driver. When the beep sounds, Lea places herself in front of the camera and allows herself to be recorded. The green indicator flashes; she can board the bus and take the seat assigned to her.

One seat per person, in a single vehicle, once per day. This is one of the measures that Europe has taken to regulate the daily flow of commuters. It's important not to miss your ride. Otherwise, you'll have to wait twenty-four hours for permission to take another.

At each stop, the bus fills with more passengers. Lea wipes the condensation from the window with the sleeve of her jacket and watches the city go by. Thirty minutes later, at the end of an avenue lit by the neon lights of strip clubs, the Gare de Liège-Guillemins, a tired butterfly with faded steel wings, emerges from the middle of a dreary esplanade. A jumble of architectural relics surround the station, various eras and styles clashing; a sad mausoleum of the outsize hopes of a city with too little means.

Hordes of commuters descend from buses, trams, and cars, rush toward the gare, and anxiously separate into lines. Lea puts on her backpack, readjusts her gloves, and checks her watch. 7:06, ten hours and fifty-four minutes until the next blackout.

The bus doors open. The passengers scramble to get off and run for their trains. Lea sprints all the way to track 2, checks the information on the departures board: *Liège-Brussels-Midi, 7:11, arriving.* She climbs the escalator, passing to the left of less-hurried commuters, and elbows her way onto the platform. A shiver runs through the horde of commuters crowded dangerously at its edge. The train cuts past, a metal serpent scintillating beneath the spotlights. Its lurching noise fills the entire station. Lea pushes to the front, shoving, trampling the other commuters. As the train begins to slow down, the third-class commuters flock in front of its passing doors, hoping they've chosen the right spot at the right time, afraid of having to ride on the outside platform between cars, without guardrails, which is often the lot of amateur commuters. Lea knows the drill by now: first, there's the faint signal as the braking starts; then you have to gauge the speed of the train and the number of doors that have already flown by: six . . . seven . . . eight . . .

She moves back a few meters, startles a man as she elbows past him, and comes to a stop with her nose in front of the door. She waits for the second-class passengers to board, swipe their AboScan cards, and take their seats. Then she swipes her own card and is authorized to board. Before, the train floors were carpeted, the seats upholstered in an elegant royal-blue fabric. All that remains of that now are the seats' rusty frames, the floors encrusted with grime, and, in the neon lamps that give off a pallid light, several decades' worth of dried-up bug carcasses. Once the car is completely full, the doors close, the lights go out, and the rising body heat forces everyone into a kind of claustrophobic intimacy. A nasal voice, distorted by the crackling of a rundown loudspeaker, announces: *"Ladies and gentlemen, welcome aboard the intercity train to Brussels-Midi. Next stops, Brussels-North and Brussels-Central."*

The train begins to move. Lea feels for the butt of her Mark III and pulls her jacket tighter around her chest. Outside, it's pitch dark. Commuting in winter is like passing through an endless tunnel.

Brussels-Midi. The terminus. The crowd comes streaming down the long concrete platforms. A fine, steady drizzle falls. The commuters walk nervously down tunnels leading into the bowels of the old station, past graffiti-covered walls and makeshift shelters. The trash cans overflow with rotting garbage. Lea has to step over a homeless man whose presence can be discerned only by the feet protruding from a heap of moldy blankets. Then she hurries to follow the line making its way toward the network of galleries that lead to the central hall, the vital organ of the underground station, buzzing with activity, worn out with the feverish passage of thousands of commuters.

But never mind the crowd. What matters is the rhythm. Lea moves in step with the man in front of her, matching her pace to his. In this way, dozens of lines form, running along tracks and into tunnels, meeting in columns, separating at automatic doors, or flowing down stairways to the metro trains, tramways, buses. Amid the urban music of squealing brakes, bells announcing the closing of doors, and the whistles of ticket inspectors, Lea is blinded by dancing headlights. She descends into the gallery that leads to metro line 2.

After taking out her passport and her work permit, she moves into the line of commuters coming from the Walloon region. On the opposite side of a plate-glass window, Flemish commuters await the same customs inspection. Just like every morning, the agent takes Lea's passport, inspects her work permit, stamps it with the date, and says in a voice even less cordial than he looks: "Welcome to the European capital."

Lea collects her papers and goes running down the slow, creaky escalator to the metro platform. A forty-second wait is announced for her train. She stands beside a row of three orange plastic chairs. The waiting commuters tap their feet, gazes flitting from their watches to the departure boards. It's a reflex, like glancing at the rearview mirror to survey the road. 8:30. Nine hours and thirty minutes until the next blackout. She is late.

A first train comes, headed in the direction of the Forest municipality. Lea moves to the front of the crowd in order to board the next one as quickly as possible. It's arriving in fifteen seconds. 8:31. Nine hours and twenty-nine minutes until the next blackout. The gray concrete, the orange walls, the dusty light that falls on the platform make the exhausted commuters look even paler and more washed-out.

Then everyone rushes to board the train in a kind of controlled stampede. A sensual female voice announces: *"Next stop, Porte de Haal; volgende halte, Halleport."* Lea is wedged beside a Flemish man with the air of a bureaucrat, reading the news on his tablet. She still remembers a smattering of Dutch—not enough to make spontaneous conversation with her colleagues, but enough to understand the article's bold headline: "The Future of the Free Quarter of Matongé: A Problem for All of Regional Europe." A jolt makes her stumble and hold on to the greasy pole beside her for balance. *"Next stop, Hôtel des Monnaies—volgende halte, Munthof."* The streams of commuters rush past, blocking Lea between the pole and the Flemish bureaucrat. He puts his tablet away in its leather case.

"Lea!"

She looks up, recognizing the voice of Jo, her colleague at the Council of Strategic Development Logics. The European administration abounds with councils, courts, bodies, parliaments, secretariats, and departments, each with a name more absurd than the last. Lea gave up trying to understand it a long time ago. She concentrates on her work. Period. The two young women push their way through the crowd to meet in the middle. Jo is wearing a little black dress, black patent-leather Richelieus, a trench coat, and a leather bag. She's from Brussels. She doesn't have to worry about being stuck on a delayed train in the middle of the countryside. Sometimes, Lea misses the days when she could wear shoes other than her combat boots.

"Ready for another day in Daedalus?" Jo asks.

Lea glances away to read the name of the next station: *Louise; Louiza.*

"I'm two points from my telecommuting license. Soon I won't have to see Vibert's old mug every day!"

The train pulls into the Trône/Troon station. Jo's face draws into a frown.

"Go on . . . have a good day," she sighs. "Say, can we meet up for lunch? My Decider has a meeting in your building."

The thought of spending her fifteen-minute break with Jo delights Lea. "Of course!"

Jo kisses her on the cheek and hurries down into the metro. She works in the old offices, in Trône. With Regional Europe's gradual rise to power, the city blocks from Ixelles to avenue Louise have been swallowed up by the bureaucratic machine. Matongé and its tenacious residents refuse to accept the same destiny. Lea gets off at Porte de Namur—renamed the Port of Insurgents by all of Europe—pushing her way off the train.

The station is nearly deserted. A few commuters walk toward the exit on the chaussée d'Ixelles. The humid, polluted air vibrates with tension. Lea pulls on her gloves, feels the butt of her gun, its safety catch off, and tightens the straps of her backpack. She trembles a little as she walks toward the exit. A police cordon blocks off the rotunda in front of the entrance to the metro. A few hundred meters away, on the chaussée d'Ixelles, barricades have been erected, slogans painted on white bedsheets in lieu of banners. Black smoke rises toward the sky. Assault divisions are stationed in front of the buildings on either side of the wide avenue, paracommando cells ready to intervene. Lea shows her pass to one of the policemen. He clears the way with an imperious air.

"Hurry!"

With four other commuters following after her, Lea runs along the gloomy, rundown edifice perpendicular to the chaussée d'Ixelles and dashes into the building where the Council of Decisional Logics is housed, leaving the besieged street behind her.

In the entrance hall, bags of sand and cement are piled at the base of the walls to protect them from possible attacks. Lea walks past the front counter, behind which Annelies, the receptionist, sits. She waves amiably and flashes a stiff smile, a gleam of amusement in her eyes. This is the paradox of Annelies: this odd mixture of composed spontaneity, of distant warmth; a flame that flickers but never burns. Lea responds with a quick, cordial *bonjour*.

"He's already here," says Annelies in her impeccable French, with its hint of a Flemish accent.

Lea consults her watch: 8:47. Nine hours and thirteen minutes until the next blackout. She curses under her breath. She already knows that, having arrived so late, she'll need to run to catch the five o'clock train, and will be lucky if she's not too far from Liège when the next blackout brings Europe to a halt. Lea sprints the few meters to the elevator and pushes the button for the sixth floor. Sebastien joins her, dusting off his suit with an elegant gesture. They greet each other with a kiss on each cheek.

"The TGV was a nightmare!" Sebastien says. He commutes from Paris every morning. "How'd it go for you?"

"No delays, no fights, I still have all ten fingers," Lea replies glibly, showing her hands.

The elevator rises into the heights of the tower. Sebastien fixes Lea with his green eyes encircled by thick black glasses and confesses in one breath: "I have an interview next Wednesday, in Paris."

Lea throws a nervous glance at the elevator mirrors and security cameras. "Not here. Tell me at lunch," she murmurs.

Sebastien shrugs, discouraged. "Who cares? Let them hear me!" And then, as if suddenly coming back to his senses, he whispers in his colleague's ear: "I can't go on like this anymore. We have to get out of here."

"I'm two points from my telecommuting license. I might have a chance—"

"That won't change a damn thing. We come here full of illusions, ambition, all of us. They break us in six months, and what's left of our motivation?"

The doors open. Lea sighs. "I know. I can't stand it anymore, either. But what can you do, Seb?"

"We were at the top of our class. They took everything from us, them and their shitty system."

A few more colleagues step into the elevator, arguing about something on the lunch menu. Sebastien throws a hateful glance at them.

"That's all we have left," he whispers. "Cafeteria squabbles."

He suddenly looks pale. His suit is impeccably cut, his hair perfectly styled, his eyes accentuated by the shape of his glasses; he has the air of a weary gentleman torn from a black-and-white photograph.

"We're worth more than this," he says before stepping out of the elevator. "You're worth more than those two points."

Lea, tired of having the same arguments day after day with Lucas, with Jo, with Sebastien, cedes with a smile of resignation. "Meet you for lunch? With Jo?"

Sebastien agrees with a slight nod and disappears, weaving his way between colleagues rushing toward their Deciders' offices, dossiers under their arms.

Lea arrives at Valère Vibert's office door, her heart beating wildly, not from the exertion of running, but from the anxiety that comes over her all at once, as it does every day, in this same exact spot. 8:47, nine hours and thirteen minutes before the next blackout; she's ready to pound her fist on the wooden door three times, *knock-knock-knock*, like every day of every week—her personal death knell. She closes her eyes and reluctantly announces the beginning of the tragicomic play she's about to act in. *Knock-knock-knock.*

A fraction of a second goes by before Valère Vibert calls from his desk in a feeble voice: "Come in!"

Lea rests her palm on the door handle. As if by magic, Valère Vibert's assistant appears at her side, blocking her way in, and stands there in the hallway, rapidly reeling off the notes from her clipboard.

"Hi-Monsieur-Valère-Vibert-would-like-a-copy-of-the-city-planning-application-because-I-don't-know-if-you-remember-we-had-started-a-procedure-with-the-municipality-but-the-constitutional-council-turned-us-down-because-of-the-delay-we-took-too-long-so-Monsieur-Vibert-preferred-we-go-ahead-without-their-authorization-but-I-don't-know-if-you-remember-the-contract-with-the-territorial-authorities-predicted-a-consultative-latency-period-a-priori-so-we-need-proof-of-the-community-agreement-except-that-we-have-no-trace-of-it-so-if-you-can-find-the-minutes-from-the-meeting-that-would-be . . ."

Lea's losing the thread but can't help staring at this little woman in her snug prêt-à-porter suit, earnestly reciting her morning soliloquy. She nods, reassuring Monsieur Vibert's assistant: "Yes, of course, I can find that in Daedalus. But I'll need the exact date and time of the meeting with the territorial authorities."

Satisfied, Monsieur Vibert's assistant starts walking, dossier in hand, toward the other backup generators arriving in the central hall, the "memos," as they're unceremoniously called, who arrive from their regions, dark circles under their eyes and coffee stains on their shirts.

Lea takes a deep breath and steps into the office. Two surveillance cameras instantly turn toward her with a metallic clicking; the microdrone that will film her for the next eight hours opens its little iron wings and greets her. Lea can see her tiny reflection in its black eye.

The musty smell of a rotting carpet permeates every corner of the room and its black and gray walls. A hard rain pelts the dirt-streaked window. Seated behind a desk from the era of Swedish reign, Valère Vibert reads an e-mail on the screen of a computer that should have been replaced long ago. The problem with technology in these past few years has been that in the time it takes to equip an entire department—to provide market studies, product comparisons, lists of posts to be reviewed, competitions to reward the most capable employees— a new model has already rendered the previous one obsolete. Valère Vibert enjoyed a certain prestige in the days when his ultralight silver laptop, branded with a bitten apple, was the gadget of the moment—but now, at the hour of spectral technology, he no longer impresses anyone. If he hasn't yet been assigned to a different post, it's simply because he's too clumsy with his own ten fingers to manipulate an intuitive program like Daedalus and to navigate holographic space.

"Bonjour, Monsieur Vibert," Lea says politely, seating herself on her rickety old chair.

It's been two years since she started working at the Council of Decisional Logics, and for lack of time and funding, they still haven't bought her a proper desk chair. One day, while she was complaining of back pains, one of her colleagues—one of the "dinosaurs," as they call themselves—burst out laughing, choking on his sludgy coffee.

"What's the memo complaining 'bout? S'been here a few weeks and already wants a comfy seat? Y'don't want a back-ache, go home to your region! I waited five years t'sit my ass down on a padded chair!"

Lea had felt too sorry for him, in his suit that matched the carpet, to bother coming up with an intelligent response. Jo, stubborn, continues to file requests every week; she bravely demands a chair worthy of the name, more stimulating tasks, the chance to learn and progress, and refuses to be discouraged by the jaded laughter of colleagues who threw in the towel ages ago. Lea admires Jo, would like to find the courage to be more like her, to say out loud what the others are thinking; but this would mean entering into endless debates at every level of hierarchy, and Lea isn't very good at argumentation. And besides, she's two points—two measly points!—away from her telecommuting license.

She positions herself in front of the rectangular crystal plate mounted on the lens embedded in Vibert's desk. At the merest touch, a bright light emanates from the lens, creating a holographic screen between her and Valère Vibert. She takes out her HUD glasses, fits them to her nose, and applies the digital sensors to her ten fingertips. Lea's hands begin to move like a spider's legs as she initiates Daedalus, the operating system that maps the deductive reasoning of the Deciders at the top of the administration. Her glasses are synchronized to the screen; Valère Vibert's mental map, which Lea has been charting for the past two years, is displayed on the bright spectrum. Her work consists of following her boss around every day, of listening to his phone conversations, attending his meetings, and beta-reading his e-mails in order to record every idea, every potential choice and opportunity that arises, to follow his thought processes and trace his changes of mind—the paths abandoned or taken up again, sometimes months later—drawing an immense labyrinth of dormant possibilities. To forget nothing: that's what Daedalus is for.

"Well," Valère Vibert says feebly.

Lea braces herself to enter the syntactic segment connected to urban projects. With her glasses on, she has the sensation of stepping into a dark hallway whose walls are covered with key words, connectives, symbols, color codes. She uses her fingertip sensors to collect the occurrences one by one, examines them as if they are precious objects, and immediately places them back, so as not to lose sight of them.

"Your assistant asked me to find the minutes from the meeting with the territorial authorities."

"Never mind."

Lea stops and looks up from the arborescence of decisions made these past few months. She moves up to the next highest branch in the arborescence and exits the syntactic segment. "Pardon?"

"Forget about the minutes. I need you for something else. You're going to insert a new scenario."

"I don't understand."

Valère Vibert laces his yellowish fingers on his desk and lets out a sigh, meaning: *Is it possible to be so idiotic, my poor girl?* "I don't know if you've been following the news, but the Council of Urban Development Logics is nearing the end of two years' negotiation with the Free Quarter of Matongé over the United Regions of Europe's purchase of the agglomeration. Okay?"

Lea nods. Though she has, like everyone else, been following the protests at the Port of Insurgents, she lets Valère

Vibert talk, for Valère Vibert doesn't like to be interrupted.

"But the Council of Urban Development Logics has un-derestimated the Matongé collective, and especially the pop-ular fervor all this media song-and-dance has created. The dossier isn't looking great and the final hearing is set for today, okay?"

Lea nods automatically. It's been nearly a year since the clashes began. Now, activists are coming from the four corners of the United Regions of Europe to support Amani Mutamba.

"And their little circus is cute, okay, but it's time to come back to Earth. Matongé can't win against Europe."

"I don't really see where you're going with this, Monsieur Vibert," Lea allows herself. "Nor what the Council of Decisional Logics has to do with it."

"The president of the Council of Urban Development Logics is a friend of mine. You are going to invent a scenario, as well as the proceedings that are missing from the dossier, and you'll file it all in Daedalus, okay?"

After a few seconds of bewildered silence, Lea blinks, takes off her goggles, places them on the desk, and says, al-ready exhausted: "I'm not sure I understand you correctly. You're asking me to create a false history? Not for you, but for the president of the Council of Urban Development Logics?"

"There's nothing to understand," Vibert replies in a dry, professional voice, sliding a thick dossier over the tabletop. "Here is all of the information you'll encode in the minutes of the six fictional meetings."

Lea can't hold back her distress: "Tampering with the history will have an unprecedented butterfly effect!"

Blood rushes to Valère Vibert's cheeks, giving them a slightly orange, waxy tint. "I'm asking you to do your *job*, so that we can be done with this so-called Free Quarter."

"It's not my job to pirate the mental map of another Decider!"

"Lea, how many points are you from your telecommuting license?"

She lets her gaze roam the winding paths of Daedalus. "Two points, Monsieur Vibert."

"It would be a real pity to get a sanction now, wouldn't it?"

Lea steels her gaze, forces herself to hide the contempt she feels. Valère Vibert's sluggish cheeks droop on either side of his dry, bloodless mouth. She thinks of Lucas, of how worried he looked this morning as she was getting ready to leave. Just two more points and she won't have to commute any longer. No more insomnia. No more walking home through the snow after the blackout. At last, they'll be able to make plans for their future. She takes off her glasses. "Yes, sir."

He grins, showing his false teeth, and slides the dossier closer. "That's a girl. There. You have everything you need right here. Be sure to backdate all the documents, okay? It's important to be consistent."

Only twelve minutes until lunch is over. In the cafeteria hall, Lea spots Jo among the dozens of administrative employees of the United Regions of Europe, her neck craned toward the giant screen where a live broadcast of the tribunal hearing plays. Just as Lea is about to greet her, Jo points up at the screen, warning: "Shhh! They're about to give the verdict."

Lea feels the tension running through her body. The Decision Room is packed with journalists, with citizens of Matongé and the United Regions of Europe. The Deciders are all gathered in the auditorium. With no suspense for Lea, the verdict comes down like a guillotine: the residents of Matongé have six hours to vacate the district. In the popular assembly where the activists are rallying, a tall black man draws Lea's attention: Amani Mutamba. When the president announces the council's decision, cries of protest mount from the four corners of the room and police attempt to contain the crowd. A furious resignation burns in Amani Mutamba's eyes.

In the hall of the cafeteria, functionaries comment on the news; the renewal of the building projects and the possibility of being transferred to new offices has everyone in good spirits. Lea sits mutely amid this buzzing crowd, unable to take her eyes away from Amani Mutamba. Jo notices her desolate expression.

"Looks like somebody had a rough morning."

Lea mixes her soup to break up the chunks of powder. "I hate Vibert!" she spits.

Sebastien joins them, setting his tray on the table. "We've all come to this!" he says in his sardonic, biting tone. "I can't stand my Decider any longer. Christ, sometimes I want to grab him by the collar of his polo and chuck him out the window."

"When is your interview?" Lea asks.

"Next week," he says, his voice suddenly sounding desperate, ashamed. "I can't stay here much longer anyway. Soon I won't be able to look at myself in the mirror."

"What do you mean?"

"The Council of Strategies has signed a secret 'cleansing' protocol. The army will enter Matongé tonight. During the blackout."

The afternoon goes by in a blur of strategic and administrative tasks. Valère Vibert thinks, Lea takes note; Valère Vibert doubts, Lea divides the syntactic segment in half; Valère Vibert weighs pros and cons, Lea dreams of the day when she'll wake after sunrise. She glances at the time displayed in the right corner of her glasses. 4:30! One hour and thirty minutes until the blackout. Lea takes off her glasses and puts them away in their case. The microdrone rotates around her, whispering metallic notes into her ear.

Valère Vibert sighs, vaguely registering the movement in front of him. "Leaving already." It's not really a question, not really a statement; it's somewhere between the two.

Lea starts putting on her jacket. Suddenly, a soft *ping* announces the arrival of a new e-mail. Lea puts her glasses back on; the lens projects the message on the holographic screen. She reads it, leaning over the back of her rickety chair, one arm already in the sleeve of her jacket.

"Ah, yes, actually, Lea . . ." begins Valère Vibert.

She doesn't know why, but these words give her a bad premonition.

From: Department of Inspection of Backup Generators
Subject: Dismissal with Immediate Effect

Dear Lea,

Today the Department of Inspection of Backup Generators noted six (6) infractions in your function's code of ethics, leading to a conflict in loyalty with aggravated circumstances. Please vacate the building as quickly as possible and leave all materials belonging to the Council of Decisional Logics behind so that your replacement can take over your dossier.

We wish you the best of luck in future endeavors.

Lea has to read the message several times before it sinks in. Her hands suddenly feel cold, the smell of the office is unbearable, and the ticking of her watch resonates like a pitiless gong. She is stunned, petrified, and it's finally Valère Vibert who interrupts her silence, in the moment between two ticks of the second hand on her watch.

"You're fired."

"But . . . why? I did what you asked me to do!"

"Open the attachment," he orders.

Lea extracts the video sequence from its zipped file. Scenes from the day play out before her eyes: she sees herself rushing into the entrance hall, late; talking in the elevator with Sebastien: *I can't stand it anymore, either. But what can you do, Seb?*" In the cafeteria: *"I hate Vibert!"*

Lea watches herself as she would an actor in a film, incredulous, eyes fixed on the microdrone. "You're not allowed to film us during our breaks!"

"What is said between these walls belongs to the Department of Inspection of Backup Generators."

Lea grabs the microdrone in midair and points the camera's eye directly in front of her. The metal wings move between her fingers like a trapped insect trying to free itself.

"Well, you know what you asked me to do today? It was illegal!"

Valère Vibert opens the second part of the attachment. An analysis report on Lea's body language throughout the day. Various photos are annotated with little white tabs—on her lips, her forehead, her eyes, her hands, her shoulders.

Valère Vibert reads them aloud in a deep, accusing voice: *"Frustration! Anger! Doubt!"* He moves on to the next photo. "Contempt, there, on your mouth, while I'm speaking to you! Your disgust is obvious, Lea, and the last straw, really, the last straw, I'm beside myself . . . there, right there, in the crease on your forehead, when you frown, there's a homicidal urge."

Lea feels this very same urge coursing through her veins

now, and Vibert can sense it. He steps back into the space behind his desk.

"The conflict of loyalty is undeniable. Clear your desk and leave the building."

Two security guards enter the office.

"You bribed me!" she spits at him. "I tampered with the history for you! I'll tell the Department of Inspection!"

"You're a memo. I'm a Decider. You have no power, my dear."

Valère Vibert watches her closely as the security guards drag her toward the exit. Her colleagues look on, stunned, as she is escorted down the hallway and into the elevator, past the entrance, and, finally, pushed out the door. The guards leave her in front of the rotunda at the entrance to the metro, where policemen observe her with suspicion.

"Go back home, mademoiselle," says one of the security guards. "There's nothing left for you to do here."

Lea is abandoned amid the stream of commuters rushing down into the station. Far away, on the other side of the barriers surrounding Matongé, the protestors are chanting: "*Udhalimu! Injustice! Udhalimu!*" It's a chant that erupts from the belly of Matongé, from place Fernand-Cocq, a chant that ricochets off the facades of the crumbling yet stately buildings on the chaussée d'Ixelles before making its way to Lea. Yes, *Udhalimu!* She trembles with a sudden rage. The commuters jostle around the growing fleet of patrol cars. The beams of their revolving lights sweep across the night sky.

Lea's telephone vibrates in her pocket, snapping her out of her daze. A text from Lucas: *Hope you had a good day. One more toward your telecommuting license. Good luck with the train.*

Her train! Lea checks the time: 4:48, one hour and twelve

minutes before the next blackout. She's lost time. She runs up the escalator, elbowing past a crush of commuters to the right, then is forced to slow her pace as she weaves her way through the crowded platform. A man presses himself up against her. She turns around, horrified, and meets his amused glance. He rubs his crotch against her butt. Disgusted, she tries to move toward the edge of the platform. The train finally arrives. People hurry to board as soon as the doors open. Once more, Lea feels the man's body straining toward her; an erection confirms his perverse intentions. She jolts forward, tries to board the train. She swipes her AboScan card, but the man gets on with her and presses her against the wall of the car. The heat, her anguish and disgust, the man's hands on her waist—it's too much, and she leaps out of the car before the doors close. The last glimpse she has of him is his satisfied smile and a lewd gleam in his eye as he shouts, "Go on, whore!"

She's sweating. She wipes her forehead. She runs toward another platform to take a different train heading toward Brussels-Midi. 4:59, one hour and one minute until the next blackout. Another car. The doors open. The stream of commuters begins flowing in. Lea swipes her AboScan card. *Access denied.* She swipes it again. The terminal displays: *This card has already been validated in metro #78–34, direction Brussels-Midi, at 4:58 p.m. To report a found AboScan card, please call . . .* The line of commuters behind Lea pushes forward. She steps out of the way, exasperated.

She looks at her watch: 5:00. Sixty minutes until the next blackout.

Lea splits in two. A primary instinct takes command of her body; anger numbs her brain. She sees Valère Vibert's cracked, dry lips repeating over and over: *You have no power, my dear.* She walks back through the stream of commuters toward the Porte de Namur station exit. The army division descends pompously on the quarter in an all-terrain vehicle with massive treads. She can't take the chaussée d'Ixelles, there are too many policemen. Determined, she walks down avenue de la Toison d'Or under a fine, icy rain. The passersby move beneath the neon lights of luxury shops, cinemas, and chic restaurants. Hard to believe that the insurgents' headquarters are only a few hundred meters away. Lea turns onto avenue Louise and its array of riches, passing women with tiny dogs and men in suits. The windows of jewelry shops at place Stéphanie shine fiercely under the streetlights. Lea walks along rue du Prince Royal. The insurgents' chant grows stronger: "*Udhalimu!*" A barrage of policemen blocks the street. She ducks under a portico and walks down a short alley that leads to a deserted parking lot. The building seems abandoned. She shimmies over a low wall, jumps down, and lands in the garden of the neighboring house under construction. She goes in by the back door and climbs through a window to make her way onto rue Keyenveld. On her right, the police barrage she's just avoided is preparing to intervene; on her left, the street hums with anxious demonstrators. Lea slips into a back alley and keeps walking until she reaches the building that appears to be the nerve center of Matongé. Wedged between two crumbling buildings, the Hôtel le Berger still has all the dignity of early-twentieth-century architecture.

This former hotel once served as a refuge for adulterous lovers. The half-timbered facade is cracked right through; torn curtains hang from what remains of the windows, velour and silk rags. The art nouveau furniture was plundered long ago, the dark rooms stripped of their secrets. A throng of demonstrators converge on this narrow street perpendicular to the chaussée d'Ixelles. Lea has to weave through them to try to enter the hotel and find Amani Mutamba. She has to yell over the noise to a man who seems to be guarding the entryway: "I have to speak to Amani Mutamba!"

Her voice is swallowed by the din of the protest. She repeats herself but the man ignores her and bursts into the hotel, shouting orders at his insurgents.

She turns to someone else, repeats: "I have to speak to Amani Mutamba!"

The chaos gives her vertigo. She follows rue du Berger and ends up on the chaussée d'Ixelles, swarming with demonstrators. No one listens to her, no one hears. "The army is coming!" she calls out. "They're going to launch an attack!" It is 5:32 and she's in the middle of a neighborhood about to be razed by the European army. There are twenty-eight minutes until the blackout, and she's the one who's made this nightmare possible. *"Udhalimu!"* Her body is thrown from one side of the crowd to the other. Fists raised, the people refuse to leave the neighborhood. From windows and balconies, from the threshold of every door, flags are hung, banners wave. Matongé will not be European. Matongé will remain *bruxellois*. *"Udhalimu!"* Lucas is waiting for Lea while she's stuck here on the chaussée d'Ixelles, unable to board a train for twenty-four hours, and she's lost her job. She's lost her job and the ground has collapsed under her feet. Only darkness before her eyes. No bearings. No perspective. A young woman crashes into her with full force.

"We have to go up to place Sainte-Boniface to reinforce the ranks!" the woman yells in a harsh, piercing voice.

"The army is coming!" Lea cries.

"We have to join the barricades to keep them out!"

Lea examines this girl with her sharply defined features, her black curls tied in a messy ponytail, wearing a frayed vest stained with blood and pointing with her bruised fingers to show Lea the way.

"Saint-Boniface, a hundred meters that way, go!"

Lea takes her by the shoulders. "No! We have to leave here!"

The girl looks at Lea as if she's just insulted her. "What are you saying? We have to stay!"

The crowd, indifferent, moves around them; the two women stare at each other like two species meeting for the first time. And yet, they're wearing the same clothes. They're not so different from one another.

"The army's about to enter Matongé and raze the neighborhood—do you know what that means? You have to leave!"

The young woman shakes herself free, disgusted. "We're already doomed! Tell me—should we eat or bathe? Which of our children should we send to school? And it's not just Matongé, it's all the Regions of Europe! It's a racket on a continental scale. And now we have proof! I can't back down. This is the only choice I have left."

Lea feels her phone ringing in her pocket. It vibrates over and over, she doesn't answer, and finally it stops. She can't turn away from this stranger's eyes.

"And you," asks the curly haired young woman, "what choice do you have?" Then she backs away, smiling faintly, and runs off toward Saint-Boniface.

The insurgents are racing to the various strategic locations in Matongé; everyone to the barricades. The army is assembling. Lea grabs her phone and calls Lucas. He answers on the first ring. She can hardly speak.

"Lea? Lea, is everything okay?"

Her lips tremble as the noise of the street floods the line, causing Lucas to panic four hundred kilometers away.

"What's going on?" he demands.

"I missed the train," she tells him. "Don't wait for me."

"Where are you going to sleep?"

The question, so pragmatic, makes the distance between them seem unfathomable. "Lucas, I'm about to do something terrible."

"Stay where you are, I'll find a way to get a car, I'll come and get you, just find a place to stay for a few hours. You're not going back there again. I don't give a shit, you'll find work *here*. Don't move. I promise you, it's over, it's the last time, everything will be okay."

Megaphones are blaring orders to the barricades, sirens exploding all through Matongé, while Lucas, so far away, tries to reason with Lea.

"Where are you? I can come get you, I'll find—"

"I'm already too far away."

She silences Lucas's pleas with the press of a button and puts the phone back in her pocket. She starts running toward the chaussée de Wavre, hoping there's still time. She looks at her watch: 5:38, twenty-two minutes before the next blackout.

At Porte de Namur, rows of protestors face the assembly of policemen on horseback. Faces hidden by scarves and foulards, they're armed with makeshift weapons: baseball bats, iron bars. Despite the determination in their eyes, they're not equipped to protect themselves from water cannons and teargas. Lea stands by what was once the display window of a fast-food chain, of which there remains only broken glass in the puddles of grease spreading over the ground. The sound of a helicopter drowns out the warnings shouted from a megaphone. The demonstrators refuse to leave, will not be intimidated. Breathless, Lea climbs the stairs of the deserted fast-food joint.

She reaches the rooftop littered with bricks and debris. Matongé stretches out beneath her feet. Out of the white smoke, police barricades rise. An annex of the Council of Decisional Logics directly overlooks the rooftop; Lea grabs a brick and uses it to strike until, fingers bleeding, she manages to stick her arm beneath the annex window and open it from inside. She crawls into the building of the European Administration. All the lights are turned off. She reaches the long hallway that leads to her office, strides down it quickly, like a thief, without crossing paths with anyone. 5:49, eleven minutes until the next blackout. She has to initiate Daedalus before they cut off the power. She enters Valère Vibert's office, praying that her access codes are still valid. She brushes her hand over the lens and applies the sensors to her fingertips. Glasses on, she plunges into Daedalus.

She follows the tortuous routes of Valère Vibert's mental map until she finds a syntactic segment where the president of the Council of Logics of Urban Development appears. She leaps into his mental map by pirating his backup generator's access, as she had earlier in the day. While she searches for the right segment, she begins to sweat. Exploring the hall of symbols, she turns to the left, moves up two branches, moves down again, feels around; colored words pass in front of her eyes, flickering on either side of her field of vision; she takes the wrong path and has to retrace her movements, leaving a silver thread behind her so as not to lose her way. In the corner of her glasses, she watches the minutes tick by: 5:53, seven minutes until the next blackout. And then she finds it: the dossier on today's hearing. She moves up the arborescence that she programmed herself as one enters a silent temple, following the branches that connect the keywords leading to the dossier code-named *Udhalimu*. The sickening irony.

She hears only her own gasping breath. 5:55, five minutes until the next blackout. She grasps the virtual threads that lead to all the false arguments, the minutes from meetings that never took place, and holds two years' worth of lies in her hands.

Suddenly, the lights go on in the office. Valère Vibert's face appears on the display screen and a police squad bursts into the room, yelling at her to remove her sensors. Startled, Lea is caught between two realities, two worlds, and beneath the surface of the labyrinthine mental map of the president of the Council of Logics of Urban Development, the silhouettes of six armed men come into focus.

"Lea, release the syntactic segment and exit Daedalus."

5:57, three minutes until the blackout. Lea stands, still holding the syntactic segment. She has only to crush it like a handful of dry leaves. The barrels of their guns do not frighten her.

"You're a liar!"

"Exit Daedalus," repeats Valère Vibert.

Lea cries out in a desperate voice: "I was just doing my job!"

She clenches the virtual words in her fists. Valère Vibert smiles. 5:58. Two minutes until the blackout.

"I'll give you your telecommuting license," he says, attempting to calm her. "The Council of Decisional Logics wants to make up for its mistake. We should never have fired you. I'll give you your two points and more. You'll have your telecommuting license and a company car."

Lea swallows. She can hear the cries of the protestors outside: *"Udhalimu!"* Her phone vibrates in her pocket: Lucas.

"Let go of the segment, Lea. And starting tomorrow, you won't have to commute. Or be my backup generator. I'll promote you to Decider of the Walloon Regional Council. You'll have a car. And you'll be able to work from Liège."

Lea's hand trembles. *What choice do you have?* Her phone rings and vibrates in her pocket. 5:59, one minute until the next blackout. Lea catches a glimpse of her future. A future of arborescences branching toward happiness, toward a vista of possibilities. At last, some stability. She lets go of the syntactic segment and takes off her goggles.

6:00. Blackout. The sound of the shot is lost among the blasts of gunfire in the street, among the cries of *"Udhalimu!"* that echo through all of Matongé. Lea's eyelids flutter. She sees nothing but the ceiling of her office and its damp stains. Warm blood flows down her chest.

Gently, her eyes close, and the light in them goes out, along with all the lights and all the hopes in Europe, everywhere, at the same time.

ONLY MUDDY STREAMS
FLOW IN DARKNESS

BY PATRICK DELPERDANGE

Rue d'Aerschot

J ust at the moment when I manage to slip two fingers under the elastic of her panties, a disturbance in the yin-yang
balance occurs. Someone is knocking, you might even
say pounding insistently at the door, each thump followed
by shouts and curses from the adjoining rooms, and Serena
Shackleford seems suddenly to awake. She realizes that her
jeans are unzipped, and that my right hand is practically inside
her panties, while the left one has been feeling beneath her red
wool sweater for quite some time now. Serena Shackleford is
from Richmond, Virginia, and she's treated herself to an all-
inclusive European tour with a group of her fellow American
citizens. She is forty-three years old, divorced, and the sort
of tourist who immediately catches my eye when I skim over
the list the agency provides. I always draw a little star beside
these names.

Whoever's at the door has not thrown in the towel; quite
the opposite. The banging is becoming more and more violent, and it's clear I'll have to open up. Serena Shackleford
understands this too. She understands that she'll have to explain the presence of the tour guide in her room at eleven forty
at night. I took charge of her group just this morning, which
goes to show how much Serena Shackleford, though perhaps
not fully conscious of it, was open to more than three days

of guided visits in Belgium when she booked her vacation. *Divorced four years*, it said on the form. Which had earned her another star.

I stand up straight, smooth out my clothes, and grab my jacket off the floor, under the anxious gaze of Serena Shackleford, who has pulled up her jeans and sits at the edge of the still-made bed, twirling a lock of her blond hair.

I wink at her reassuringly. Spreading peace around me is what I'm paid to do, in addition to the lectures and museum visits. I've learned to remain at ease, come what may, thanks to the path of the Buddha. When Megan Elizabeth Peyton twisted her ankle leaving the Cathedral of St. Michael and St. Gudula, I carried her in my arms to the car, all 175 pounds of her, while her husband, Rodney, stood there and watched. (Megan Elizabeth Peyton received no star from me.) When Steven Dale Gross's wallet was stolen with his twelve credit cards and three thousand euros inside, I was the one who brought him to the police station to file a report.

"Serena!" someone yells from the hallway. "It's me, Tina! Wake up, please!"

Now Serena Shackleford jumps up, panic-stricken. This Tina is her best friend, as far as I've been able to observe since this morning. Tina Marie Kinworthy had gotten a star on my list, a star I crossed out once I'd met her. As I understand it, she's on a honeymoon or an engagement trip—accompanied, in any case, by a certain Scott Burdett. He guards her like a rottweiler, constantly hugging her waist with his beefy arms, to the great enjoyment of Tina Marie, who throws little mischievous glances at Serena whenever this occurs. It's the first time I've heard of an engagement trip taken with a group, but the lessons of the Buddha have taught me to be surprised at nothing.

I station myself beside the door and lower my voice to declare in my most lilting, Yankee-accented English: "Don't you worry, Miss Shackleford, this can happen to anyone."

Then I open the door and act surprised to find Tina Marie Kinworthy standing there in a slip, barefoot, her hair tousled, visibly beside herself.

I smile at her with Buddhist serenity, then glance back at Serena, still in the half-darkness of her room. "Don't worry," I say to her over my shoulder, "I'll take care of everything. Get some sleep now. We have a very full schedule tomorrow."

I close the door behind me before Serena comes into view, then put a hand on Tina Marie's waist, as she seems to appreciate, and pull her aside.

"Can I help you, Miss Kinworthy? Is there a problem?"

She's still a bit stunned at seeing me leave her friend's room, and takes a moment to recover. "Scott's disappeared!" she finally blurts out.

I raise an eyebrow to indicate my concern. "You mean he isn't in his room?"

"*Our* room!" whines Tina Marie. "When I got out of the shower, he was gone."

"He probably went out for some fresh air."

"I've been waiting for two hours!"

"Hmm . . . yes, that is a long time."

My words seem to throw her into an even greater panic. "I'm sure he was kidnapped!" she says. "Oh my God, how will I pay the ransom? Do terrorists accept credit cards?"

I pat Tina Marie Kinworthy's plump little arm and walk her back to her room at the end of the hallway.

"Calm down, Miss Kinworthy. I assure you Mr. Burdett has not disappeared. Wait for me a moment, I'll be right back."

I leave her and go down to the hotel bar. The waiter is

busy putting glasses away behind the counter. Scott Burdett isn't here. I lean toward the barman, smiling.

"I've lost one of my Americans. You wouldn't have seen him here, by chance?"

He hesitates a moment. "What sort of guy is he, your American?"

"Burly, with a face like a bulldog."

He nods. "He downed a double whisky, then told me he wanted to go 'window-shopping,' if you know what I mean. I pointed him toward rue d'Aerschot. Don't know if I should've."

"Okay."

Outside, a fine, cold rain has begun to fall. I pull my jacket collar up high and take off in the direction of the Gare du Nord, not far from the hotel. Rue d'Aerschot isn't mentioned in the travel guides, and yet quite a few tourists are aware of its existence. The gentlemen in particular, I must say. My gaze is drawn to the first neon lights that flash in the darkness. There's a line of cars on the street, practically at a standstill, with the drivers leaning in to get a look at the shop windows. Girls—very young girls—writhe slowly beneath the red and blue lights in nothing but lingerie that emphasizes their assets. One of them beckons me with a motion of her index finger. But the lessons of the Buddha showed me long ago that this sort of invitation owes nothing to my charm, and so I remain as Zen as a moss-covered stone in a windswept garden.

Of course, there's more at stake here than my ability to resist sexual temptation. If my American has ventured into one of these establishments, he's not only in danger of coming out minus a wad of cash—which wouldn't be *so* bad in itself—but also of ruining his engagement trip and causing Tina Marie one hell of a nervous shock. All of which would be a serious pain in my ass for the next three days. I'll do whatever I can to avoid that.

I walk into the Blue Star, a café/bar between two red-lit windows. It's so dark in there that you have the feeling of entering a cave deep in the woods. The only source of light comes from a string of tiny bulbs draped around the bar counter. Two guys are seated on stools, sipping their cocktails and talking in low voices in what sounds like a language from the deep steppes. The barmaid turns around, pointing at me an impressive pair of breasts that no longer owe much to nature, held only by some miracle inside her skintight, half-unbuttoned blouse.

Her eyes blink for a moment, fixing on me. "Well, what do you know?" she says. "Didn't think we'd see you around here again, my ol' Pat. Thought you'd straightened yourself out once and for all."

"Hey, Sonia," I reply. "I'm here for professional reasons. Don't go imagining anything."

She starts to laugh. "I'm not imagining a thing. You're the artist who had enough imagination for two, aren't you?" She lets out another little mocking laugh.

Yes, this girl and I were involved in a kind of relationship awhile back. But that was before I discovered the path of the Buddha. Without getting into details of doctrine that would only lead us off course, I can assure you that the spirit of Zen doesn't quite square with the pastime we engaged in.

"How 'bout a bourbon and soda, Pat?" she asks, grabbing a bottle of liquor from behind her. "As usual?"

"Stop calling me Pat," I say. "I always hated that. And I've quit bourbon. Well, I've quit drinking so much." I wait until Sonia has placed my drink on the counter before continuing. "I'm looking for one of my tourists . . . an American. He's got it into his head to visit the neighborhood and I don't want him to get lost, you know . . . A big fellow with the face of a pit bull."

I raise my hands above my head to give her a sense of the guy's height. With a discreet movement of her chin, Sonia points to a corner of the bar near the restrooms.

My eyes are so unaccustomed to the dark that I hadn't seen him when I'd first come in, besides which, he's half-hidden by a curtain hung from the ceiling that forms a sort of alcove. Considering the shoulder breadth of the patron seated there, it must, indisputably, be Scott Burdett. Just as I'd hoped, he'd gone into the first café he saw upon arriving in the district. I take my drink and go to join him, acting casual.

He's deep in conversation with a girl sitting across from him. Or rather, he's talking to himself and the girl is listening, a vague smile on her lips, which she parts every so often to drink from the glass of champagne in front of her. The bottle juts out from a bucketful of ice and appears already half emptied. It takes Scott Burdett a moment to register my presence. He rotates his bull-like torso and sizes me up and down without a word.

"Brussels by Night is on Wednesday," I tell him, sitting down on the banquette beside the girl. "You're ahead of schedule, Mr. Burdett. And the Blue Star wasn't on the itinerary."

He makes a gesture in my direction, followed by a remark, neither of which leave room for interpretation, and it's only the mastery of my nerves, acquired through rigorous training, that keeps me from responding in a similarly crude manner. The thickness of his muscles—his biceps in particular—must also be taken into consideration. In the pallid glow that bathes the alcove, he looks like a grizzly bear wearing a too-small shirt.

I consider a few of the koans I've meditated on over the past few weeks before placing a hand on Scott Burdett's forearm and saying: "When the wind stops, the flowers still fall."

I pause for a moment to let him grasp the subtle character of these few words, but Scott Burdett is obviously not moved by the poetry of Zen. He suddenly grabs me by my jacket collar and pulls me over the table, toward him.

"Piss off," he grunts. "I'm talking with this girl, can't you see?"

I don't think he knows who I am. He must believe I'm just some asshole, when in fact I'm simply doing my job. But it's strange that he doesn't recognize me, since our faces are now only a few centimeters apart, which allows me to appreciate his remarkable features in detail. He finally lets go and I fall back onto the banquette, trying to smile, to show him I'm not offended by his macho attitude.

"Tina Marie is in a hell of a state," I say as soon as the air can move normally through my lungs again. "She thinks you've disappeared."

"Tina Marie?" repeats Scott Burdett, as if he's never heard the name before. *"Pfffff!"*

He makes a mildly disgusted face while the girl pours herself another glass of champagne, with the clear intention of emptying the bottle as quickly as possible.

"We really should get back to the hotel," I say. "I'm telling you, you'd better get some rest. Otherwise you won't be in shape for my lecture on the Flemish primitives tomorrow morning."

"I don't want to see her ever again!" cries Scott Burdett. "She annoys the shit out of me, she's worse than the bubonic plague. I wish she'd go fuck herself!"

"Tina Marie Kinworthy?"

"Who else?"

"You're not engaged anymore?"

In lieu of a response, he waves his hand to get Sonia's attention and orders another bottle of champagne, as well as a bourbon and soda for me, which I find a thoughtful gesture on his part. "I never should've let myself get involved with her," Scott Burdett says once he has a full glass in front of him again.

"But you seemed so much in love today."

He looks at me without answering. "She's loaded," he finally says. "She's just inherited a ton of money from her dead banker husband. She pays for everything, for herself and for me. And she gave me this, when we were in Paris." He holds out his wrist to show me a watch with a silver band. The thing must be worth a good dozen years of my tour guide salary, if I know the price of a Cartier.

You'd think the mere exposure of the watch to open air had captivated the attention of the entire bar. In any case, a second girl has just materialized out of thin air. Fidgeting in her minidress with its neckline plunging down to her navel, she sits next to Scott Burdett and immediately cuddles up to him, causing a wide grin to spread across his craggy face. He starts serving glasses of champagne on the fly and the girls laugh while I drink my bourbon and soda, telling myself that to get Scott back to the hotel, the best strategy is probably using the enemy's own strength against him, as the Buddha teaches us. In other words, since he wants to drink and enjoy himself, I'll do all I can to help him at it, and once he's out of commission I'll pluck him like a daisy in a field after a rainstorm.

It's at this point that things begin to grow hazy.

It seems to me that Sonia keeps coming back to our alcove, maneuvering bottles and glasses. She flashes me a sly wink each time she refills my bourbon and soda. Beneath the gruff exterior, Scott Burdett reveals himself to be a truly charming guy, and the few stories he tells us—rollicking tales of ass-kickings in the suburbs of Richmond, Virginia—certainly don't make us like him any less. Now the two girls are sitting on his lap and I think, though it's hard to be sure in this poor lighting, that their hands have slid beneath his shirt and even started unbuttoning it, coaxing Scott's torso to reveal itself in all its glory.

"So . . ." I say to him at one moment, trying to catch hold of my glass, which has a nasty habit of sliding toward the edge of the table. "So, old Scotty, what do you think of Brussels?"

"I love it!" he roars.

"Shall we go out for a stroll, then? There are some other places I'd like to show you. You can bring your two new friends, of course."

On rue d'Aerschot, the line of cars is just as long as before. The drivers are still in search of true love, which is to say a girl with long legs and a tight ass who'll agree to give them a little human warmth in exchange for their cash. Scotty studies the shop windows with the look of a kid who's been left overnight in a Toys "R" Us. He staggers a bit, but *you* try to walk in a straight line with two girls hanging from your biceps. As for me, I move with a slightly swaying step between the clients meandering down the sidewalk, their noses in the air, examining the merchandise.

As I'm looking for the bar where I used to while away the hours, back when I hadn't yet found the path, I hear a guttural cry behind me: Scott Burdett is suddenly brawling with several opponents, a dozen arms and legs thrashing wildly, all clearly set on relieving my American friend of a piece of his fortune and his personal effects.

The two girls run off without further ado. I throw myself into the fray to pull Scott out, but it's hard to know how to go about it discreetly, and when an elbow slams into my nose and the side of my mouth, I understand that even transcendental meditation has its limits. And so I retaliate with all the strength and precision I have left after the barrel of bourbon and soda I've just imbibed.

Eventually, our little group skirmishes its way off the sidewalk and onto the street. The drivers here are so distracted that we risk being flattened on the asphalt without anyone even noticing, so absorbed are they in examining the silhouettes of the girls on display. The strangers who have just ambushed Scott Burdett seem well aware of this. I can make out, in the glow of the streetlamps shining down on us, two heads emerging from the crowd. At that moment our attackers evaporate like the dew at sunrise, and we find ourselves alone, Scott and I, sprawled out on the ground. It takes us a moment to realize that I'm biting into his calf muscle while he's pinning me down with his right elbow. We manage to untangle our limbs, only to break into raucous laughter and throw ourselves on one another again, this time in righteous celebration of our friendship that has only been strengthened by this manly adventure.

We decide to make a stop at Shalimar to drink to the occasion. The bar has been run for ages by an old friend of mine who bears an uncanny resemblance to Yul Brynner in *Taras Bulba*—well, he wears an astrakhan hat, at least. When he sees me coming into his place with Scott, he howls in surprise and immediately fetches a bottle from his cabinet, a liqueur whose name I've never been able to remember, distilled with some rare herbs gathered by the proprietor's own grandmother and brewed according to a recipe that's been kept secret, no doubt for the sake of world peace.

And then, without the faintest idea how this could have happened, I find myself slumped in the hall of my tourists' hotel, my back to the wall next to the reception desk, wearing plaid golfing pants. (While golf is a respectable sport if ever there were one, I've never played it in my life.)

I know that part of this story seems to be missing, but I beg you to believe that it isn't my fault. Address your complaints to Taras Bulba's grandmother.

I have no clue what time it is. My watch reads 2:32, but considering the state of its face, that must be the moment when a foot crushed it earlier in the evening.

I manage to stand up and, leaning casually on the edge of the desk, observe the night watchman seated on the opposite side. After a moment, he looks over at me and nods sympathetically.

My professional conscience forces me to make sure that Scott Burdett has found his way back to his room. And so I go up to the third floor. At the end of the hallway, I see a body lying on the carpet. Beside it, an empty suitcase and piles of clothes in a jumble. Scott lets out a snore that leaves no question as to the state of his health.

Reassured, I begin to walk away when I hear a noise coming from his room. I press my ear against the door's varnished wood. I've guessed right: someone is crying in there.

I knock twice, and the door opens immediately. Tina Marie Kinworthy is in tears, her face damp, her features ravaged by grief. She recognizes me and calms down a bit, then looks behind me at the mass of Scott's sleeping body. She nearly chokes at the sight. "The son of a bitch! Oh, the bastard!" she hisses, releasing all her fury.

"Shhh," I say. "Can you tell me what happened?"

"He wanted to . . . he wanted to . . ."

"Yes?"

"He came back here at four in the morning, completely drunk, with a . . . a . . . with a woman of ill repute!" she finally spits out. "Do you realize? When we've just gotten engaged!"

I gaze at her for a moment with my most compassionate expression. "Men are bastards," I say.

Tina Marie nods in agreement, a sorrowful look on her face, once again on the verge of tears. She trembles slightly in her negligee.

I take her by the waist, I lead her gently to her room, I close the door behind me with my foot, and I whisper in her ear: "Tell me everything, Tina Marie. That's what I'm here for. You'll feel much better afterward, I'm sure of it. Only muddy streams flow in darkness."

I don't know why, but I have the feeling tomorrow's lecture on the Flemish primitives—or rather, today's—is going to find itself slightly shortened, to my great regret.

RITUAL:
DIARY OF FLESH AND FAITH

BY KENAN GÖRGÜN

Anderlecht Abattoirs

*Cities, like forests, have their caverns in which all the most wicked
and formidable creatures which they contain conceal themselves.
Only, in cities, that which thus conceals itself is ferocious, unclean,
and petty, that is to say, ugly; in forests, that which conceals itself
is ferocious, savage, and grand, that is to say, beautiful. Taking one
lair with another, the beast's is preferable to the man's.*

—Victor Hugo

1.

The Feast of the Sacrifice: along with Ramadan,
the most important holiday of the Muslim year.
The events I am about to relate took place during the last Eid al-Adha. In Turkish, the language of
my ancestors, the festival is known as kurban bayrami;
bayram *means "holiday" and* kurban *means "sacrifice,"*
*but refers also to the sacrificed animal, as if the act and
its consequence had become one, as if crime and victim
were no longer distinguishable. It all began with my desire
to film reportage on this unique celebration: on the same
day all around the world, thousands of believers slaughter
thousands of animals, literally spilling their blood. Do you
know of many traditions that have remained essentially
unchanged for centuries? I'm not talking about primi-*

tive rites or obscure ceremonies, but a ritual observed by more than a million individuals. Laborers, artisans, businessmen, researchers, musicians, politicians, diplomats; Muslims today hold positions in just about every sector of society imaginable. And once a year, they cut the throats of millions of beasts and celebrate their faith in a bath of blood. No part of this ritual has given way to its symbolic representation; preserved in all its original violence, it is, I believe, the only major religious celebration that has not become a romanticized version of itself. Blood is spilled today as it was in ancient times. There is no dramatization here, no playacting. Here, as in the recording that follows, everything is real.

So begins the letter I found in my mailbox yesterday morning. A letter, accompanied by a DVD, which continues:

A more or less obscure journalist with no job security, I was motivated, in part, by the need to advance my career. To make a name for myself. Nothing reprehensible, nothing transcendent. I told anyone who would listen that I wanted to film behind the scenes of the festival as no one had before. I would start at the market where the animals are bought and sold. With my camera on my shoulder and its focus set on eternity, I would immortalize the killing of these creatures. Already I could see the rough, textured shots, the close-ups of shanks and intestines, the hides ripped from layers of fat, entrails spilling everywhere. I wanted to film the squalor of this celebration and leave the beauty outside the frame. Considering that I'm of Turkish descent, and that my family is Muslim, there's reason to think I'm settling personal scores. I've always been against bloodshed, even if I don't mind a plate of lamb chops—the hypocrisy of all urban meat eaters who can't stand the sight of blood, coupled with the latent disdain of a Muslim child tired of explaining what he believes in, and why he is often tempted to believe in nothing. And, in the end, I did what I set out to do . . . but for one detail. But for one detail, I was given all that I wanted. Only, I hadn't imagined the atrocity would go so far. The atrocity, and my comprehension of it.

K., my "guide," asked me if I wanted to "film something interesting." I had no idea what he meant by this. What I did know was that I wanted to tear the mask from the face of ancient Islam, to show that When-the-World-Is-in-Such-Miserable-Shape-It's-Disgraceful-to-Unleash-So-Much-Violence-on-Innocent-Animals. And if I felt I was disturbing the ghosts who sleep nestled in the cradle of legends, I soon came to see that this darkness was not specific to Islam, nor to Muslims, but to human beings in general. I found myself confronted with more masks; that of the Christian, and beneath it another, that of the ancestral Jew. Was it all a farce? A mirage? These sons of man multiplied: white, black, yellow, red, flatheaded, slant-eyed, all murmuring in a single, muted, obstinate voice: "We are legion, and we have been here since the beginning. Our differences are nothing but smoke and mirrors. We are all made of the same clay; our fears and our lies, too, are the same. Since the dawn of time, we have given our blood and taken the blood of our brothers. We have heard this blood crying out to us from the ground. It begged us to stop. Stop what? If you are among the suffering, then you already know. If you are among the oppressors, then it happens that you forget, as you've forgotten *how to put yourself in another's place. For a moment, the blood that flows in the veins of the living and the blood that springs from the veins of the dying are no longer alike. Do not forget this illusion of difference between those who leave and those who remain. Blood knows that it is the same everywhere, that man alone perceives a difference: inside his body, it is life; outside his body, death. This illusion lasts only a moment, the time it takes for your final breath to leave your body. 'What have you done to one another?' This is what our blood cries out, and we have refused to listen."*

I quote K.: "Jews, Christians, Muslims; we have all betrayed God, but the Muslims' betrayal is the most serious. For we are the last ones, and we ought to have known." As I read these words, I felt a shiver pass through me. No sane person would make such claims. I should have known better, I should never have agreed to be his witness.

2.

The text you are about to read is the transcript of a documentary. The package containing the letter and the DVD was neither stamped nor postmarked: it was slipped discreetly into my mailbox. After watching the film, it took me some time to decide what to do about it. I was tempted to consider this work the fruit of a deranged mind, intent on exploiting religious tensions for profit. Then I realized I had it all wrong; the film is an unflinching account of the violence of our time, and how this violence, in its encounter with false idols, threatens our humanity itself. It is both a terrible indictment and a desperate plea. The date on which I received the package might be a clue as to the mental state of its sender, the filmmaker, presumably (who remains anonymous, never turning the camera on himself): two days before the Feast of the Sacrifice, while the Muslim community was bristling with excitement, I discovered these unbearable and nevertheless fascinating images. The footage, according to the letter, dates from last year's festival. Why would he have waited so long? *I finally came to accept their truth. For it was well-founded. Not moderate—radical, to the contrary—but just.*

What truth? That of K., his guide, and of K.'s family, more traditional and fervent than most I have known; yet, *but for one detail,* he was given all he wanted.

Two days before Eid, the investigators are working against the clock, fearing the reprisals these images might provoke, should they fall into the wrong hands—for what they show us, as outrageous as it seems, happens every year. In forty-eight hours, millions of believers will celebrate their faith. In forty-eight hours, the horrors exposed by the film will be repeated.

3.

The camera moves along an ordinary street paved with loose, uneven cobblestones. The buildings are narrow, five or six stories high, with single-glazed windows, their cracked facades crisscrossed with bare cables. Under the cornices, the leaden sky casts a pallid light on the windows, where clouds are reflected in wavering pools like the milky whites of gouged-out eyes.

"I grew up here—these streets were our playground. Where have all the children gone? I don't see any. And yet, compared to the middle-class neighborhoods, where reproduction is a carefully planned affair, this is where fresh blood hums—on these streets bordered by the Anderlecht and Molenbeek municipalities, the working class watches its dreams pass by, along with the barges

on the Charleroi canal. Children, we would throw garbage bags into its greenish water. One morning, we pulled up a blue-faced Moroccan—a father, himself an orphan—bloated and dead. Another time, it was my cousin who surfaced, as though regurgitated, tied to a car that had carried away part of the balustrade. His face beaten beyond recognition, his anus burned with cigarettes, he'd been tortured by former business partners. Cocaine trafficking. No one had suspected him of being a dealer. The last time the canal showed me a glimpse of the hidden face of things was on a night when some friends and I saw a man hurl his bag into the water; it came open in midair and out flew three revolvers, three blackbirds diving into the murky depths. And since that night, death has followed me wherever I go, swinging its scythe, cleaving bodies from souls. Those who live here share an aversion to the world, and the world returns the sentiment."

We see two men dragging a sheep by a rope tied around its woolly neck. One of them addresses the camera: *"What do you think you're filming, eh?"* The sight of men towing a sheep in the street is generally considered anachronistic. A question of context.

"I learned this in school: a woman wearing a bikini on the beach draws attention only in proportion to her good looks. On an avenue, the same woman in the same outfit would be the object of everyone's attention, as though she were walking on the beach in a tailored suit and heels. Good journalism attempts to find the false note at the heart of an unremarkable score. These men and their sheep, here, in the city, are a perfect example. There is a certain violation of intimacy, of an unspoken pact; things we aren't supposed to see are momentarily exposed on the street under the pressure of circumstances: the parking lot was full, no spots left near the exits, and so they had a greater distance to travel between the protected spaces of car and covered market. In a Muslim country, this same

tableau provokes no particular reaction: men hold their sheep on leashes as though they were walking dogs, while two blocks away, a nervous steer attempts to escape its owners. The animal runs back and forth from the sidewalk into the middle of the street, hooves skidding as drivers honk and shout from open windows. His pursuers hurl insults from one end of the street to the other, like a soccer team changing strategy midfield. The cow sees all possible escape routes cut off; terrified, it attacks. One man throws himself beneath the animal, while another lashes him repeatedly with a cane. Once they've managed to beat it into submission, these same men joke among themselves: such are the hazards of the festival! Muslims will ask me: 'And so what? You don't eat meat?' It's not the consumption of flesh that disturbs one, but the immediacy of the violence, the return to a time before industrialization, when animals were slaughtered by hand rather than by machines that deliver them ground and boneless. For many, the presence of bones and joints is intolerable. More so even than blood, it reminds us that our portion of meat comes from a larger whole—bones, joints, flesh, and all—that was the living animal itself."

In a wide-angle shot, we see the entrance to the Anderlecht abattoir. Filmed from the other side of rue Ropsy Chaudron, the impressive dome reaches a height of thirty meters, making the slaughterhouse a site as recognizable as the Atomium with its nine steel-clad spheres. Two massive statues of bulls flank the entrance, looking ready to charge. As a child, I had to walk down this street on my way to school, and this facade always intimidated me, especially the bulls with their bulging muscles; I sensed in them a terrible anger, petrified in the bronze. From its perch on the brow of one of the bulls, a pigeon contemplates the animals in their pens below, living but hardly any freer than the statues, the ground beneath their hooves covered in straw and feces. The market's passages swarm like those of a medieval city-state, bustling with men in search of a bargain. At the intersection of two alleys, a group of around twenty stands engrossed in debate, their chatter mingling with the music played over the loud-speakers. A man with a cigarette hanging from his lips walks over to the group. He carries a cardboard tray with cups of coffee, tendrils of steam rising and dancing with the smoke of cigarettes. The camera follows the movement of the spirals; instead of dissolving, they grow thicker and thicker, soon filling the frame. Then, a series of spliced shots: a jet of steam escaping from a vent; a duct pipe; a kebab cart; strips of meat cooking on the grill. Two men assemble sandwiches one after another: meat, lettuce, and garlic sauce, accompanied by a carton of *aryon* (a yogurt-based drink, nearly impossible to find ten years ago, now served at every self-respecting Turkish snack joint in the city). One of the customers inadvertently drops a slice of kebab.

The timing is perfect, as they say: the camera zooms in on this piece of meat while a customer stops in front of the caravan, holding a billy goat on a leash. The goat sees the meat, stretches out his snout, sniffs, draws back, sniffs again, then strongly exhales, as though sneezing, or trying to expel the odor of a fellow creature's flesh.

Cut.

Then, eight sheep hides hung out to dry. One can easily distinguish the parts that covered the thighs, the back, the shoulders. Seen from the front, these hides resemble men who've been ordered to put their hands up, or insurgents before a firing squad, frozen in horror. Farther away, other hides are drying on the ground, their humanoid forms even more striking, calling to mind the white chalk outlines that police trace around bodies at the scene of a crime. When a customer has the animal butchered at the market, he can choose to keep the hide or leave it with the vendor. Most will take the fur, at the request of their wives. At home, the wool is cleaned in a bath of scalding water, then used to stuff mattresses. I slept on such mattresses throughout my childhood. And yet my dreams were never haunted by the souls of the animals flattened out beneath me.

A man in blue work overalls walks in front of the camera and unlatches the door to a pen. It creaks open on its hinges, and the sheep back away. The man grabs hold of one of them. *"This one?"* The customer, standing in the alley, points at another animal stamping its hooves on the ground. The vendor unceremoniously drags this sheep over by its wool. *"Three hundred fifty euros. A handsome animal. Hardly any fat on him."* The customer takes a long look without stepping into the pen. *"You said that last year . . . We threw out several pounds of fat."* The merchant pats the sheep on its side; not affectionately, only to show its heft. *"Three hundred twenty, last offer."* Here, vendors hawk their wares as slave traders once did. They speak of race, of weight, of pedigree; they urge you to feel the back muscles, to examine the teeth. At this market, men do to animals what not long ago they did to their brothers. Nothing guarantees that, tomorrow, they won't enslave one another again. At this point, the filmmaker cuts to a long shot of the abattoir: beasts and men.

"My objective was to show that men, like animals, form herds. The pen does not, in fact, create the flock, any more than the market creates the human crowd. The flock creates the shepherd. By this same instinct, men create dictators. And prisons, office buildings, football stadiums, military bases, housing projects—all of these communal spaces in which the constant repetition of an action is enough to make it seem acceptable, when in reality it is anything

but: it's easier to shoot a man if hundreds of soldiers around you are doing the same; it's easier to believe in the unseen if thousands of others swoon before its beauty; to point your finger at a sheep and watch him pass into the hands of a butcher, while you would be incapable of hurting it if you met it on a path in the countryside. I could go on for a long time. Instead of complaining about his lack of freedom, man should ask himself if he is capable of living free. He declares his own goodness at the top of his lungs, when it would be much more convincing to simply be good."

The camera, hidden, films a group of men at knee level. Gathered around a vendor, they haggle over the price of a steer and the distribution of its meat among them. One of the potential buyers has backed out, raising the cost of each share. *"That comes out to more than two hundred fifty euros per person—it's too much." "We won't go over two hundred." "You've seen the animal, he's superb,"* says the vendor. *"You'll get more meat per person! . . . All right, fine, go find someone else and come back and see me . . . I'm not going anywhere."* Several pairs of legs move toward the bargaining circle; we wonder if someone is going to join the pool. Then another pair approaches, bends, crouches down: K., the future guide, enters the frame, face angled downward, as if he were tying his shoes. He has brown, close-cropped hair; bony, well-defined features. His starched white shirt collar is folded out over his black coat. K. turns discreetly toward the camera. There's a dazzling light in his green eyes, as much from their iridescent color as the intensity of his gaze. Then K. smiles faintly, winks, stands up, and becomes a pair of legs once more.

"I'll discover these images only later. For the moment, I remain standing there, without even glancing at him, for fear of confirming his suspicion: namely, that a camera is filming these men without their knowledge. K. remains silent, alerts no one. He too has a

hidden agenda, and is setting the stage. I take the plunge and ask: 'How much to join the pool? I wanted a sheep but they're too expensive and not big enough.' The steadiness in my voice surprises me; it does not tremble with excitement at this chance to take my film in a direction I could not have hoped for. 'I have a hundred twenty euros on me.' 'We put in two hundred each.' 'Two hundred fifty,' the vendor says. The discussion drags on, the vendor is getting annoyed. 'I can lend you eighty euros, if that's all you need.' K.'s intrusion into the affair unsettles me. His deep, velvety voice has an entrancing quality, but one senses it could become threatening if not taken seriously. I don't yet realize that by offering to help me, he's advancing a pawn. 'If . . . it's not too much trouble,' I say. 'No, not in the least. God wants us to be generous to our brothers, after all.' A murmur of approval greets this platitude. I accept K.'s offer.

"The group of men finally follows the vendor, who leads us toward the area of the market reserved for butchers, far from the produce stalls, the kebab carts, and coffee stands. I expect them to search me, to confiscate my film; I prepare to make off with my camera between my legs. But such chaos reigns in these hours before the festival. Everyone's shouting and bargaining, tying up animals and dragging them from their pens, and rarely do they give in without a struggle. Sometimes the fight becomes a spectacle, with all eyes on an animal determined to go out in glory. Several men might be needed to restrain it, but not as a father holds his child back during a tantrum, summoning all his patience to console the kid. No, this is a fight to the death, never mind that the animal is acting out of fear. Everyone knows that its resistance is in vain. With each moan, it is saying farewell to this life, to these men who surround it, and among whom, it hopes, there might be one who objects to what they're about to do to it. After all, has it not been loyal and obedient, has it not used all its strength to serve man, to spare him from ruining his health with hard labor? The animal asks not for pity, but for recognition. Barely two years old, our steer weighs 714 kilos; raised in the open air, in one of the country's most pristine regions, it comes from a stock known for the tenderness of its meat. While my companions calmly fulfill their duties as good patriarchs, eager to observe the edicts of their faith, I stay in the background for two reasons: to keep my camera at the best angle for viewing them, and to not come too close to the animal. I do not fear it will attack me; I'm afraid of looking into its eyes.

"But the animal does better: rolling its immense head on its muscled neck, it looks away. I feel as though I am standing at the entrance again, watching one of the bronze bulls above the gates come suddenly to life. Its mouth is dribbling saliva, its nostrils flare, exhaling plumes of vapor in a sigh whose meaning escapes me: Is it one of resignation? Or of a warrior who knows he must return to battle? I hear one of the men say that this animal, chosen to satisfy God, is blessed. We say the same thing about suicide bombers. The vendor is joined by two men in bloodied aprons. One sharpens his machete on the rim of a toothed wheel. Several knives of various shapes are laid out on the block beside him. His gestures are precise and mechanical; he works quickly so that we won't have to wait long. The other approaches the steer. No sooner do I realize he's holding a syringe the size of my forearm than the needle is sinking into the animal's neck; the plunger, pushed all the way down, injects the sedative. Then the butcher starts to lay into the animal. One-two, left-right, a boxer warming up on the bag, softening its leather. By instinct, the steer follows the butcher's movements with its eyes. Its own innocence does it in; it grows tired within seconds. Then the butcher pushes forcefully against the animal's flank, as if he were trying to flip a car over onto its roof. The steer resists with all its strength, but its knees finally give in. It emits moans at random, a foghorn launching its last distress signals before a shipwreck; engulfed in a sea of darkness, the steer is sinking, its enormous body collapses. This time, there's no doubt; it is a sigh of resignation. What awaits it is beyond its comprehension; killed twice over, its corpse desecrated, hacked into six parts to be carried off in six different directions, in the hands of six predators who will never see each other again. I can no longer bear it; I close my eyes. (But the camera films everything.) I hear the clatter of horns on concrete, the sound of the blade against the sharpening device, the prayer that precedes its assault on flesh and bone; I hear these men murmuring, 'Allahu akbar,' and I wonder if this is really what God wants. Then someone flicks a lighter—a cigarette? They're ready to smoke, to enjoy the show. I hear a braying, more human than animal, and the butcher's voice asking his partner to help him 'hold up the head.' Behind my eyelids, I see one of my cousins lying on the floor of our living room, shaking with convulsions. My father holds his head to keep him from choking on his own vomit. He'd swallowed pills. To die. His wife, too beautiful for him; her red mouth, her black curls, her eyebrows like arrows, and the looks men gave her. My father had arranged their marriage so that this nephew would be able to regularize his situation in Belgium. The violence between this man and this woman: Did it come from love? From hate? For each other, for themselves? It was unspeakable. And their death, three days later: two strangers broke into their apartment, stole nothing, and killed them in their sleep, two bullets each, in the chest and the forehead. We will never know just what they were mixed up in, only that their executioners came from Antwerp.

"I hear the butcher order us to step back, and a few seconds later, the sound of a jet of blood spurting from the steer's veins like water from a ruptured hose. I hear crackling noises I can't identify. Perhaps they're lighting a fire to smoke the head, as my father used to do during festivals when he would force me to participate in the sacrifice; to tie the animal's hooves together, to hold it back as it struggled against the slashes of the knife. The crackling of that fire has found me here. I feel a moist heat exhaling from the area that surrounds the steer, as if I were standing on the threshold of a hammam. I know it is coming from the animal's opened body. When I dare to look, I see the steer's head lifted at an unnatural angle and its neck exposed: a gash beneath the chin reveals the quivering muscles of the throat. The butcher is straddling the animal, one arm held tightly around its neck, the other pressing the knife handle over the veins spurting blood. I throw a glance at the inner courtyard, spattered with rain and hail. I walk toward the exit. Outside, men and sheep are lurching like cats in the downpour, and into the open gutters of the Anderlecht abattoir flows the blood of beasts and of men I've seen killed by bullets, fire, and drowning, the blood of those who kill themselves—last month in Schaerbeek, where most of the Turks in Brussels live, three young people, whose parents are from the same village as mine, found asphyxiated in their car in a locked garage—they'd let the motor run. No letter, nothing. Just death, at barely twenty years old. And every forty seconds, someone on this earth puts an end to his life. The abattoir did not invent suffering, death, or sacrifice; man, already disposed to dance with death, comes here to kill freely.

"'Would you like to film something interesting?' The voice is not yet familiar to me, but it's no longer unfamiliar. It shouts against the drumbeat of the rain. K. stands right beside me. With raised arms, he shields himself from the thousands of arrows that fly at us from above, sent by an army in position behind the clouds; the rain forms a thick screen of mist in front of his face. There is something unreal about K. 'I . . . I don't have your eighty euros anymore.' He smiles amusedly at me, then turns and begins fighting his way through the crowd."

We hear the filmmaker running and the image turns

shaky; K. is jostled from head to toe. The setting becomes a flurry of disjointed signs. Near the gates, the camera stops to film the bronze bulls standing guard. The rain slides over their chiseled muscles, their slanted brows and grimacing mouths. In the street, chaos ensues; people dash across the pavement, cars zigzag in and out of lanes.

"*K. leads me down rue Ropsy Chaudron. We're not far from rue Liverpool and the neighborhood where I grew up. There was Francis the barber, who'd been racist at first, then a little less so. Jeff and his dog Faruk. Nathalie, the princess of my childhood, whom I saw again one day on the 63 bus, and who'd gained so much weight that she now took up a row of her own. Giovanni— Belgian mother, absent Sicilian father—who still sucked his thumb at twelve. Who knows where they've all gone, the playgrounds replaced by dealerships exporting cars to the Balkans. K. stops beside a Ford Transit. He opens the passenger-side door and turns toward me. He senses that I'm nervous, hesitant. 'What did you come here for? To film a different world, right? Well, do what you set out to do!' He gets in on the driver's side and looks hard at me. I climb in. It's an almost unconscious decision, and an irrepressible one. Through the rain-lashed windows, the world is a smeared painting. As K. starts the car, I hear the sound of stamping hooves; behind me, the floor is carpeted with newspaper, straw, and minced herbs; at the back of the van, a plump young sheep trembles and defecates black pellets. Fear.*"

Then cut to black. An ellipsis of time and space that complicates the work of the investigators, who continue to study the images for clues to where they might have been shot. Any typical elements of setting—streets, businesses—could help them to trace his route and identify the zone of residence of K.'s family. Difficult to imagine that such footage would not exist; the only explanation is that the filmmaker edited it out.

When he gets into the car with K., he has no idea what awaits him. But he knows that by cutting to black, he's letting the rain wash his own tracks away.

4.

In a world forsaken by the gods, the camera films a man with a thick mustache. K.'s father is dark-skinned, with hazelnut eyes and thick, lustrous eyebrows, of the type that one grooms with a small comb. He drinks tea. Clasped between his thumb and forefinger, a rosary. There are two kinds: the long string of beads, ninety-nine in number, is meant for prayer, while the shorter string of "worry beads" is used by men to calm their nerves. They finger the amber beads and, once at the end of the string, twirl them around like pistoleros. Other men talk and drink tea in the father's company. The doorbell rings, the guests continue to rush in. K.'s father is the eldest, and families always gather at the home of the eldest. This reunion is being held here for other reasons too—reasons linked to the festival, certainly, but to a unique conception of it.

"We are nearly thirty, most of us of an age to be parents. Yet I am struck by the absence of children. By 'film something interesting,' was K. suggesting this family's tribute to the blessedness of carnal pleasure? And do they expect me to immortalize their shindig with a home movie? For the moment, they allow me to walk around, filming. Everyone has been informed of my presence, of my camera—they all seem to know more about it than I do. They force themselves to act naturally as I weave through the vast living room. I approach the large picture window to film the garden and the tableau it offers: K.'s mother, a basin balanced on her hip, stands in the company of seven living sheep. After having seen hundreds of them at the market, it's the whiteness of their wool that's striking. Without touching it, one knows how soft it must be. But

what are seven perfectly healthy sheep doing here? Like brothers around a campfire, they huddle near the basin. The camera zooms in and films its contents: a mixed salad of zucchini cubes, celery sticks, lettuce, tomato quarters, and shaved carrots. 'Today marks the seventh year that my family has bought a sheep on the day of the festival . . . and sacrificed none,' says K., who appears with two steaming cups of tea. 'Why buy them, then? To do as everyone else does?' 'It's more complicated than that. But I will try to explain it to you. It's time.'"

In a long, unsteady shot, the camera scans the spines of several books, classics of various literatures: *Memed, My Hawk* by Yashar Kemal, Hardy's *Jude the Obscure*, Hugo's *Les Misérables*, Edward Bunker's *Beast* trilogy, essays on ethnology and the social sciences, including René Girard's *Violence and the Sacred*. (The presence of this last work gives pause, considering that Girard took mainly Judeo-Christian texts as the basis for his study.) This succession of images—the antique and modern volumes, and the classical music added to the montage—bring to mind a scene from *Seven*: on the eve of his retirement, Detective Somerset (Morgan Freeman) locks himself in the library and gives us a glimpse into his research methods. He peruses works that might shed light on the motives of the killer who plagues the city, staging elaborate murders based on the seven deadly sins. A conscious reference on the part of the filmmaker? Indeed, for he goes on to say:

"*Seven. One of the great modern tales of the darkness of our souls. This investigation of the violence that engulfs us all, following on the trail of a harrowingly lucid serial killer, remains unforgettable even after several viewings. K. and I had spoken of it. Hard not to take Brad Pitt for a moron in the role of Detective Mills. But why blame him? He who doesn't know doesn't know, and he who knows can no longer pretend not to. The veteran detective played by Morgan Freeman knows. And it keeps him up at night. It's so humid in this city swarming with mortal demons that he sleeps with his window wide open, and wakes in the night to hear God murdered in a blind alley. A wave of darkness is spreading over the world. He doesn't know whether he should speak of it, or how. He doesn't know if anything can be done to reverse it. His doubt is so great, in fact, that in the end, when the killer insists that he and Somerset are more alike than different, the detective finds it hard not to agree with him. And when the moment came, I too would find it hard not to agree with K."*

K. speaks with a fervor that transfixes the camera: "*I studied all the texts, questioned every resource. Every night, I dreamed of death. Always, it was barbaric. I sank into a depression. My family wanted to call an exorcist. I told them it would solve nothing—I was tormented not by jinns, but by man. Man who had committed the irreparable and condemned us to perish, not in some unfathomable afterlife, but here, on Earth, where we would soon unleash a living hell.*"

In this room that serves as a library, a row of framed portraits in black and white, of young men between the ages of twenty and thirty, decorates a wall. There are seven of them, youths whose expressions are kind but distraught, as if they knew things one shouldn't know so early in life. The black and white lends an old-fashioned air to these faces, a timelessness, a charming patina. Seven portraits in a row on this memorial wall. Here, the only dissolve in the film occurs. A dissolve is a progression of frames from the end of one shot to the beginning of the next. A dissolve can be rapid. It can also be drawn out, so that the viewer has the brief impression of looking at a single, larger image. This effect usually seeks to provoke an emotion, to establish a link between two things, drawing attention to their similarities or contrasts. Here, the image of the seven portraits dissolves into that of a sheep. Then the camera zooms out and gradually incorporates the six other sheep into the frame. We are at the back of the garden. The father, crouching, digs a hole in the ground with a stainless-steel bowl. The sunset reflects an indigo light on the clouds behind him. Breathing heavily, the father scrapes and throws the dirt, digs, scrapes, and throws. With the flat of his hand, he smooths over the walls of the hole: the gesture is so care-ful, you would think he was consoling the earth. On a napkin, he has laid out two clean knives and a sharpening stone. Dif-ficult not to think of the butcher's instruments on display at the abattoir. Except that there is only love in the father's eyes.

"*It is into this hole that the blood will flow, once I've severed the vein. The blood must return to the earth. That is one reason I never arrange for sacrifice at the abattoir. There, the blood is drained away in onyx gutters. Stripped of its poetry. The earth must absorb the blood, commemorating the lives that it sustained.*" He takes hold of the larger knife. "*Son, there is nothing more important, at the moment of sacrifice, than the condition of your tools. The knife must be perfectly clean and sharpened. Otherwise the blade will tear at the flesh. And the victim will suffer longer than necessary.*" "*The sacrifice is an ordeal, then?*" The father addresses the cam-era with a playful look. "*Death is never a bed of roses. Even if it is desired. Even if it is justified . . .*" "*You seem to be acting against your will.*" The father mops his forehead with the back of his arm. "*You don't know yet what I'm going to do.*" He points to the hole. "*But what must be done, must be done. From now on, each of us must bear his responsibility.*"

5.

"*If God sent the ram to Abraham, then we wouldn't have to sac-rifice our sons . . .*" "*What do you mean, if God sent the ram?*"

K. walks toward the picture window. In the garden, his father rises to his feet. Father and son exchange a look. *"There are seven sheep outside,"* he murmurs. *"And seven portraits in the room next door. One of them is my brother. My best friend, until the day he left us . . . We have always known how to mourn those we've lost. What these portraits have in common is that they live in our hearts, and, by substitution, in our garden. Each day, we care for our sheep as though they were our children."* "You . . . what are you saying?"

The filmmaker is poised to revolt. From every corner of the house, the guests observe him warily.

"Eight years ago, tragedy struck our family," says K. *"We lost one of our own under horrible circumstances. He left home and began visiting people who claimed to worship our God, but were nothing at all like us! We've all read the Koran, we have kneeled before God in prayer, but he kneeled before other mortals who have networks right here, in Brussels. Imposters of the faith preying on the youth groups and Koranic schools of our neighborhood, they stole from us one of our bravest sons. The only time we had news of him, it was to learn of his death in a suicide attack in London, eight years ago. This loss was the most difficult of all to mourn. For the first time, we did not even know how to comprehend a death. Not only had he put an end to his life—already difficult to accept, considering our beliefs—but he'd done so in the worst way imaginable: by turning his own body into a bomb, and using it to murder as many people as possible. And so we were forced to ask ourselves a seemingly simple but essential question: what really happened between the father, the son, and God, on that night when the father, in order to prove his faith, agreed to sacrifice his son, and when, at the last moment, convinced of the father's devotion, God sent him a ram and allowed him to sacrifice the animal instead? This myth, common to the three religions of the Book, whose protagonists are*

Abraham/Ibrahim and Isaac/Ismael . . ." K. is joined by another man of around forty, elegantly dressed. "*We have always deplored the recourse to violence,*" the man says, coming to K's side. "*But the day when one of our own strapped a bomb to his back, we were suddenly in a position to see this act for what it was. The fog cleared and we had, before our eyes, the truth of what it means to send a son to his death while invoking the name of God, like these 'peddlers of Islam' who recruited our cousin!*"

"*Can you begin to see, now,*" asks K., "*why his death cast us back to that night when Abraham, on the point of sacrificing Isaac, was deterred by God's provision of the ram? Abraham sees this sacrifice as a supreme act of love: to give to God what he loves most in the world. This aspect is crucial. And God, seeing him sincere, is satisfied with the intention alone. In the history of myths and symbols, stained by centuries of human sacrifice from the Aztecs to the Romans, Abraham's renunciation of Isaac's sacrifice should have marked the immemorial end of human sacrifice, certainly in the name of God. Yet the plague of suicide and violence continues to spread, and there is no longer an end in sight. They are dying by the thousands, in the prime of life, convinced that their act has its place in the divine order. Not only do they go where God Himself spared Abraham from going, but the essence of the ritual is annihilated: the act of love is transformed into an act of hate. God gave us a means of renouncing this violence and protecting those we love, and we have desecrated it.*"

"The ram in the myth of the sacrifice . . ."

"The scapegoat, yes. The Feast of the Sacrifice was supposed to be a reminder of this pact, and as Muslims, we were the last to assume the duty of honoring it. But look at the world: is it not full of the bloody evidence of this betrayal? What purpose does the festival serve if the pact itself is broken, if the reconciliation it was supposed to offer has been undone? Terrorism, then, would appear

to be only the most spectacular symptom of what is, in reality, the
slow death of our dogmas and our rites, the spiritual collapse of our
world. Our violence weakens us, makes a mockery of our hopes
for the future! Born of the agendas of politicians and religious lead-
ers, it has escaped their grasp and become a monstrous ballet of
violence, without rhyme or reason, without nation or God!" "But
that's a horrible—" "It could be worse! And if Abraham had killed
his son? If God had left us to murder one another? Would not this
version of the myth be truer to our world? There would be no more
betrayal, for God would already have abandoned us; our religions
would have lied to us in order to hide the atrocious truth: that there
is no redemption."

K. stands, and the others follow him. Through the large
windows, the father's solitary silhouette can be seen standing
at the back of the garden. He's waiting for them to join him.
Moving closer to the camera, K. asks:

"How are we going to survive this?" "I must leave here. I'm
not ready—" "What could it mean to you, atheist, nonbeliever,
delivered of all spiritual concern? Why did you come here, if only to
feed your contempt? Why did you follow me, if only to profit from
what you despise?"

"I am still trying to conceive of what all this has been leading
to, from the moment K. offered to lend me money, when I hear the
call to prayer. I say, 'Aziz Allah,' as is the custom when the call
rises from the minarets, this call that makes all of us equal before
God. It has been years since I last prayed or set foot in a mosque,
but I have never been able to remain unmoved by this chant. Well
recited, it can make the soul tremble. K.'s father bursts into the
prayer and carries it beautifully."

The sequence that follows left the police no choice but to
contact the Turkish Islamic authority of Brussels. In this Euro-

pean capital, one-fifth of the population is Muslim. The Turkish Muslim community, regulated by the Diyanet, an advising body of the Turkish Minister of the Interior, is the most active religious group. The mosque is located on the chaussée de Haecht in the Saint-Josse municipality, at the heart of the neighborhood known as Little Turkey—where everything is, in fact, *alaturka*: from the grocery stores, bakeries, restaurants, and pizzerias, to the travel agencies and brokerage firms. In the weeks leading up to the Feast of the Sacrifice, one of the Diyanet's most time-consuming tasks is collecting donations for Muslims who lack the means to pay for the holiday meal, often those living in faraway countries. We—myself and the investigators following the case—are desperate to stop this from happening again in just a few hours, this rite we have witnessed, incredulous and . . . not disgusted, for it goes beyond revulsion. And the imam we've summoned is every bit as stunned. We are in urgent need of his wisdom, but the man remains speechless.

And here is that final sequence, which for me brought together atrocity and comprehension. We are in the cellar; a wavering brightness like firelight enters through the small, round window. In this flickering light, the walls are like those of a cave on which platonic shadows dance—the shadows of K. and his mother, the former crouching, the latter standing and pouring water from an earthenware jar over her son's head (we can hear it lapping in the basin where K. sits). She has resigned herself to her role: to accompany her child. To make sure that he'll smell sweetly when the angels breathe him in. She washes him and prays—her voice faintly echoing the ethereal prayer that reaches us from the garden, where the father leads the family in reciting the blessing. A close-up at waist level shows K. pushing his hair off his forehead so that we can look into his green eyes.

"If God truly did send the ram to Abraham, then, by our bombings and our disregard for the divine order, we have broken the pact, and we must pay for our carelessness. If God did not send the ram, then the present form of the ritual is still void, and our faith demands that we honor what was asked of us: an act of supreme love, the gift of what is most precious to us." The water from the jar washes away all tension from his face. "In mythology, that which is sacrificed is always of great value. If it is an animal, it must be in good health. If it is an object, it must be a treasure. If it is a child, it must be the favorite child. If a human group relies on these members to perpetuate itself, to sacrifice them is to forfeit its greatest chance at survival. Those who preceded me were not chosen at random. By sacrificing them, we know we are denying our family its most fertile elements and allowing it to perish. We accept this, and, in so doing, reveal the work of violence in this desecrated world: to deprive humanity of what should assure its permanence. You see: it all makes sense. You film, I confess. Like the candidates for martyrdom, like my cousin . . . each of us prepares his own death." He takes his mother's hand. "Do not blame my parents. You'll always be welcome here. And do not blame me. I don't matter anymore. Tonight, I am every man and every man is me. When I join my father and lie down before him, my neck bare, I will be all the sons of the earth. And believe me, their suffering will cause me more pain than the knife!"

Outside, the prayer grows more fervent, as though the family were reaching a state of trance.

We see a wide-angle shot of the garden and its occupants. Earlier, the air was misty because of the heat and the heavy rains. But the evening sky is clear, limpid: the garden is lit by flaming braziers planted in the ground. The sheep, now eight in number, pass beneath a tree.

The assembly of nearly fifty men and women stand with their backs to the camera. The angle and the distance from the subjects add to the sense of voyeurism. The prayer is drawing to an end. They're waiting for the one who must come, as the ram came to deliver humanity, or so we long believed. It's K. who comes. He stops at the edge of the garden. We see his legs and his bare feet. His parents, his uncles and aunts—his family—turn toward him. K.'s feet sink into the grass, into the earth, still humid from the morning rain. He is as naked as he was on his first day, his body as white as a cloud, as the sheep that have become his family's sons. The father contemplates his child as he walks among his own. Some hold out their hands. K. touches them lightly. His father welcomes him into his arms. And we watch, from a distance maintained by the camera, as the family slowly closes in around father and son. *"The knife must be perfectly cleaned and sharpened. Otherwise, the blade will tear at the flesh. And the victim will suffer longer than is necessary." "The sacrifice is an ordeal, then?" "Death is never a bed of roses. Even if it is desired. Even if it is justified . . ."*

6.

I spent a whole year with these images, watching and rewatching them, editing them, searching for the meaning in each shot, asking myself over and over how to put them to use. And all this time I continued, on the surface, to lead the life I had known before my encounter with K. Beating my fists against the glass walls of a coffin of solitude, not knowing how or with whom to share what I knew, finally turning to the only ones in a position to understand me—K.'s family, which became my own. Today is the Feast of the Sacrifice. At dawn, I went to the Anderlecht abattoir. I examined the sheep. Choosing one's animal is an art in itself. This sheep must not stand out from the eight others in the garden, just as my portrait must appear in its proper place next to K's. *Each of us prepares his own death*, he said, guiding me carefully toward his own. It's the Feast of the Sacrifice but now more than ever, a mournful holiday; seated beside K.'s father, facing YouTube, I tremble, appalled: a hooded specter, all in black, cuts the throat of a man in orange clothing. For love of God, Abraham/Ibrahim was prepared to offer Him his child. What do these butchers of the self-proclaimed Islamic State believe they are accomplishing in the name of Allah? Claiming to lead us back to the origins of Islam, they have nothing to offer God but their own hatred and blindness, and the martyred souls of the brothers they mistake for their worst enemies. They betray us all, and will not be forgiven. *We are hopelessly right*, says K.'s father. *And we so hopelessly long to be mistaken.* The force of our love has become a force of hatred. And hatred will never win the approval of the gods.

PART II

SUR(REALISM)

A FRACTION OF A SECOND

BY PAUL COLIZE

Palais de Justice

I pull up the collar of my raincoat and set out across place Poelaert under a driving rain. In spite of the downpour, I can't help stopping in the middle of the square.

It stands before me.

A hundred meters tall, the building looms over the Marolles district and seems to challenge wrongdoers.

By spending so much time within its walls, I've finally come to know some of its secrets.

For several years, it's been covered in scaffolding to the point of appearing disfigured. The renovation was started without a permit and is now at the center of an interminable legal battle. A rather surreal situation, considering that it's supposed to be the emblem of our justice system.

I'm soaked to the skin, but I stand still, facing my old enemy. This morning, it appears to me in a new light.

A gust of wind sweeps across the square.

My eyes blur with water.

There were three of them.

If it hadn't been for the screams coming from every direction, I might have found them amusing, with their long coats and carnival masks.

They burst into the supermarket a few minutes before closing, the Giant leading the way. He yelled out an order and they scattered. One made a break for the cash registers, the other ran down an aisle toward the back of the store. The Giant came right for us in slow, measured steps.

My father stayed calm, as if he knew what was about to happen. He pointed to the space beneath a shelf. "Under there!"

I obeyed. I got down on my knees and crawled in between the rows of bottles.

He smiled weakly at me. "It'll be okay—" His words were lost in a hail of gunfire. He disappeared from my field of vision, as if he'd been wrested away by some superhuman force.

The Giant drew nearer.

I was terrified. I could see only the bottom of his khaki coat, his boots, and the barrel of his gun. He leaned toward me.

For a fraction of a second, I glimpsed his eyes through the holes in his mask. An ineffable gleam shone in his pupils.

He raised the barrel of his gun.

More cries rang out as a series of shots sounded from the other end of the store. I hugged my rag doll to my chest and closed my eyes.

I climb the broad, imposing staircase.

When I come to the top, I make my way through the forest of columns and down one of the passages. I walk through the glass door into the main hall, so vast it's dizzying.

The month of May has brought the first tourists of the season. A group of them gathers around a guide whose voice echoes through the cavernous space.

I recognize Maarten's accent. He's from Anderlecht and speaks seven or eight languages. I've crossed paths with him many times in my comings and goings here; he knows the place like the back of his hand, has explored its every nook and cranny. When he's not in Brussels, he leads tours through the canals of Bruges, the Citadel of Namur, or the Waterloo battlefield.

He likes to throw numbers out at his audience, rolling his r's for effect. "This building covers a surface area of twenty-six-thousand square meters; it is more vast than the place Saint-Pierre in Rome. Unveiled in 1883, it was the largest edifice built in the world in the nineteenth century. It has 245 rooms including this one, the main hall. The dome measures 104 meters from the ground and spans over 3,600 square meters."

Each superlative elicits murmurs of admiration.

I check my watch. According to the plan, I have an hour left to wait. The longest one.

Later, after more cries, after more gunfire, after the blaring of sirens and the patter of footsteps, a policeman crouched down and lifted me out of my hiding place.

He was pale and his voice quavered. "Come on, little one."

I was still hugging my rag doll. The man wrapped a blanket around me and took me in his arms. I wanted to look back over my shoulder at the place where my father had been standing just before he disappeared, but he covered my eyes with his hand.

At the end of the aisle, a man was slumped on the ground, back to the wall. His T-shirt was bloodstained and he breathed with difficulty. A pinkish foam dribbled out of his mouth and nose.

I left with the policeman. An indescribable chaos reigned outside. Police cars were parked all around the building, revolving lights flashing. People were talking rapidly, screaming, crying. They said certain words over and over.

Poor little girl.

The mad killers.

The policeman fought his way through the crowd. I held onto his shoulder and buried my head in his neck.

On that night of September 27, 1985, I didn't know who these people were talking about. I didn't know who the Mad Killers of Brabant were. I had no idea that earlier in the evening they had murdered three people, and just now five more.

Including my father.

Apart from the cluster of tourists hanging on Maarten's every word, only a few people are milling about in the hall, some accompanied by their lawyers, their footsteps resounding on the marble floor, their black robes floating around them.

I head toward the tables lining the perimeter. They're equipped with antique lamps that cast a dull glow around the lawyers who pore over their dossiers.

I find a corner table, behind the newspaper stand. An elderly couple is seated at the table beside me. They lean toward each other and whisper, their hands covering their faces.

Standing beneath the dome, Maarten gesticulates like a Shakespearian actor. "Someone dubbed it the acropolis of Brussels. The building has ninety-four stone staircases, with 4,320 steps in total. The forty-one wooden staircases have 630 steps, and the twenty-nine new iron staircases have 991. A smaller replica of this courthouse was built in Lima, the capital of Peru."

I shiver.

In the days that followed, I was approached by many people. Most of them spoke gently to me, without ever raising their voices.

They asked me how I was doing. They wanted me to speak about my experience, to exorcize the images that haunted me. They said that it would do me good, that I would feel better afterward. Others wanted me to tell them about the Giant, to describe what I'd seen, to give them details.

I said nothing. Only my mother saw me cry a few silent tears. Cut off from everyone else, I thought of my father, of his last smile, his last words.

It'll be okay.

I'd hear the sound of the explosion and begin to tremble all over. Then came the fraction of a second.

When I wasn't reliving this nightmare, a happy memory returned to me, and I watched it like a film sequence played in slow motion. There were so many images of him to choose from, but my memory fixated on these brief moments of joy.

A few weeks before, we had gone to the cinema, the three of us. The film had made us laugh. My mother had hummed to herself. Papa was in a good mood. As we left the theater, he picked me up and set me on his shoulders.

It was the first time he'd ever done this. I had goose bumps. I was caught between a diffuse fear, like a fog, and a sense of invincibility. After a few minutes, I understood that there was no danger, and my fear faded away.

Perched on his shoulders, I was a princess. I looked in people's eyes with arrogance and condescension.

On Thursday, I attended the funeral.

At the moment when he disappeared into the grave, I dropped a white rose on his coffin and swore to him that I would find his murderers.

Six weeks later, on November 9, the Mad Killers of Brabant struck again. The Aalst massacre was the last attack, and the bloodiest. Eight people were slain.

In total, the assassins had left behind twenty-eight dead and forty wounded.

After this final massacre, they vanished.

I know he's there, somewhere in the bowels of the old building. I've studied his schedule. They woke him at six thirty this morning and brought him his personal effects. If his family hadn't provided him with fresh clothes, then he must have put on the ones he was wearing at the time of his arrest.

He got up, shaved, and combed his hair in order to look respectable, as his lawyer had surely advised him.

At seven thirty, they came to collect him. They handcuffed him, marched him out to the courtyard and into the Black Maria.

A police car led the way, siren blaring, and another brought up the rear. The convoy arrived at its destination around eight. The police vehicle entrance is at the back of the building, on rue de Wynants.

The officers escorted him out of the van and delivered him to the security guards, who led him to the jail cells in the basement. The eighty cells, spread over four floors, are often all occupied. Sometimes two or three detainees cohabitate for several hours in a space scarcely larger than a telephone booth.

The inmates are constantly agitated, especially if there are women in the neighboring cells. They call out to one another, send messages by tapping on the wall, provoke and insult each other, the atmosphere quickly breaking down into cacophony.

For him, this will not be the case. He will be put in solitary confinement. Perhaps he might eventually be able to earn a few basic privileges.

* * *

I woke up in an unfamiliar world, gray and cold.

In the space of a few days, I passed from childhood to adulthood. I never experienced that period they call "adolescence." My carefree years had come to an end one autumn evening, in the aisles of a supermarket. A fraction of a second was all it took for me to be propelled into another life.

My silence worried my mother.

She brought me to see psychoanalysts, healers of the soul, ecclesiastics, prophets. Some put forward a diagnosis. They spoke of the disturbed mourning process, of internalization, of selective mutism, of social anxiety, of God's will. According to them, my father's death had brought me to the edge of sanity.

No one understood that my father's death had made me sad, only sad, desperately sad.

My grades at school became mediocre. When I came home, I would neglect my homework and turn on the TV, switching from one channel to another, completely absorbed by the news.

Belgium was undergoing its worst years of violence, a decade that will long be remembered as a cursed moment in its history.

After the Heysel Stadium disaster, in which hooliganism caused the death of thirty-nine people and wounded more than six hundred, the curse continued to plague the kingdom.

In addition to the blind attacks perpetrated by my father's murderers, the country had seen a wave of bombings incited by the CCC, the Communist Combatant Cells. At the same time, it came to light that an extreme right-wing group was recruiting soldiers to prepare a coup d'état, and that several organs of law enforcement had been infiltrated by the CIA.

During the summer of 1991, a former minister was killed

in Liège, and there were rumors of a possible political conspiracy.

The horror would reach its height five years later, when the country, mute with disbelief, would learn of the kidnapping, torture, rape, and murder of several young girls by a deranged monster.

I stayed glued to the screen for hours. For nothing in the world would I let a political program or a headline escape my attention. I took notes, recorded programs. When I wasn't in front of the TV, I was listening to the radio. My allowance went to buying daily newspapers and magazines.

Gradually, I formed my convictions. I was sure that certain links existed between these incidents, and that I would be the one to uncover them.

When I celebrated my eighteenth birthday, the hunt began.

The couple rise to their feet.

It seems they've reached the semblance of an agreement. They hesitate, hold out their hands, hesitate again, take each other in their arms. Tears come to their eyes.

In the center of the hall, Maarten's show nears its end. The working-class Marolles was substantially demolished to make space for the Palais. Furious at the architect, the townsfolk opened a café at the corner of place des Renards and named it De Skieven Architek, "the crooked architect."

My phone vibrates in my pocket. I check the time.

If the roll is respected, the case will be heard in thirty-three minutes. Starting at nine o'clock, the defendants will go before the court one by one, in the order chosen by the presiding judge. Each case is given approximately eight minutes.

I close my eyes, count the seconds.

These preliminary hearings are closed to the public. In

general, they do not exceed the allotted time, but for one reason or another, a case might take up to two hours.

The knot in my throat tightens. I draw in a long breath and slowly let it out. I glance at my watch again. Barely three minutes have passed.

To my mother's surprise, my first decision as an adult was to bring forward a civil suit.

I knew that the process would allow me to meet the examining magistrate, to ask her permission to consult the dossier, and, if necessary, to suggest further investigative action.

She seemed disconcerted when I first stepped into her office, and only more so once she'd interviewed me to evaluate my knowledge of the case.

From that day forward, I set myself the task of going through the thousands of pages that made up the dossier. It was a tome, but my father's murderers remained at large.

Ten years after the incidents, the press continued to mention the case from time to time—whenever new evidence emerged, new witnesses came forth, or new suspects were apprehended.

Over the years, I had the occasion to explore the various hypotheses that were put forward.

The left-wing press accused the extreme right; this type of militant operation was its signature. Others were convinced that the robberies and random killings had been used as a smokescreen for the deliberate assassination of a few targets.

A third theory alluded to a Mafia racket. The fact that the majority of victims were attacked in supermarkets belonging to the same chain was cited as evidence. Finally, there were those who clung to the idea of the petty criminal motive.

As the months passed, a wave of vague speculations would arise, such as the one that cast the killers as shooting enthusiasts, thrill-seekers who had decided to leave their gun clubs and go after live targets, killing for amusement.

In ten years, several associations for victims' families were created, but they always grew frustrated with the investigation's lack of progress. I came to understand that I could only rely on myself.

I became a regular at the Palais de Justice and its many annexes. The people I met there didn't take me seriously at first, even if they were impressed by my confidence and my determination.

One day at a time, I built my network of allies: victims, police, witnesses, journalists, attorneys, judges. In two years, this turned me into a phenomenon. I was the girl who never gave up, the Joan of Arc of the case of the Mad Killers of Brabant. We forged lasting connections among ourselves.

I owe them all so much.

One of them in particular.

I stand and walk across the hall, waving to Maarten as I pass.

He smiles at me.

I glance at the wall clock and rush through the double doors, then down the large marble staircase that leads to the first basement. When I get to the bottom of the stairs, I quickly take in my surroundings.

A man is standing in the middle of the hallway, a telephone pressed to his ear. He speaks loudly, in a language I don't know, and paces like a caged lion. A sign points the way to the restrooms. I turn right and walk a few meters, then step into the ladies' room.

It's deserted. I lock myself in one of the stalls, take off my raincoat, and get undressed.

The first idea was to disguise myself as an officer of the

security forces. The service employs twenty-five thousand people throughout the country, including many women, and the rate of turnover is very high.

Another option was to try to pass for a cleaning woman.

After much consideration, I decided to dress as a lawyer instead. Dozens of members of the bar roam the hallways all day long. They hail from every corner of the country, and a good number of them have never met.

I emerge from the stall and look myself over in the mirror. Under different circumstances, I might find myself comical, with my long black robe and white band.

In September 2005, I stepped back and took stock of the twenty-year investigation. I knew the dossier inside out.

When a journalist wanted details on some aspect of the case, I was the first person he or she would contact. I had spoken on several radio programs, and had more than once been the guest on a television show.

I met regularly with the examining magistrate assigned to the case. We would talk at length, and I would pass on the information I had gathered since our last visit.

After two decades, my heart would still skip a beat when a new witness came forth following years of silence, or an unexplored hypothesis emerged.

In two decades, I've seen several suspects arrested.

Each time, the press was enthusiastic about the developments. Newspaper headlines were promising. Journalists referred to formal evidence, devastating witness statements, imminent confessions.

In two decades, I've seen just as many suspects released.

By September 2005 I had to face the facts: the investigation wasn't going anywhere.

Many of my close friends advised me to let it go, to turn the page, to finally think of myself, to begin to live.

If I hadn't met Jean-Pierre, I probably would have followed their advice.

I leave the restroom and keep moving down the corridor.

The entrance to the council chamber is some twenty meters away. In addition to the steel-reinforced door and employee badge reader, a sign discourages the curious: *Restricted area—authorized employees only.*

I climb a few stairs and approach the end of the corridor, passing two out-of-service elevators. A narrow hallway leads to a metal escalator; I walk down it, taking care not to step on the pleats of my robe.

I reach the second basement. The air is heavy.

To my left, a door opens into a control room that looks like a cemetery for discarded safe-deposit boxes. To my right, another long corridor disappears into darkness. Thick silver heating pipes run up the walls and along the ceiling; large blue and red circular valves jut out from all sides.

I lower my head and pick up my pace for another twenty meters, feeling as if I'm descending into the depths in a submarine. I make my way in the complete darkness. The farther I walk, the more unbearable the heat becomes.

I feel a switchboard on my left, and stop in front of a metal door. A strip of light filters through the gap, weakly illuminating my shoes.

I turn the handle, my heart beating quickly. The door is open. I go into the boiler room. The air is suffocating.

My phone vibrates, startling me. I check the screen: *Four minutes. I love you.*

* * *

I met Jean-Pierre in 2007. I had just turned thirty. He was thirty-two.

My romantic life had been uneventful for some time. I'd had a few relationships over the years, but none had passed the fateful six-month milestone.

He was a lawyer, fascinated by the Brabant case, in particular the lapses in the investigation, the errors committed by the police, the overlooked leads, and the witness statements forgotten at the bottom of a drawer.

I had heard about him. He had heard about me.

A journalist invited us to discuss the case, hoping to elicit our opinion on the recruitment of an FBI-trained profiler.

By analyzing the killers' mode of operation, the scene of the crime, and the clues left behind, the journalist aimed to put the police on the right track. She was committed to providing them with information as specific as the killers ages, marital and social statuses, living environments and psychological makeup.

Jean-Pierre and I agreed on one thing: whether a profiler, a psychic, a crime novelist, or a voodoo sorcerer, anyone who might be of use to the investigation was a welcome ally.

That same night, he asked me to have dinner with him. We fell passionately in love.

Jean-Pierre was a whiz with computers. He saw in the Internet a way to expand research beyond geographical confines. In 2008, he developed an online forum that would address the case and investigation.

In less than three months, over two hundred people had joined the community. Every aspect of the case was meticulously examined. The smallest detail was analyzed, dissected. Some nights, more than one hundred messages were posted.

In a few weeks' time, the site had become a meeting place for the most fervent truth-seekers.

Among the members, we counted witnesses, victims, police, mobsters, but also paranoiacs, compulsive liars, and the inevitable conspiracy theorists.

Jean-Pierre played his role of administrator to perfection. He facilitated the conversations with complete objectivity, privileging no particular theory, nor rejecting any of them.

As for me, I stayed in the shadows.

I studied the members' reactions. I noted the subjects on which each of them commented, the nature of their remarks, the names they cited, the frequency of their participation.

It was a Herculean task, but I was guided by the theory that a murderer always returns to the scene of the crime.

I had to suffer in silence for six years.

Finally, the day arrived.

I hike up my robe and climb the narrow ladder that leads to the control room.

We had only a short time to prepare the operation.

Appearances before the court must be made, at the latest, five days after a suspect is served with an arrest warrant. For four days, I have drifted through this labyrinth of corridors, staircases, galleries, and landings. And yet I can still hardly manage to find my bearings in this place.

Fortunately, we found a few people who were willing to help us: former police officers, some colleagues of Jean-Pierre's, my friend Maarten, and a reformed burglar who agreed to take up his tools again in order to open a few doors for us.

I arrive at the top of the stairs.

I position myself behind the door, my ear pressed to the metal.

Normally, there is the incessant sound of footsteps coming and going.

Normally.

He called himself Ghost.

It was the screen name he'd used to register, but he changed it regularly, as if he were afraid of being identified. He logged in frequently, but seldom commented. When he did, it was on subjects related to the killers' mode of operation and the weapons used.

I took a closer interest in him.

Occasionally, he seemed to find a perverse pleasure in refuting certain statements without offering explanations or alternate versions of the story. Rumors, inaccuracies, and hap-hazard guesses seemed to unnerve him. More than once, his comments became malicious.

At the beginning of the year, I visited the examining mag-istrate and spoke to her about this member. I suggested she try to identify the person who was hiding behind these different pseudonyms.

She accepted.

Afterward, she would not speak to me of the matter, responding to my questions only with an enigmatic phrase: "Things are taking their course."

Until five days ago.

Each court chamber has two entrances.

The first is a padded double door designated for magis-trates and defense lawyers. These men and women stand around in a vast hallway, waiting their turn. Jean-Pierre slipped in among them today.

The second entrance is situated at the back of the room.

It is assigned to defendants and prisoners. They reach it by way of a network of staircases and windowless corridors. From the jail cells, they have to walk some hundred meters to arrive at their destination. Handcuffed and surrounded by security officers, the journey takes one to two minutes, depending on the case.

Shortly before entering the chamber, they pass in front of the control room's double-locked door.

Only a few people have the key.

Now.

That afternoon, I received nearly fifty text messages and just as many phone calls.

The police had arrested a man. All the radio stations were talking about it. Journalists anticipated a confession.

I began to shake as if seized by a sudden fever. I didn't know if I should weep, scream, or rejoice. I called the examining magistrate. It took me an hour to finally reach her.

I asked her only one question: "Ghost?"

A few seconds went by. I knew that she had taken an oath of silence, but my question was deliberately vague.

"Yes."

I went on: "If it's him, I'll be able to recognize his face."

Her tone changed, became cold. "I know. You've already told me. Now, be reasonable and let us do our work. You were eight years old; that was almost thirty years ago, it lasted only a fraction of a second, and he was wearing a mask. What would your testimony be worth? Any lawyer would make a mockery of you."

I hung up.

I open the door at the moment the man passes by. He's escorted by two guards. They pause and glance at me disapprovingly, but seem more surprised than concerned.

The man is stoop-shouldered and walks with a slight limp. He's about to continue on his way, when the object in my hands attracts his attention.

He slows his step, his eyes fixing on the rag doll. He glances up at my face. Then he turns his head and keeps walking away.

I close my eyes.

The rest of the world will probably have to wait months, even years, to find out what role he played in the crimes, and whether he is guilty or innocent.

As for me, a fraction of a second will have been enough.

Author's note: This fictional story is based on actual events. I am grateful to Patricia Finné for the time and assistance she contributed to my research. She allowed me to paint the backdrop of this story and to add personal elements. Léon Finné, Patricia's father, was murdered by the Mad Killers of Brabant on Friday, September 27, 1985. For over thirty years, Patricia has left no stone unturned in the search for her father's assassins. A relentless, opinionated, and determined fighter, she has never stopped hoping that one day someone will come forward and bring the truth to light.

THE OTHER WAR
OF THE MAROLLES

BY SARA DOKE

The Marolles

I wake at dawn, at the foot of the statue of Peter Pan, curled up between Tinker Bell and Wendy, in the gardens of the Palais d'Egmont. There's no sign of what might have led me here. I'm not missing anything; my clothes are in perfect condition, not the slightest crease betraying this little nap on the grass. Dry and untouched by the morning dew.

But I remember nothing.

When I stand up, my legs feel a bit stiff. I leave place du Petit Sablon by the carriage gate, waving to the bronze guildsman atop the wrought-iron fence; flash a smile at Notre Dame de la Chappelle and her illustrious, eternal host; and find myself on rue Haute, trying to piece together my forgotten night.

Seated on the red spiral bench in the middle of place de l'Epée, my back to the glass elevator that ascends to the monstrous place Poelaert, my gaze lost in the silhouette of the Jacqmotte coffee emporium, I try to sort out my few impressions of last night. The day's first beer slowly warms in my hands. I wonder if the taste of alcohol can revive memories of past drinking bouts.

Where did I start out the evening? Which bartender poured my first golden faro? I could make the rounds, ask each one of them, but I'd rather not draw attention to the state of my beer-soaked brain cells. Above all, I don't want to show any signs of weakness. The beasts in this jungle have some serious fangs, and aren't afraid to use them.

I crawl from one watering hole to the next, passing the time before nightfall. The neighborhood is in the throes of gentrification. Place du Jeu de Balle, between rue des Renards and rue de la Rasière, has become the frontier of the working-class district. Near place de la Chapelle, the houses are elegant, the businesses flaunt their wealth, attracting tourists and bourgeois bohemians, and the architecture, from its Spanish gables to its historic cinemas, is picturesque. South of rue de la Rasière, poverty is still widespread; the Marollien, whatever his origin, recognizes his history and culture here, in the crumbling ruins of his all-but-forgotten childhood. The Bon Bec, the preferred sweet shop of the local *ketje*, now stands empty, its sign faded to a dirty gray that blends in with the sky. Only one small area, across from rue aux Laines and the remnants of the hospital for the poor, has somehow avoided bankruptcy and even sprouted several upscale boutiques. But on the main thoroughfare, the last thriving businesses are restaurants and bars, from the trendiest to the most working class. I stop in at a few of my locals, chat with the owners, order myself a beer, soup, steak tartare with chips.

Evening comes on, faster than I'd expected.

Outside, the darkness is deep, a bluish glow on the deserted cobblestones. The last bobo restaurants have lowered their metal curtains, and the secret, nocturnal Brussels begins to creep out from back alleys and underground passages.

Chic cafés and lounges give way to the taverns that fuel the city's lurid, indigenous nightlife. The sounds we make change; you might say we speak a different language altogether.

If you don't live in the Marolles, you're advised to stay

away after dark. Strange creatures prowl here, creatures you wouldn't want to come across in the moonlight. Not even the homeless of Saint-Pierre dare to venture far from their meager territory, and they're wise to keep their distance. Those who emerge from the forgotten dark corners of rue Haute, loping down the streets from Jeu de Balle to the sophisticated rue Blaes, are often not quite human.

Rat-people deformed by misery, cat-people with gleaming fangs, hyena-people who can kill with a single glance.

At midnight they start to come out, with the hope of finding an imprudent tourist, thrill-seeker, or rich girl looking to misbehave. They lead her to some back room, aroused by her fear, her curiosity, her repressed desire. They're careful to hide their spoils from the aging Lost Boys, who've swapped the child who wouldn't grow up for the *zwanze** of the prankster Pitje Scramouille. Their eyes are cruel, their limbs lithe. And not all who dare set foot on the cobblestones of the old town are welcome to their nocturnal dance.

The new masters of the Marolles rule with a vengeance: they've reduced the mermaids of place St. Catherine to sexual slavery, threatening to bring a drought on the land; raised taxes on the junk vendors' stalls at the Jeu de Balle flea market; forced the owners of our bars to hand over the better part of their profits. Everyone must take an oath of allegiance. Some refuse, but the lords of this new feudalism have a well-trained army at their command, ruthless in its cruelty. Their games are lethal, their chief ferocious; Marolliens are powerless under his control. So much has changed since the fall of Peter Pan, whose joyful anarchy was hospitable to all.

The bric-a-brac dealers have yet to set up on the outskirts

---

* *A typical* bruxellois *spirit of mockery, derision, and self-deprecating humor.*

of the market. Between midnight and four o'clock in the morning, the streets belong only to predators and forgotten ghosts.

And so I wander from bar to bar, nod at familiar faces, exchange a joke with the regulars, a handshake with the doormen who pretend to be assuring the security of all. Mich has found himself a pretty redhead and is smugly persuading her to finish the night in his bed. Manu mocks him, trying to throw him off his game. The lady resists, wide-eyed, in awe of this foreign world and its exotic dangers. Mich won't speak to her of the bloodthirsty creatures who would hunt her if he left her alone on these streets. He prefers to lavish her with little falsehoods that make him sound like a great adventurer of the night. She doesn't see the two switchblades her gallant one-night stand is packing; if she looks any closer, she's bound to get scared. I know them so well—Mich, Manu, Scal—their stories of wild nights in bars, of concerts and parties that exist nowhere but here.

I'd been sure they would offer me a clue, some anecdote to jog my memory. But no one utters a word. Perhaps I didn't meet up with them last night, after all.

I move on to another place, hoping someone will notice me lingering at the bar, remember seeing me last night with the girl I've forgotten, help me to grasp onto my slippery memory.

A tap dancer with a clear and joyful voice comes traipsing up rue des Capucins, humming, swinging hands with a child. As they draw nearer, I recognize Mickey la Bourgogne and Little Ka. Her too-big eyes, her too-red mouth arouse my suspicions. She has a violently hungry look that's better not to acknowledge. She smiles at me, ravenous. They're making their way back from the Bazaar, which closes its doors promptly at midnight.

"Well, Steph, are you recovering from your little tryst?" Ka asks me.

I look at her, surprised, fumbling for an appropriate response, not wanting to say too much, show too much vulnerability. "After a night like that, it's better to forget everything."

"Your mermaid would be shocked if she could hear you."

Mermaid?! Where would I have met a mermaid? They're usually too scared of poachers to come around here.

"Hey, where did we part ways yesterday? I'm drawing a blank."

Mickey la Bourgogne stops hopping around for a moment and smiles. "With all that you knocked back, that doesn't surprise me. We left each other at la Porte Noire, you were going to take her to l'Arrosoir. You'd picked her up at la Fleur en Papier Doré."

"What was I thinking, bringing her to l'Arrosoir? That's no bar for a mermaid."

"She wanted to see the slums," Ka replies, her full, red lips smiling wolflike.

"You charmed her with your ghost stories," adds Mickey, jeering.

Oh God! I can be so stupid when I'm trying to impress a woman. L'Arrosoir is not the most well-reputed café this side of the Marolles, either. Its patrons are boorish, known for their macabre sense of humor.

"We tried to talk you out of it. Big Catherine even insisted. But your mermaid wouldn't be bossed around and you were already too wasted to refuse her."

I know that gleam in Mickey's eye; he's mocking me and my wayward memory.

Ka bursts into fiendish laughter. "You don't remember *anything*?"

"Nothing. I woke up at Peter Pan's feet, alone, unhurt, my pockets full, my memory blank. And no mermaid in sight."

"We told you yesterday," Mickey presses, "the Lost Boys took back l'Arrosoir. It's definitely not a bar to bring a lady to anymore."

"I don't even know what happened to her."

"You're going to have to retrace all your steps, Stepheke," says Little Ka. "Make sure nothing happened to her."

I agree, nodding my head without letting her see the fear in my eyes.

I walk from rue Haute to rue des Alexiens, slowly making my way down to la Fleur, the last neighborhood bar to keep its old-world charm. Tourists are rarely seen there. They prefer la Becasse, Au Bon Vieux Temps, or l'Imaige Nostre-Dame, hideously remodeled by investors.

The interior of la Fleur is cluttered with antiques, its walls decorated with relics of various eras, all jumbled together, clashing: surrealist illustrations and maps of old Brussels hang side by side.

There's hardly anyone here tonight, but the owner gives me a warm welcome. I sit near the bar, order a half-and-half instead of another beer; the mixture of faro and lambic goes right to my head. So much for sticking to one type of booze. Mireille, always the mother hen with her customers, walks over and sits beside me.

"What's going on with you? You rarely come by like this, two nights in a row." Her Anderlecht accent always has a soothing effect on me.

"Well, I'm having a hard time remembering what happened last night." I know I can trust Mireille. She considers me one of her own, would never do me any harm, not even to please the new rulers of the territory. We're from the other side of the boulevard, she and I. They don't have the same hold on us.

"She was a pretty one, the mermaid you brought here. That's all I can say about that, but I doubt she's a man-eater. What'd you do with her?"

"That's just it, I wish I could remember."

Mireille laughs brazenly, gives me a big slap on the shoulder. "I've never known you to be a forgetful drunk, Stephy. What happened to you?"

"I'm trying to remember. According to Mickey la Bourgogne and Ka, I went by la Porte Noire after I left your place, then took the mermaid to l'Arrosoir—to impress her in that cloud of testosterone, I guess."

"What a silly idea! That doesn't seem like you. You must have a serious crush, my boy!"

"I must. Well, I'll have to keep trying to jog my memory."

"If the Lost Boys didn't steal it from you."

"They can do that?"

"With Pitje in power, fairies and boys can do whatever they please. There are no more taboos."

"I thought it might've been the Rats, or maybe the Hyenas."

"They're still loyal to their chief; they don't come near rue Haute anymore. The Marolles are no longer safe, my little Stepheke."

I finish my drink, hug Mireille, and walk back up the street toward la Porte Noire, the favorite haunt of role-players and goths.

The door is indeed black, the stone staircase still poorly lit, and the basement room looks the same, with its long tables and benches. Pierrot le Zinc is at the bar—standing in front of it, not behind—his customary glass of whiskey in hand, and I don't know how many others under his belt. He calls out and offers me a drink. I climb up onto a stool. I stick to white wine; I'll avoid beer for the rest of the night.

I exchange a few jokes over the counter with Pierrot, wait for him to ask me about last night. He doesn't, preferring to tell me all about the novel he's just finished reading, to bore me with gossip about the regulars at his bar on the other side of town.

I sip my wine and remain silent, hoping he'll take the hint. He looks about ready to strangle me when he catches on, his face suddenly breaking into a grin.

"Ah, so you dreamed away your memories. I was expecting you to come in here like some *dikkenek** with your mermaid story."

"I can't even remember what she looks like! Let alone where I left her."

"She wasn't in your bed this morning? Or you in hers?"

"No, I woke up on the palace lawn."

"You can't hold your beer anymore, brother Steph. Are you getting old on me?"

"Mickey la Bourgogne and Little Ka say I brought my mermaid to l'Arrosoir to satisfy her curiosity."

"Bad idea, l'Arrosoir. You want me to come with you?"

"Well, sure, but I don't want to be a pain."

"Why not? I feel like throwing some punches tonight."

You can always count on Pierrot to be up for an adventure, with his flat cap pulled tight over his shaved head, frayed leather jacket on his Irish longshoreman's shoulders, his shoes well-shined. He abandons his glass of Jameson and I swig the rest of my wine.

We walk back up toward Jeu de Balle, passing by rue du

* *Someone who acts pretentious (literally, "fat-neck").*

Saint-Esprit and its youth hostel, then along rue de la Chapelle until we reach rue Haute. We turn the corner past the
Samaritaine theater and find ourselves at the blue and orange
door of Pitje's bar.

Inside, the Lost Boys take up the tables near the bar; apart
from them, a group of punks huddle together around their
cheap pilsner. Their favorite waitress, the petite one who
sometimes offered them a house-brewed beer along with her
smile, stopped working here after the change of hands. Vince
le Rouge brought them off the streets, found them shelter,
clothes, and shoes. Now he lovingly takes them out drinking,
but manages to keep them from getting too sloshed.

Sam the Rascal, with his odd air of an English cabbie, is
working the bar tonight. Pierrot greets him coldly, quickly scans
the room, and moves up close to the bar. We order calmly,
nothing too strong; we have to keep our wits about us.

The Lost Boys watch us with their wild eyes. Pitje le Scramouille is nowhere to be seen. Leaving the back room, we're
surprised to see Till, a glass of jenever in hand. He joins us at
the bar. His dialect has improved unusually quickly since he
left his native Flanders for the capital.

"I didn't really think we'd see you back around here so
soon, Stephy!" he shouts at me, rolling his r's. "You looking
for your mermaid?"

"I suppose."

"Bad idea. Tchantchès doesn't like to share."

"That *liégois* has no business in our Marolles!"

"Since Pitje took him in, he's like me, your lord and master."
Pierrot laughs softly.

"Nowhere else do we mix so freely. Brussels is nothing but
zinneke!* Till Ulenspiegel of Flanders, Tchantchès of Liège,

---

* *Diminutive of Zenne, a name given to bastard dogs and* bruxellois.

and Pitje le Scramouille: that's quite a few pranksters for one bordello."

"Careful what you say, Zinc, the boys might be lost but they aren't deaf or blind and you're on their turf," Till hisses.

"We've just as much a right to be here as any of these *ketjes*. I've worn out the seat of my pants on the benches of every bar in this town!"

Till stifles a malicious laugh. "You had what none of them has ever known, Stephy. Parents. A mother and a father who didn't abandon you."

"They fell from the roofs of Lycée Dachsbeck in the last police raid."

"But you knew them. And you remember."

Pierrot rests his hand on my shoulder to keep me from losing my calm. It's better not to challenge the tricksters here, in their lair, in front of their henchman. But my hands curl into fists. I lost more than just memories, and now a mermaid has disappeared because of me. They rarely venture far from place du Marché aux Poissons, for fear of the horrors that await them here.

"Where did Tchantchès bring my mermaid? What does he want with her?"

"You should be happy he didn't leave her to the boys. He brought her to the baths. And you don't have permission to go down rue Blaes."

I'm seething inside. This prohibition is absurd, but I'm at least partially responsible. Oh, I can take rue des Renards, or even rue des Tanneurs—the baths are on rue du Chevreuil, for that matter—but only in the daytime. At night, rue des Brokelots and place du Jeu de Balle are off-limits to me. It all goes back to a depressing story of a brawl in a pub with some shady characters. But it's the pirates' territory, and many of us are forbidden to go there at night. Even the Lost Boys avoid it after dark. Only the three tricksters have permission to come and go as they please, and they had to use all their force to get it.

So Tchantchès found the ideal spot to hide my mermaid. I don't know who will be able to help me now.

In the time of the one who wouldn't grow up, the rat-, cat-, and hyena-people united under their chief, regularly accepted visitors to their territory if the reason was good, the beer stout, and the discretion infallible. Today, their vigilance is unrelenting. It's almost impossible to outwit them.

Till moves away from the bar, leaving me to my thoughts. Pierrot's hand still rests on my shoulder, comforting me. I know I can always count on him for support. I don't want to worry him about my memory, but I need his help to come up with a plan to save my lady.

The mermaid whose face I've forgotten might be safe in the Brussels baths, since they've stopped chlorinating the water, but I wouldn't give her—or her scales—much of a chance in Tchantchès's hands. The trickster of Liège has particularly violent sexual habits.

But first I have to let my anger subside a little, to grab hold of the memories that are still drifting around l'Arrosoir. Somehow, the walls of this place seem to preserve the memory of everything that happens here, of all those who pass through. I try to match my breath to the rhythm of the music and the clinking glasses. I keep my head lowered while taking in the room around me: the long bar, the worn leatherette benches sagging under the weight of one too many patrons, the mirrors reflecting a panoply of images and colors, the yellow door that leads to the back room reserved for the master of the house, the red door that leads upstairs.

Gradually, as my breath becomes easier, memories start to surface: the mermaid's little cries of delight at the premonition of violence that seeps from the walls; her insistence on visiting the upper floors, and how impatient she is to find the cursed room; her fervent sighs as she discovers the stench of the tortured cadaver that haunts the house; her eyes lighting up as she counts the rusty nails in the framework; how she jumps in surprise at the sight of the ghost-dog running past; my suspicions that force me to lead her back downstairs despite the excitement rising through my body, filling me with desire; the tricksters' laughter as we descend the staircase; this mermaid who reeks of pheromones; Pitje, Till, and Tchantchès who watch me with contempt, who look her up and down, grinning.

I try to convince my mermaid to let me take her somewhere else, to end our night in a quieter, less crowded place. But all the attention she's getting only fans her flames. She doesn't sense the danger. Her feral smile reveals the sharp teeth of an aquatic predator, but she acts the lady, bats her eyelashes, gliding from one man to another, from one boy to another. She wants to play. It wouldn't take much for her to start singing. She refuses to listen to me. I take her by the elbow and try to guide her toward the door. She resists, orders a Screaming Orgasm from Sam the Rascal, and pouts at me, saying that she wants to make the most of this, to let these admiring gazes wash over her, to feel the eyes of the three powerful tricksters on her pale, green-speckled skin.

Vince le Rouge's boys try to come to my rescue, but he holds them back. Till and Tchantchès laugh at my boldness. Slowly, without rushing her, I steer my mermaid away from the bar, toward the street and the night that awaits us behind the immense door. But she uses all her charms to resist me. Pitje approaches her, slowly runs the tips of his fingers over her transparent skin, adorning it with finely braided plant motifs in the art nouveau style, to the delight of this lady of the sea. I avert my eyes, do my best to hide my anger—and yes, my fear—but the look in my eyes, the tension in my body give me away. It's the mermaid's turn to laugh at me. She teases me for worrying, tries to wear down my resolve with little caresses. The lure of so many glances, of so much feverish, unsatisfied desire, is even more powerful than my need to protect her. She glides toward the bar, where the *zwanze* flows as freely as the booze. That's when I lose her completely.

I make my way over to the bar, try to convince Pitje to let her leave with me, appealing to our shared memories, our common struggles. He responds only with a cruel laugh.

The Lost Boys stand up and close in on me, trying to pull me away. Fortunately for me, Vince le Rouge intervenes, sending his protégés over to help me. They carry me away from this den of shadows, but not before Till slips a glass of beer into my hand; it's as amber as my lady is blond. Without thinking, I drink it down in one gulp.

So that's how I lost my memories! How Vince le Rouge and his men came to lay me down at Pan's feet. Hoping, per-haps, that he would be wakened by my suffering. That he would finally be able to escape the gardens where the three pranksters imprisoned him.

As the events come back to me, my mind is flooded with thoughts, with unfamiliar sensations; all at once, I know that a part of my being is inhabited by the conscience of another. *I wonder if it's him. If he can help me. If I might somehow, in the smallest way, be of help to him.*

Slowly, I regain my footing in reality. The presence of Pier-rot at my side becomes palpable, and I sense the invisible rope of trust that binds us. I sigh. It takes some effort not to let my shoulders drop, to keep my head held high. I force myself to sit up straight on my stool.

I can hear the ghost of the hanged man moaning through the staircase. Does he, too, sense the presence of the exile? Is he trying to communicate? To wake me?

The tension in the room is thick. Everyone is looking back and forth between me, Vince le Rouge, and Till, the only lord among us, wondering how we will react.

I grab Pierrot by the arm, lean on the invisible rope that binds us, and signal to him that we have to leave, to go somewhere else and talk it over. Perhaps we can round up some allies to help us free my spellbound mermaid. But first—right now—we have to leave this den of shadows.

In the end, I lead him toward the Palais d'Egmont; something draws me back to the place where I regained consciousness. Is it him, in my head? No matter, the calm of the park will help me recover from the chaos of the bar.

Pierrot asks no questions, is content to support me in silence. His presence and his strength reassure me; even in the face of my distress, he is calm. When I stumble, he holds me up with a swift movement of his arm. I gradually find my center, and my breath becomes slower, deeper.

When we arrive at the statue of Pan, I let go of Pierrot's arm and lower myself carefully onto the grass, resting my head on the pedestal. For an instant, I close my eyes. The stone quivers beneath my head, the ground beneath my body; it trembles softly, almost like a caress. I let go completely, abandon myself to the sensation. At the edge of consciousness, I can see Pierrot crouching down beside me. He doesn't touch me, but I know in my bones that he'll stay—no matter what happens.

I came back. I brought you my memories, they won't disappear again. Did you wait for me? Where are you? I can feel your spirit in me, all around me. Where are you?

I feel a shudder run through my entire being. Is that even possible? My body becomes tense. Pierrot's distant voice soothes me. The trembling intensifies, and suddenly it's as if I'm trapped in a vibrating cocoon. My bones pulse, about to break. The clamor of an explosion bores into my eardrums. Scraps of metal and dust fly everywhere. I feel a shock against my chest, my stomach. A twisting pain. I open my eyes.

Pierrot helps me to my feet, dusts off my jacket with his hands. At the same time, he manages to hold me up, to support me when my legs give way. His breath warms my face; I feel the strength coming back into my limbs.

The sound of panpipes turns our heads, and we see the exile standing there, escaped from his bronze prison. Tinker Bell flutters around his crown of auburn curls. Wendy is holding a rabbit, a squirrel perched on her shoulder.

Pierrot and I both nearly fall backward. The boy who wouldn't grow up laughs with unrestrained joy. The tiny fairy has just covered us with a scintillating dust. The wise young girl approaches, intent on comforting us. Pierrot and I exchange a bewildered glance, then break into raucous laughter, stumbling around.

As we finally collapse side by side, out of breath, I try to get my thoughts in order. I hiccup, I stammer. Peter leaps into the air, turns around, shakes himself off like a young fawn.

"How?" I can't keep myself from asking.

"What does it matter?" he laughs. "We have a mermaid to save, a neighborhood to take back, tricksters to chase off! Comrades, let the adventure begin!"

"But . . . but, how?" I feel profoundly awkward, ridiculous.

Am I stupid? What did I think? That the prince of Never Never Land was going to fret over his strategy? The size of his army? That he'd want to take time to reflect?

"There aren't enough of us," I say. "We can't take back the Marolles like this! Don't forget who you're dealing with!" I shout, eyes brimming with tears of laughter and disbelief.

"Not for long! All the statues are waking: Manneken Pis is racing up rue des Grandes Carmes, his little sister Jeanneke, rue des Bouchers; Madame Chapeau is taking rue de la Roue, the Water Carrier has already crossed la Barrière de Saint-Gilles with her pails across her back . . . Children, peasants, nobles, guildsmen, animals—they're leaping down from their pedestals, from their horses! They're racing up rue des Grandes Carmes, up rue des Bouchers! They're coming from Saint-Gilles, from Notre Dame du Sablon, from Jeu de Balle, from everywhere! So we're only five now, but just wait, by the time we get to la Chapelle, we'll be thousands strong. All of Brussels will come to our call, even the *meiboom* will pull up its roots and join in the march. The bars and the cafés are emptying, the brasseries too! And all along the Senne, that river that will one day rise again, *pei* and *mei*, *ketje* and *keeke*, *bomma, bompa,* and *zinne*ke call out to each other in solidarity. *Walloons, flamoutches, bruxellois*—they're all marching to meet us. Don't you feel our city coming to life?"

Oh yes, I do. I feel it. *Pan!* Let's bring them to their knees.

THE OTHER HALF OF A LIFE

BY AYERDHAL

Gare Centrale

T his isn't any ordinary train. It's a train you catch on the fly, when you have time to spend hours staring into the eyes of cows. It never travels faster than 120 kilometers an hour, a speed it only reaches twice—when passing fields of beets and potatoes along a stretch where the land is farmed rather than lived on. (There isn't much to life there, anyway, except for the winds that change with the seasons and the rains they sweep along with them.) Then come more brick houses, bell towers, train stations, and bridges that straddle the lazy canals and rough roads. The cars rattle over switches, the wheels screeching against the rails; a few passengers step off and many more rush to board, in greater numbers as the train approaches a city, especially from Antwerp onward.

Jeroen boards a few stops after Rotterdam. A young woman is seated alone in a four-seat compartment, facing against the direction of the train, a tablet asleep on the table in front of her. He greets her in Dutch with a Flemish accent and asks if she'd mind if he sat across from her. She responds in English, apologizing for not being able to speak Dutch very well. She understands it but can't speak it, finds the sentence structure confusing. Jeroen assures her, in English, that this doesn't bother him in the least. She tilts her head to the side and her eyes brighten.

"French works for me too," she says.

Jeroen greets this remark with an oblique smile. "My accent?"

She corrects him: "Your intonations. Typically Francophone. I can't hear them in Flemish, I haven't had enough practice. But in English, they jump right out at me."

"Never could get rid of them. But I'm not Francophone, not really. I grew up speaking both languages, Flemish at home, French at school—and *brusseleir* in the bars, of course."

His smug way of letting her know he's from Brussels. She smiles tautly, out of politeness.

"Sun Hee," she introduces herself.

"Jeroen . . . or Jérôme. I never really had a chance to decide."

"Well then, I'll call you Yerroon." She corrects herself: "Jeroen. How is my pronunciation?"

"It was fine the first time."

"That's nice of you, but I know my limits."

"I was being sincere."

Her eyes tell him that she doubts it; she looks out the window for a moment before turning to face Jeroen again.

"What does your name mean?"

Jeroen grimaces, embarrassed. "Etymologically, it means *sacred name.*"

She bursts out laughing, but immediately stops herself. "Excuse me. I'm in no position to mock you. In Korean, Sun Hee can mean a lot of different things, but my parents meant it in the sense of *fairy of hope.*"

"That's very poetic."

"It's not an easy name to carry—and I'll spare you the other interpretations."

The car is nearly empty, the countryside a vast open space. A vaguely overcast sky hangs above tall white turbines, their blades turning slowly. To ward off boredom, Jeroen has only his e-book reader in his backpack on the seat beside him; Sun Hee, the tablet in front of her still turned off. Conversation is an alternative they attempt as one might explore an old-fashioned amusement park. It's a haphazard stroll, a game without stakes, a momentary excursion. The questions are innocent; the responses, superficial, do not prompt further questions, are simply stated and acknowledged. Jokes serve as punctuation, reflected glances out the window as line breaks, cues to change the subject.

Sun Hee is from Busan, the second largest city in South Korea, and grew up in a neighborhood where Russian was spoken almost as much as Korean. She started her studies in biology before focusing on molecular genetics, and received a scholarship that allowed her to continue her university work in Europe.

"And you chose Brussels?"

"Brussels chose me. A unit of Erasmus Hospital recruited me to join a project with a laboratory in Den Hague."

"A private lab?"

She nods and turns her gaze toward the window.

Jeroen, for his part, is *bruxellois* as far back as his family can remember. He's been procrastinating at university, switching from one concentration to another within the department he finds crudely named "social sciences." Everything interests him, nothing fascinates him. He piles up unfinished dissertations. He accumulates multiple undefended master's.

"You don't have a project?"

"Not exactly. For the moment, let's say that I'm learning and trying to understand. I'm sure I'll find something to do with it later."

The countryside passes by, the stations grow closer and

closer together, the car gradually filling with passengers. No one asks Jeroen to move his backpack, or dares sit beside Sun Hee. It's wrong to interrupt young people sharing the details of their lives with the curiosity of children, especially when there's a certain tenderness about their shy complicity. They've created a bubble around themselves that the slightest intrusion would burst. They would become simple strangers again. They will, of course, as soon as they step off the train—that's in the nature of these ephemeral encounters—but no one feels the right to deprive them of this almost-intimacy.

Already, they look at each other differently. They *see* each other. Their gazes meet every so often through the reflection in the window, and they begin to smile at this code they've established in order to maintain their distance. She's the one who finally looks away after refusing to answer a question.

"I never talk about the studies I participate in. What happens in Brussels or in Den Hague stays in the labs."

"Military secrets?"

"Commercial ones, actually, but that's not the problem. You'd have to be a specialist to understand, and we don't make a mystery of our work. We can't, for that matter, if we want to receive outside funding." She lowers her voice. "What do you think of GMOs?"

Jeroen remains speechless for a moment too long. She smiles at him sadly.

"Now you know why I avoid saying that I work on the development of genetically modified organisms. People don't understand. Not the reasons, the causes, or the consequences, let alone what drives me—and *that* I don't even discuss with my colleagues. We all have secrets. This is mine, and I keep it so well that not even my thesis director has the slightest clue."

"You're talking about your motivations?"

"Yes, Jeroen. I can't hide what I do . . . That would be absurd. But I don't want to have to explain my reasons."

"I won't ask you to."

"I wouldn't answer you."

Sun Hee's eyes remain fixed on Jeroen's. She no longer needs or perhaps no longer wants to be distracted by the landscape, now increasingly urban, passing by in the window. The train is approaching Brussels. All that's left is to say whatever will allow them to go their separate ways, satisfied to have exchanged a little more than platitudes, to have confided what cannot be shared except between strangers, with the exhilarating certainty that this will have no tomorrow and no consequences. They've already tacitly agreed not to exchange phone numbers, not to try to see each other again, to accept that they might regret this in a few hours or days—when it will be too late—precisely because they don't want to look back. To do so would be to forfeit the freedom they've granted themselves.

Jeroen lets everything out at once: "I wasn't trying to dodge your question so much as to articulate an honest response. For me, GMOs bring to mind a catastrophic time bomb whose fuse is constantly being shortened by corporations for the sole purpose of lining their shareholders' pockets. If you think you can convince me that reality isn't as bleak as I see it, I'm listening."

He expects her to clam up; instead, she sighs.

"My area of expertise is genetic engineering, not forecasting. Trust me, we already know more than enough to address questions whose answers are not at all categorical or definitive. In the matter of research, everything is progress. Every mistake, every impasse, every recorded failure contributes to the evolution of knowledge. At the risk of sounding cynical, I would add that so too does every catastrophe, and in a sense it's all growing increasingly removed from the Darwinian definition of adaptation."

Jeroen takes a moment to reflect. He has the feeling that Sun Hee has just distilled for him a part of the secret she never shares with anyone.

"So selection is becoming less and less natural, is that it?"

"By forcing ourselves to control it, we've entered the era of a synthetic evolution, which we must adjust to at a rate that is constantly accelerating. If, paradoxically, this is a consequence of evolution, it demands that we adapt more rapidly than any species has ever had to do. In terms of cost—and I'm not talking about money so much as research time—it's becoming less expensive to modify the human population to adapt to the conditions it imposes than to maintain a viable ecosystem for us to live in today. But we're not ready for that investment. Our reasoning is not only short-term, it's illogical."

Jeroen is staggered. "You're talking about genetically modifying human beings?"

"Does that shock you?"

"You might say that, yes."

"And yet we've been doing just that for a long time, if only with pesticides, antibiotics, polluting agents, vaccines, and many other deliberately harmful vectors."

"And GMOs."

"That's a chapter in the dissertation my thesis director doesn't see coming."

Jeroen strokes his chin. "Didn't you say that you wouldn't talk about it?"

"I only said I wouldn't answer questions concerning my

motivations." There is more than a hint of mischief in Sun Hee's smile. "My work raises ethical issues that are impossible to resolve within an ethical framework. And this is the fundamental dilemma that genetic engineering presents. Knowledge cannot be unknown, and it's unrealistic to think that we can limit it to rational use, because it generates its own reasons."

"Okay . . . and what do you do work on, exactly?"

"Chimeras."

Described in a few simple terms, Sun Hee's chimeras turn out to be rather unexciting and much less fantastical than those envisioned by Jeroen. To his travel companion's surprise, he doesn't seem to take offense. Nothing truly shocks him anymore, he who has over the past year calmly watched his world expand beyond the confines of rationality. Sun Hee plays the sorcerer's apprentice, mixing genes to create improbable organisms. And so? Jeroen's world tipped over into improbability on the day a certified letter informed him that he was the sole inheritor of an abandoned house in the middle of Uccle. He, a drifting, penniless student who was living in a tiny basement room between the Gare du Midi and the Parvis de Saint-Gilles, found himself the owner of a crooked little farmhouse that had been in use through the middle of the twentieth century, and a small, enclosed plot of scrubland. A reversal of fortune, in a sense, fortune with its inevitable hidden face, and the madness that lurks in its crevices, waiting for the moment to come forth and thrive.

Sun Hee has not fully revealed her secret, but she's given Jeroen enough material to imagine what it might be. He can trust her with his. He feels the need to tell her before their paths diverge. Not knowing how to begin, he asks: "You want to hear about something even more demented than your genetic chimeras?"

She studies him carefully. "You'll have to be brief. I get off at Gare Centrale."

"Me too." Reading the suspicion on her face, he quickly adds, "And I have no intention of following you out of the station to finish my story."

She relaxes. "Well then, I'm listening."

Jeroen takes a long breath and begins: "I live in a house that's bigger than the space it occupies. I have no idea how many rooms it contains or how they're laid out. It seems to me that that they're constantly being rearranged—"

"You're right, that *is* demented." She grins skeptically, a little peeved.

"Not all that much."

"In books, perhaps, Jeroen, but not in real life."

Jeroen knows he should quit now. He just doesn't want to. "I stopped placing boundaries on reality after I moved into this house. Knowing that what I'm telling you can be explained away by psychiatry doesn't keep me from experiencing it as completely tangible."

Sun Hee raises her eyebrows. "But that doesn't make it real."

"If you didn't modify the genes of different organisms, would your chimeras even have a chance to exist?"

She contemplates the question for a long moment before responding: "Infinitesimal. What are you getting at?"

"You construct a reality that wouldn't exist without your manipulation. Perhaps my brain is doing the same thing. I live in a house that seems infinite, I talk with ghosts, and my only true friend is a five-hundred-year-old fictional character."

For the first time, Jeroen has told someone everything. He expects nothing to come of it. So he turns toward the window to put an end to the conversation, but meets Sun Hee's reflection once again. She must have turned her head at the same moment. He makes a face, shrugs his shoulders. She imitates him. They smile halfheartedly.

The train slows down and clatters over the switches. Sun Hee stands to take her small suitcase down from the overhead compartment, stuffs her tablet inside, throws on a cardigan. The journey is over; the spell has been broken. All that's left is to exchange a polite goodbye.

Sun Hee surprises Jeroen: "What is your friend's name?"

"Till Ulenspiegel."

"I don't know of him, but I'm going to do some research."

"Research?" Jeroen is bewildered, but since she nods her head, he adds: "In French, his name is Till l'Espiègle—*the merry trickster*. You really take me seriously?"

The train comes to a stop.

"I take your analogies seriously."

She starts moving down the aisle. Jeroen grabs his bag and follows her.

"My analogies?"

She turns around and looks at him strangely. "Your house is just as immeasurable as my field of research. Chimeras or ghosts, the reality we construct depends on how we change the one we live in. Now I just have to find *my* trickster, Jeroen. For that and for your company, I thank you."

She turns back around, leaving Jeroen to his astonishment, and slips into the stream of passengers exiting the train car. He lets two people move past him, then steps down onto the platform, scans the crowd from right to left, finds her in front of him. She had stepped aside to wait.

"I'm taking the metro, line 5," she says. "I guess you have to take the tram."

"The 92."

"Not the same exit."

"No."

They're equally embarrassed.

"I . . ." he begins.

She stops him, shaking her head. "I'm happy to have met you. I thank you again, Jeroen, and I hope you find your way." She nods at the escalator a few meters to her right. "Mine leaves you here."

He does his best to smile knowingly. "May the force be with you, Sun Hee. Light or dark, no matter, since you make your own midi-chlorians."

She acknowledges the joke with a smile, rises up on her tiptoes, and quickly kisses him on the cheek before hurrying toward the escalator. He watches her for a moment, hoping she might turn around, then gives up and walks toward the staircase nearest his exit, the scent of cinnamon on his skin. Beneath the cinnamon, he also detects clove, nutmeg, and a hint of pepper. Jeroen imagines he'll remember this each time he seasons certain dishes.

As he reaches the staircase, he feels an emptiness in his chest, a pang of regret foretelling many more that will accompany those same dishes. An urgency. He reaches for the handrail, trembling, and grips it firmly to brace himself against the irrational feelings that rush over him; he laughs at himself, takes a deep breath, and leaps with all his strength up the stairs, four at a time, struggling not to bump into anyone, excusing himself when necessary. He is too young to be haunted by regrets.

* * *

Jeroen doesn't like the Gare de Bruxelles-Centrale, which, for him, prefigures the architectural horrors of *bruxellisation*, but he knows its history—from its original design by Victor Horta to Metzger's recent renovations—as well as its every nook and cranny, its hallways, shops, and galleries. He could run through the station with his eyes closed, if it weren't for the nearly two hundred thousand passengers crowding its six platforms every day. Even today, a Saturday, at this hour of light traffic, he has to hug the walls, weave through the crowd, and jump over the suitcases passengers drag behind rather than beside them.

Finally, he arrives at the foot of the main hall and the three staircases that climb toward the departures board. Ten steps, one narrow landing. Ten more, a second landing. And the last five steps up to the hall itself. There aren't many people on the staircase. Twenty or so. Sun Hee's slight silhouette is easy to pick out. She reaches the second landing, her tiny suitcase in hand.

Jeroen stops, hesitates. In a few seconds he could catch up with her. He feels both relieved and ridiculous; bold enough to risk everything and incapable of forming a sentence; his thoughts racing but the words eluding him; wiser than he's ever been, clumsy as an adolescent.

Then everything slows down, even his heart, which only beats harder. His field of vision blurs and widens, distorting into a kind of fish-eye lens; his brain swims, as it does whenever this happens to him. A bit more than the other times, in fact. Probably because he's remembering the events linked to each previous incident, and the trauma that followed. Jeroen forces himself to calm the anxiety roiling up from his subconscious. He breathes gently, deeply, and the scene comes into focus, piece by piece, until he can see what it is that caused him to panic.

Above him, to the right of a staircase, a man on a mountain bike leans against a column. His helmet looks more like a motorcyclist's than a regular bicycle helmet, with an opaque visor covering his cheekbones and most of his nose. His visor turned in Sun Hee's direction, the man plunges his hand into his half-opened jacket.

Jeroen's vision returns to normal; the scene accelerates. He runs up the staircase as the man bolts away from the column. Sun Hee begins walking up the last flight of stairs.

The cyclist's left hand emerges from his jacket. His arm points toward Sun Hee, elongated by a gun that thunders twice in the direction of the Korean student.

The bike continues to race toward the exit on rue de l'Infante Isabelle.

Sun Hee flies backward.

Jeroen reaches the second landing, opens his arms, catches the falling young woman, leans forward to keep from being thrown back along with her, and kneels down as Sun Hee collapses, her head on his lap.

The cyclist has disappeared. Two young people who tried to stop him each took a bullet in the head and lay lifeless on the ground. Several more shots rang out in the street. Jeroen looks only at Sun Hee, can see nothing but her chest covered in blood, can do nothing but try to keep the glimmer of life in her eyes from fading as they look into his.

People rush toward them, some taking out their cell phones to call the police or emergency services. Others stand there filming or taking photos. Normally, Jeroen would have cursed them out. Now, he doesn't give a damn; Sun Hee is dying.

She raises her hand, he clasps it in his.

She smiles, he holds back tears.

She looks serene, he hides his despair.

They are just as they were in the short time they knew each other. Day and night. Yin and yang. For her, they are two forces in equilibrium, perfectly complementary. For him, they are a universe that will not have had time to expand. She opens her mouth slightly, a trickle of blood comes out.

"I was sure, you know."

"The cyclist?" he guesses.

A clot of bloody mucus stifles Sun Hee's laughter. "That you wouldn't give up."

"I won't give up."

She can no longer speak without coughing; she has to communicate with her eyes, and seeing the resignation in them, he responds with even greater determination.

"I won't give up," he repeats.

Sun Hee's eyes tell him he's only trying to convince himself, that she wishes she were able to fight with him, that she thanks him. Then they close. She is still here, with him, but she has no more strength. Life is leaving her.

Jeroen squeezes her hand a little tighter to remind her that he won't give up, but it's a promise anchored in helplessness. They're alone in the middle of a crowd that neither one of them hears or sees any longer, a crowd the security guards have started to disperse as they cordon off the area to allow access to the paramedics. The sirens are still far off; death is near.

There's nothing more Jeroen can do, only close his eyes and plead with the ghosts that Sun Hee took as metaphorical, try to summon the first one who had intruded on his life, until then so full of certainty; the one who'd been watching over him long before he became a spirit. His grandfather.

* * *

Bompa, help me.

But Bompa doesn't hear him. Bompa only appears, only has any influence, in the house without end, in Uccle, so far south of the city.

Bompa, please.

Suddenly, a presence fills his spirit.

I don't know how to help you, ketje.

His grandfather's voice rings false to Jeroen. It holds true sadness for him and compassion for Sun Hee, but Bompa's words are deceiving. When he says *know*, he doesn't only mean *can*, as any Belgian would; he also, secretly, means *want*.

You don't want to. Why not, Bompa?

I'm sorry, ketje. I can see that you're sweet on this stranger, but what you don't know about her isn't worth the price you'd have to pay.

The young Korean's hand is growing cold in Jeroen's.

What don't I know, Bompa?

Look at her, ketje. She accepts her death like someone settling a payment.

You mean she doesn't want to live?

No, she loves life. Today, she loves it more than anything. It's the gift you gave her, and she doesn't want to waste it.

What gift?

How do you expect me to know? I can only feel her emotions.

Jeroen understands that his grandfather is trying to stall for what little time Sun Hee has left, to put off answering his grandson.

What do I have to do, Bompa?

He replies with a sigh.

Bompa!

Nothing less than to offer her half the life you've left, ketje.

I don't understand.

I don't know a better way to tell you. It's something you must draw on deep within yourself. A heartbeat, a pulse—all of your strength. Make it into a ball of lightning and project it into her.

Jeroen doesn't need to summon the strength his grandfather's ghost evokes—it's already rising up out of his desperation.

Ketje, it's inevitable. You'll die in the same second, halfway through what would have been the rest of your life.

I don't believe in destiny, Bompa.

And I never believed in ghosts or balls of lightning. You don't know what you're giving away. You don't know what you're losing—in months, in years, in decades. Do you think I enjoy being nothing more than a specter? Do you think I have no regrets?

Jeroen is no longer listening; he doesn't want to hear anymore, but can't keep himself from remembering that he never knew his father's mother, who died before he was born, and that the one he called Bomma passed away on the same night as Bompa.

You did it!

Not me, ketje. Bomma. And it pains me to think of what I stole from her by accepting her gift.

Between his stomach and his heart, the ball of energy continues to swell and finally overwhelms Jeroen's spirit. Sun Hee's hand tightens around his, then goes limp. Jeroen leans over her, rests his forehead against hers, and lets out, in one breath, half of what would have been the rest of his life.

Sun Hee's back arches, her hand grips Jeroen's fingers, her eyelids open. She suddenly breathes in the air her lungs were missing.

Jeroen sits up, smiles, caresses her forehead without taking his eyes off hers, winks at her.

"I don't know how to give up," he whispers. "That's my secret. One day, perhaps you'll tell me yours."

The sirens have stopped wailing. The emergency paramedics are rushing between the security cordons, immediately followed by police. One of them asks Jeroen to move aside while two paramedics kneel down by Sun Hee.

"Stand up, sir," insists the policeman. "She's in good hands. We'll let you visit her at urgent care as soon as possible."

A paramedic supports Sun Hee's head in order to allow Jeroen to stand. He does so, reluctantly.

"He's coming with me," says Sun Hee. "He's my trickster."

THE KILLER WORE SLIPPERS

BY NADINE MONFILS

Place du Jeu de Balle

H ick in the daytime and pinup at night: that was the life of Jefke Vanwafels, a.k.a Mimi Castafiore after dark. No one in all of Brussels would have suspected this affable retiree of supplementing his pension by giving blow jobs in the Bois de la Cambre, dolled up like a whore in flea-market frocks.

Jefke spent his days in sweatpants and slippers, quietly tending his garden full of plaster gnomes. He was well-liked in his part of the Marolles; the local shopkeepers were fond of him, and he willingly lent a hand to his elderly neighbors. He even helped some of the merchants to pack up their goods at the end of the market day; then they'd go and throw back a few Mort Subites at Willy's or la Clef d'Or. Since Marcel's joint had disappeared, they were left to carry on wherever a bit of the city's soul survived, knowing that one day soon, Brussels as they knew it would be as good as gone, thanks to those asshole real-estate developers. Sometimes, he visited his mother at the Bergamot nursing home in Schaerbeek, and brought her tomatoes he'd grown on his balcony (the garden, of course, being reserved for the gnomes). *Oh, little lamb . . .*

"You oughta wash your hair with pigeon poo, my Jefke, that'll make it grow back and you'll have pretty curls like when you were little," she told him each time.

But Jefke couldn't have cared less. When night fell, he put on his blond wig . . .

He'd led a calm life, working at the factory. At forty years old, he had still lived with his mother. Oh, there'd been a woman, but Mrs. Vanwafels hadn't liked her, because she wore nail polish and that "made a bad impression." Finally, he realized he preferred football to the ladies. And he became a staunch fan of Standard Liège.

When the time came for his mother to leave their house on rue Blaes, he found himself all alone and, being an insomniac, grew a little restless. He bought a small car, which allowed him to hang out in a variety of seedy bars at night. It was around then that he first saw la Grande Bertha, an ex–truck driver, covered in feathers and sequins, impersonating Mireille Mathieu onstage at Chez Maman, a popular drag club in the city center. Jefke had fallen head over heels. He'd discovered his calling.

And so he'd taken his savings to the shops around place de Brouckère and bought the perfect pinup outfit, from false eyelashes to stiletto heels. With his platinum curls, his rhinestone necklace, his slinky black dress and lime-green shoes, he found himself simply divine. Sure, he had hair on his legs and chin, and his love handles, pinched by the waistline of his dress, formed a buoy around his stomach. But at night, all dreams are possible. You just have to find your corner of the dimly lit side of the room.

Mimi had learned all of Dalida's songs by heart. She sang horribly off-key, but that didn't matter, as the audience was distracted by her huge tits. To whoever would listen, she'd explain that they weren't silicone, and that she'd taken hormones—until the day she was shimmying onstage and her falsies slipped, ending up caught on one of her stiletto heels.

But the real problem was, all these frills and baubles were expensive! That was what made Mimi Castafiore decide to put her singing career on hold and start getting her knees dirty in the Bois de la Cambre. It paid better, and since she kept her dentures in her purse, Mimi could apply two different rates: fifty euros without teeth and a hundred with, because of AIDS.

In addition to the dentures she'd worn since a catfight with la Grande Bertha, Mimi had acquired a crowbar, an indispensable tool when walking alone in the woods. One night, while she was dozing off in a pile of dead leaves, she heard a harrowing cry. It was her friend Brigitte calling for help—she'd shoved a bottle of whiskey too far up a client's ass.

"Mimi, quick! Go get your crowbar from the trunk of my car. I can't pull the neck out any farther!"

Like Jane coming to Tarzan's rescue, Mimi went leaping into the thicket. But just as she was approaching her friend's car, she got nabbed by some cops and, lickety-split, off she went to the station. As for the client, he found himself at Hôpital Saint-Pierre on rue Haute.

Despite Mimi's adventurous life, Jefke was not completely happy. He always had the feeling he was missing out on something. As soon as he met someone the least bit cultivated at a bar, he felt out of his depth. Just plain stupid.

One day, seated among his garden gnomes, for the first time in his life he began to reflect. Aside from the magazine *Modes et Travaux*, which his mother subscribed to, he'd never read much of anything. He thought he'd better get down to it, even if his old lady had always said, *Don't go sticking your nose in books, they'll only bring you misery.* One of her friends had a son who'd decided to study literature and moved to America, abandoning his poor mom, and she'd been scared to death of all printed matter ever since.

Jefke went to visit Phillipe, the owner of l'Imaginaire, the used bookstore on place du Jeu de Balle, and asked him to recommend a book "that makes you cultured," without too many pages, and in large print. Gathering that Duras probably wasn't the best place to start, Philippe gave him *Ma Tante chez les Nudistes* by a certain K. de Mongeot (no relation to Mylène).

Jefke left with this precious volume in his backpack, but on rue du Chevreuil he was cornered by a thug who grabbed his bag and took off running. Jefke tried to catch him but collapsed, breathless, after only a few meters.

Given his aversion to the pigs, he obviously wasn't going to file a complaint. After all, aside from his depleted wallet, a photo of himself in slippers, and his new purchase, there had been nothing of any real value inside.

And so Jefke returned home, a bit shaken up certainly, but not devastated. And he spent the evening in front of the TV, as he always did on his nights off from performing.

The next morning, walking by a newspaper kiosk, he caught a glimpse of *La Dernière Heure* with his photo on the front page. In bold letters, the headline proclaimed: "Killer in Slippers Rapes, Dismembers Banker." Jefke couldn't believe his eyes. He raised the collar of his jacket to hide his face, and quickly read that his bag had been found, containing his ID and a "pornographic" book, at the scene of the crime. It was the only piece of evidence—there were no fingerprints. And since he hadn't gone to file a report of the theft, he was up to his stilettos in shit creek.

Jefke couldn't go back home, not now that the cops had his address. So he went to Brigitte's on rue de l'Economie, hoping he might be able to hide out there, but she sent him packing, convinced that he'd bailed out during her misadventure with the whiskey-loving client. Try as he might to explain that it wasn't his fault, she wouldn't hear a word of it and slammed the door in his face. As for la Grande Bertha, it wasn't even worth thinking about—they hadn't spoken since she'd smashed his teeth in for "borrowing" her mascara.

If only he hadn't gone to the bookstore that day, Jefke would never have been robbed and then accused of murder. All because of a book, he'd found himself on the street, threatened with life in prison.

And so he went into a shop and stole a wig, a dress, and some high heels, and killed off Jefke forever. Mimi Castafiore swore never again to disobey her mother. She was right: books, they'll bring you nothing but misery!

THE VILLAGE IDIOT

BY Edgar Kosma

Rue de Flandre

The American

In the neighborhood around rue de Flandre, no one knew his name and everyone called him "the American." The fellow who answered to this nickname was endowed with quite singular physical characteristics, and so was easily identifiable. He was a sturdy little person who stood no more than five feet tall but weighed about 135 pounds, who was missing as many teeth as he had fingers (nine, since he'd lost one in the bread slicer as a child), and whose remaining stumps were preparing to jump ship, one by one. He could, at least, be grateful that this unkempt mouth was partially hidden by his disheveled beard.

As for his attire, the American had the particularity of being completely impervious to fashion, and always wore the same clothes: a green nylon track jacket covered in a red argyle pattern, too large for his small torso, with brown velour pants too long for his short, chubby legs, and a beige and gray flannel shirt, more or less fitted to his atypical build. On his head sat a navy-blue baseball cap with the logo of a second-tier American team. The most plausible hypothesis was that his nickname came from the perpetual sporting of this headgear. It was, however, a fair bet that he wouldn't be able to locate the United States on a world map.

What could such an odd little person's everyday life be

like? The American didn't work, but wasn't unemployed, either, and belonged to a third, rather unenviable social category: those who are disabled by at least 33 percent, and receive a monthly allowance from the federal government. His handicap bore the disreputable name of *debility* or *mental deficiency,* terms that varied according to different medical studies and eras.

Despite his exceptionally low IQ, the American got by on his own, in a small apartment at the end of rue de Flandre, where, by force of repeating the same routines day after day, he managed to maintain a stable lifestyle. The American could, in this way, be considered an *autonomous person,* according to specialists on the subject.

In the morning, he took care of the basic household chores, then went to the supermarket to buy himself a loaf of white bread, a package of sliced, garlic-flavored salami, a can of Coke, a jar of cornichons in vinegar, and, if necessary, some other essential, or a little treat. Then, at home again, around noon, he consumed his purchases while watching, on a French cable TV channel, game shows in which he would never even dream of participating.

In the afternoon, the American would hang out at the neighborhood bars, most often the Laboureur, a café at the corner of rue de Flandre and rue Léon Lepage, whose dark wainscoted walls and old Belgian beer posters hadn't changed since it had opened in the 1950s. It was a place where aging card-players, barstool philosophers, and young, hip architects rubbed shoulders, where Francophones and Flemish speakers came to drown their petty linguistic quarrels.

But it wasn't to drink that the American went there. As it happens, he had become an employee of the café without anyone having asked him. In concrete terms, he brought the empty glasses from the booths to the counter, and in exchange for this service, the waiter offered him a Coke. This no longer seemed to shock any of the patrons, and in view of the high cost of labor in Belgium, the owner didn't object to a little help from a good old chap who could make do with such a humble salary.

To pass the time, the American practiced an additional activity that would have made the most cynical person smile, and the most fearful tremble: he photographed girls during his daily walks in the neighborhood. From the front? No, the American was too shy for that, and would never have dared ask their permission. Considering his appearance, it was unlikely that the girl would consent, for that matter, or that she wouldn't run for her life, crying bloody murder. No, the American was a deceitful little person who always photographed them from behind. Which, incidentally, was preferable for the mental health of his ignorant victims.

His modus operandi was as simple as his mind-set: when he saw a girl walking toward him on the street, he would rather obviously pretend not to have noticed her, then, a bit farther on, he'd stop, take out the disposable camera from its caddy, make a sharp turn, step up his pace in the girl's direction, stop again no more than five meters away from her, and, if all the conditions were right, click on the shutter. Then, with the satisfied air of a fisherman who has just caught a trout in a polluted river, he would put away his camera and retrace his route without turning around to look at the girl. Like a good old American going off to win the West with his well-oiled gun and his belt loaded down with ammunition.

Justine

In the neighborhood around rue de Flandre, hardly anyone was aware of her existence, certainly not her name. In her defense, Justine had lived in Brussels for only a few months, and hadn't yet had the occasion to meet many locals.

She had come from her native Île-de-France in order to study physical therapy in Brussels. Not for love of the flat country, where she'd never set foot until now, but to avoid the impossible entrance exams and exorbitant tuition costs of French schools.

This ambitious nineteen-year-old already imagined herself, years later, practicing her chosen profession on the fragile bodies of the aging bourgeoisie in a private office in the 16th arrondissement, which—according to her preliminary estimations, confirmed by her accountant father—could earn her as much as eight thousand euros per month, as early as the first year, excluding expenses.

Justine had ended up in the neighborhood near rue de Flandre thanks to an ad she'd found on a rental website. A certain Marie, twenty years old, was subletting a room in her apartment there: *Well lit and spacious, in a small urban village, young, vibrant, and multicultural, in the heart of the city.* Justine had contacted her from Paris, and the deal was quickly done.

The first few months in Belgium only confirmed what Justine had read on the travel blogs: Brussels was a friendly city, full of kind, open-minded, approachable, warm people, always ready to meet up for a beer and chat with their goofy accents and their expressions that made you piss yourself laughing.

In the neighborhood, the temptations to go out were many. And even if the prices at the bars were far cheaper than those in the City of Light, once she'd paid rent, credit cards, the phone and Internet bills, and covered the cost of restaurants, sandwiches, movie tickets, clothes, and all her other basic needs, there wasn't much left of the measly thousand euros her parents sent on the first of every month. And if there was one thing Justine hated above all, it was being stripped of her buying power.

One cold night in November, during a party with her classmates where everyone had gotten a bit too sloshed, Charlotte, another French girl whom Justine had befriended, told her about a lucrative activity she'd been practicing for nearly a year. Considering her physical assets, Charlotte thought Justine would also be suited to it.

"So what does this involve, exactly?"

"It's easy: you meet men, you give them a little pleasure in as short a time as possible, and you get as much cash from them as you can!"

"But . . . that's prostitution, isn't it?"

"In a certain sense, yes . . . Well, you can call it whatever you want. But it brings in enough cash to let you pay for school without working yourself to death twenty hours a week at some fast-food joint and smelling like grease all day . . . This way, you can give yourself every chance to succeed!"

The argument had percolated all night in the half-conscious brain of the postadolescent.

The next day, Justine sought more information from Charlotte, who was thrilled to bring a new participant along on this rewarding adventure.

As soon as she'd returned home from class, Justine sent her phone number, along with a picture of herself in her underwear, to thegermangay@gmail.com. It took no more than five minutes for a certain Boris Umanov to respond with a link and a password that allowed her to create a profile on www.studandmeet.be. Justine followed the instructions and chose the worldly yet unassuming pseudonym of Natacha. Not for love of Russia, but because it was the first name that came to mind, and one that she could easily imagine belonging to a whore. Her registration was quickly confirmed, and Boris sent her another, more personalized e-mail, in which he advised her to fill out her profile with a few charming photos and risqué quotes. In conclusion, he predicted that she would find success in this new endeavor and, in an attachment, provided a list of practical recommendations: the most important ones, in bold, at the top of the list, were to buy a cell phone with a prepaid card and create a dedicated e-mail address to be used exclusively for this professional activity.

In just a few days, the machine was set in motion, and the first requests flooded her new Hotmail inbox. The formula was simple: interested clients contacted her via the site, Justine accepted them or not, they agreed on a meeting based on her availability, and the men came to her place at the appointed hour. Justine made sure this was always at a time when her roommate wasn't home, which was easy enough since Marie was usually holed up at her boyfriend's house. These mostly affluent middle-aged men were excited to find themselves in that atmosphere, tinged with nostalgia and eroticism. It reminded them of the golden days when they could get hard over the smallest thing, without the least anxiety. Before the session began, they paid her in cash, an amount agreed upon in advance, of which Boris took a 10 percent commission, to be transferred into a PayPal account within forty-eight hours. Justine set her prices according to a fixed rate, asking, on average, for two hundred euros for a complete service, which could not exceed an hour. She added a small fee of fifty euros at the start of each additional quarter hour, which was paid at the end and not subject to the commission. And in this way Justine, working sometimes less than an hour a day, earned nearly as much as her two parents combined, who did not, for that matter, have reason to complain, given their three-bedroom Parisian apartment, their brand-new Citroën, and their second home in Upper Normandy.

Justine and the American did not meet through www.studand-meet.be, for the simple reason that the American had no Internet service, no cell phone or landline, did not really know what all that fuss was about, and lived relatively well without them.

On that night, Justine was at the Laboureur with a few French friends who were in town for the weekend. As she approached the bar to order another round of the beers that her friends found very good and, more importantly, very cheap compared to the bland five-euro drinks they were used to imbibing, the American greeted her with a timid *bonjour*. But with the deejay blasting oldies and playing the harmonica at the same time, everyone was shouting to be understood and no one could hear a thing.

"What's your name?" he went on, surprised by his own sudden boldness.

This time, Justine registered his presence and looked disdainfully at him, as one observes a fly who has lost a wing and whose life will be snuffed out in a matter of seconds. Undeterred, he repeated his question. She reflexively gave him her pseudonym and immediately wondered why she'd responded to this pathetic creep who was shorter than her fifteen-year-old brother.

Of course, the American latched onto these first words like a mussel to a pier. "You want a Coke?"

"No thank you."

"C'mon, it's on me!"

"If you've got enough to buy me a glass of champagne . . ." she said, so that he'd leave her alone.

"Oh, yes, I've got a little here." The American pulled a wad of fifty-euro bills from his pocket. "And if that's not enough, I've got more at home . . ."

Justine turned toward him with the look of a slot-machine player on a casino cruise.

"And what are you doing with all that cash at home?"

"On TV, someone told me banks are nothing but robbers."

"And you believe that?"

"Isn't it true?"

"And you're not afraid to leave all that cash at home?"

"Have I done something bad?"

"You have a lot more, then?"

The American held his hands about two feet apart, to give her a sense of the amount.

"Seriously?"

"That's a lot?"

Justine told him it was decent, then explained that she couldn't talk much longer, since she had to go join her friends who were waiting for her at the table, but that he could call her sometime, if he wanted to. He said yes, so she took out a Bic from her purse, wrote her ten-digit number on a beer mat, and handed it to the American, who couldn't believe his eyes. In the seconds that followed, he felt a strange throbbing sensation deep down in his stomach. He stopped bringing empty glasses to the counter and preemptively headed for the restroom.

Having no notion of the complex rules of the game of seduction, the American dialed the ten-digit number first thing the next morning, in a phone booth at a Pakistani call center beneath his apartment. Five seconds later, Justine's cell phone began to vibrate on her nightstand.

"Hello?"

"Natacha?"

"Who's this?"

"It's me."

"*Who?*"

"Uh, me . . . you told me to call you if I wanted to . . ."

Her sleep had been too short and the beers too many. Justine closed her eyes and immediately remembered the hoarse little voice like a sick child's, and asked herself why she'd given her number to this guy, before recalling his wad of bills. Then she glanced at her alarm clock and realized it was only nine in the morning.

"Why are you calling me so early?"

"It's early? I didn't know. When does it stop being early?"

Justine said nothing and sat up, leaning on her elbow in such a way as to turn her back to the guy asleep beside her, about whom she didn't remember much.

"Do you want to go to the movies with me?" The American had asked this since, in the American films he'd seen, first dates often took place at the cinema.

"No, I'll come to your place tonight, around nine," she said, with the courage of those who know that you have to burn a little midnight oil to get ahead in life.

The American gave her his address and Justine hung up first, before asking herself how much she could get from him, and if it would be enough to buy the new iPhone 6 to replace the iPhone 5 her father had given her for Christmas, whose screen was already covered in scratches.

Justine showed up at the American's place an hour late. She didn't apologize, and he didn't give her any grief. With her short dress, tall boots, and black eye makeup, she looked at least twenty-five. As for the American, he was dressed in his usual outfit, but had just taken off his hat.

First Justine walked through the apartment like a prospective tenant, and the American followed her without saying a word, not for one second taking his eyes off her ass. She sat down on the couch at the end of the living room, and the American grabbed something from his caddy near the front door. Justine suddenly had a bad feeling. Fortunately, when the American stood in front of her again, she realized it was only a stupid disposable camera.

"Can I take your photo?"

Justine refused, having no desire to be enshrined on his fireplace for years to come. "Couldn't we get to know each other a little, hmmm, instead of playing with your little toy?" she asked, patting the space beside her on the couch.

Like a good dog obeying his mistress, the American nodded and perched beside her.

Convinced she had enough information to establish her client's commercial profile, Justine decided to price her services à la carte.

"You want to see my breasts?"

"Yes," said the American.

"If you give me fifty euros, you can see them."

The American nodded.

"And if you want to touch them, you'll need to give me another fifty."

The American nodded again.

"And I'd prefer to have it before I start . . ."

The American got up and began walking toward the kitchen. Justine followed him with her eyes. A few seconds later, he came back with a small wad of bills and handed them to her. She immediately stuffed them in her bag, without counting.

In order to reward this good behavior, Justine took in the situation and began by showing him what she had promised. The American's eyes grew wide. She grabbed his hairy hand and placed it on one of her breasts. At that moment, he felt a pressure through his underwear, and it was as if he couldn't breathe. Justine told him to calm down, that everything was going to be okay, and started taking off his belt. The American did not blink once, and suddenly saw his pants pulled down to his knees, which usually only happened when he was in the bathroom. Justine found his skinny legs very ugly, but, always conscientious, she stayed focused on her work. She plunged her hand down his underwear and discovered, with surprise, a relatively large penis for such a small body. This reminded her of a funny joke about midgets she'd heard on the radio in her parents' car, on the way to their summer home one after-noon when she was a little girl. Then Justine started stroking it, slowly at first, then faster and faster. The American's face grew increasingly red and Justine, afraid he might suffocate, slowed the pace of her movements. His erection was strong, and she had the idea of taking him in her mouth, but just as she was lowering her head, the American let out a gasp that signaled her time was up. By good luck, Justine had dodged the projectile. She slipped her shirt back on, thinking that she hadn't had to do much, that it was easy money, especially in comparison to the fifty-year-old guys she sometimes had to jerk off for several minutes before they got hard, and who took twice as long to ejaculate.

While the American slowly returned to his senses and his face regained its normal color, Justine went to wash her hands in the bathroom. As she entered back into the living room, she didn't see him on the couch, instead finding him in his room, lying stretched out on the bed. She lay down next to him and wondered how long it had been since his sheets were washed. After a moment of silence, the American stood up, left the room, and reappeared a few seconds later with his camera.

"Now can I take your picture?"

Justine said nothing and pretended to be asleep. She could sense the light of the flash on her closed eyelids but didn't react, thinking that the poor guy had earned his photo, after all, and if he wanted to put her in a frame, well, it wasn't her problem. At least, with him, she could be sure of one thing: there was no chance the photo was going to end up on Facebook.

Then the American went back to bed and fell asleep in less than five minutes. It was the moment Justine had been waiting for to get up and quietly leave the room. First, she tiptoed into the living room and found her purse. Then she made her way to the kitchen and began to dig through the contents of the buffet table. In the top drawer, she found a case containing hundreds of envelopes full of photo prints. Justine opened one at random, and looked at the first image, the second, the third . . . *but what the* . . . what kind of a sicko was this guy? Without knowing why, she stuffed an envelope into her bag, as if it might be of use to her later on. Gathering her courage, she went on with her search, and finally, in the cabinet below the sink, she found the goldmine. And when she discovered the contents of the plastic grocery bag, Justine couldn't keep herself from blurting out: "Holy shit, I've never seen so much cash!" Then she thought she heard the sound of a door opening in the hallway.

Marc

In the neighborhood around rue de Flandre, everyone knew him and everyone called him "FotoMarc," in reference to the rather unoriginal name of his camera store.

In 2014, running a camera store mainly meant selling digital cameras, memory cards, and useless gadgets, and no longer really developing film. For that matter, since people had started to post their photos on Instagram rather than gluing them into a dusty album they unearthed once a year at a soporific family dinner, even digital printing was becoming rarer.

Marc's world had changed a great deal, to be sure, but there were still a few customers who came to develop their film: the dreamy, nostalgic ones, and the digitally challenged ones. The American, who had been coming to FotoMarc every week for several years, was one of these customers, and needless to say, he belonged to the second category.

"But why don't you get yourself a camera, instead of buying all these disposable ones?" Marc had asked him one day. "I have a good one for less than 150 euros, it'll save you money in the long run . . ."

The American had responded, in simpler words, that he was afraid to buy a camera that might stop working, that this way was very practical, with the film already inside, and he really didn't see the point in changing.

Though far from being a close friend, Marc was still one of the people in the neighborhood who knew the American best, and certainly the only one so familiar with his odd fixation. A good storekeeper, Marc never passed judgment on this activity which had already made him a nice little profit, but he couldn't keep himself from wondering what the American might be doing with all these photos of young girls. Sometimes, he imagined him alone at home, at night, sorting them into little plastic boxes according to a classification system only he could understand: ass size, arm length, flat shoes or high heels, hair color, skirt or pants . . . Or perhaps he taped them all to the walls of his apartment, in chronological order?

Marc had to admit, the whole thing seemed a bit shady. At the same time, it was probably just a hobby, and there was no reason to be alarmed. Had the American been an artist, would these photos have been interpreted as a body of work worthy of interest? Perhaps. But since the American was just a guy in a baseball cap who picked up empty glasses at bars, it was better for him, and for Marc, that this oeuvre remain a secret.

A few days after his evening with Justine, the American brought in a new roll of film and left with the previous prints, as well as another disposable camera. Marc developed the film that afternoon and, as usual, checked the prints as soon as they came out of the machine. The first photos he looked at were unsurprising. Some were blurred, or even completely black, and, always the good shopkeeper, he didn't charge for any that hadn't come out well. It was the twelfth image that got his attention: darker than the others, it showed for the first time a girl not from the back but from the front, lying inert on a bed, eyes closed, her skin translucent. Who was this girl? What was she doing there? Where had the photo been taken? Was she dead? Locked away? *Had he killed her?* This seemingly harmless dork—was he in fact a sick pervert? Feeling lightheaded, Marc stepped outside to take a deep breath of fresh air. He obviously couldn't ignore the questions that assailed him like a meteor shower out of nowhere.

Freddy

In the neighborhood around rue de Flandre, those who knew him called him "Inspector Freddy," and, at the station, some of his junior officers called him "Inspector Mustache," in homage to the impressive tuft of gray hair that covered his upper lip and most of his lower one, and acted something like an air filter when he spoke in his baritone voice tinged with a Brussels accent.

Freddy had worked at the Brussels police department since 1975. If all went well for him, he would collect his pension in 2015. But this was without taking into account the current far-right campaign to reform the retirement plan for public servants, and neither Freddy nor anyone else knew where all that would lead.

Freddy was in his office, on the second floor of the station, polishing his new work boots, when his spiral-corded landline phone rang.

"Hello, Freddy?" It was Marc, the photographer on rue de Flandre. "I took the liberty of calling, as I feel I ought to speak to you about something . . ."

Freddy recognized a certain gravity in his voice, and concluded that he'd better take the guy seriously.

Half an hour later, the inspector walked through the door of FotoMarc. Marc thanked him for coming so quickly before leading him to a small office on the first floor, where Freddy sat down without being invited.

"I don't know if I did the right thing, calling you here for this," said Marc, handing him the photo, "but . . ."

"It's always better to be safe," offered the inspector, who no longer knew quite how to finish that sentence.

Freddy took off his glasses to examine the photo in closer detail. Without pausing, Marc explained the reasons for his concern, going several years back to the time when he'd first seen the American walk through the doors of his shop.

"This photo was actually taken by the American, then?" asked the inspector, once Marc had finished his story.

"Yes, I think . . . In any case, he's the one who has them developed . . ."

Freddy pinched his mustache between his thumb and forefinger. "Have you seen this girl anywhere before, and do you have any idea who she might be?"

Marc had never seen her, and had no idea.

"Is this the first time she's appeared in one of his photos?"

"Hard to say. Like I said, they're always taken from behind . . ."

The inspector grimaced and clasped his hands together. "Do you think she could be his girlfriend?"

Marc raised his eyebrows in a way that Freddy took to mean he had just asked a dumb question.

"I see . . ." said the inspector, who didn't know the American terribly well, but well enough not to believe just anything with regard to him.

"You think she's . . . *dead?*" Marc couldn't help blurting out. It was, for him, the one and only question that had any bearing in all this murky business.

"Impossible to say, based on a photo alone," replied the inspector, who, throughout his career, had seen plenty of live bodies that looked quite dead, and plenty of dead ones that looked alive. Then Freddy looked Marc straight in the eye, and the silence grew heavier. "You, who've known him for so long, do you think he's capable of the worst?"

"No, no, I don't think so. But at the same time, I don't know him as well as all that . . . and he's a very peculiar person. He's always nice, but, well, what does that really mean, after all?"

"Not much, you're right," concluded the inspector before taking leave of the photographer.

Twenty minutes later, Freddy called Abdel into his office to tell him everything he had just learned.

Abdel was the inspector's new right-hand man, named to this post after the departure of Jean-Marc, who had decided to finish his career in the central administration. He was a young recruit who still had much to learn, but Freddy had a great deal of faith in him.

"And what do we do now, chief?" asked Abdel.

"Well, first you're going to scan this little photo and send it to forensics, then make copies and go looking for the girl . . ."

"Okay, chief!"

"As for me, I'm going to try to get my hands on this damned American."

Abdel walked toward the door, and just before stepping over the threshold, turned to Freddy with a worried expression. "Tell me, chief, do you think she's—"

"I don't know, Abdel. Experience tells me that if he'd killed her, he probably wouldn't have gone to get the photo developed."

"Ah, that's not a bad point . . ."

"At the same time, this might be his way of revealing his true nature," added Freddy.

"You mean with this sort of guy, anything is possible?"

"Unfortunately, yes. These men don't always think rationally, and it's often very hard to discern their intentions. But come on, enough chitchat! The main thing, for now, is to find him . . ."

Freddy had no trouble getting ahold of the American, since, after going to ring the bell at his apartment, he found him, like most afternoons, at the Laboureur, bringing empty glasses to the counter. Freddy approached him, introduced himself, and quietly asked him to step outside.

"And my Coke?"

"I'll buy you another one . . . Come on, follow me and don't make a scene."

The inspector and the American left the Laboureur under the amused gaze of the bar's regulars, who weren't on their first beers of the day, nor their last. They walked side by side, and Freddy said nothing to him of the matter until they'd arrived at the station, a few blocks away. He brought the American into a brightly lit room near his office, and pointed to a chair where the latter sat down without batting an eyelid.

"You know why we're here?"

The American did not seem to understand the reason for his presence in this place. Freddy took the photo out of his pocket and set it down in front of him.

"You know this girl?"

"Natacha!"

"Natacha what?"

"But that's my photo!"

"Natacha what?"

"How do *you* have it?"

"Natacha what?"

"Just Natacha."

Freddy told himself it wasn't impossible that he didn't know her last name, and changed the question. "Who is she, this girl?"

"She's Natacha," responded the American who, for the first time, seemed visibly annoyed.

"You're the one who took this photo?"

"Yes, that's *my* photo."

"And where did you take it, this photo?"

"At my apartment."

"Natacha was at your apartment?"

This time, the American only nodded his head.

"And can you tell me what she was doing at your apartment, this girl?"

"She came to my apartment to see me."

"To see you," repeated Freddy, laughing. "But of course . . . And how long have you known her?"

The American seemed to be genuinely searching for a response to this question, but dates and days of the week, like many other things, had never been his strong point.

"You know where she lives?"

"No."

"And can you tell me what this Natacha whom you don't know much about was doing at your apartment, lying down with her eyes closed?"

"She was sleeping," said the American, before releasing a nervous little laugh that led the inspector to suspect he was less stupid than he'd first seemed.

"And since when do you take photos of sleeping girls, huh?" Freddy cried, pounding his fist on the table. "It's not already perverted enough to shoot them from behind on the street? You need more, more, more?"

The American went pale as photo paper that had been exposed to the sun.

"And who's to tell me you didn't drug her and rape her, then kill her and take her photo, like hunters do with the heads of their prey? Eh? Who?"

The American curled up on his chair, took his head in his hands, and started to breathe like a horse at the entrance to a slaughterhouse.

"Listen to me, American: I'm not your enemy and I'd like to believe whatever you tell me, but as long as you say nothing and we don't find her alive, I can't let you leave here . . . You understand what I'm saying?"

The American spread his hands and made a strange movement of his head that perplexed the inspector.

Freddy asked a security guard to make sure the American didn't leave the room, then went back to his office. A few moments later, the ringing telephone interrupted his thoughts.

"I found some stuff on the girl, asking people in the neighborhood," said Abdel. "Some of them recognized her face, and one woman had even seen her go into the building on 156 rue de Flandre. So I went there myself—there was no name on the doorbell, but I knocked on the super's window and he let me in. I showed him the photo, and the guy confirmed it was one of the two students on the third floor . . . I headed up . . . there was no one there, but since it was an old door, I went ahead and pried it open without causing too much damage . . ."

"Bravo, respect for the procedure," said Freddy. "And then?"

"I looked around a bit, and it seemed just like any other student's apartment, with two rooms, single beds, and two desks covered with textbooks . . . Anyway, in the smaller room there was a photo of the girl, the same girl in our photo, and I told myself that it must be her room . . . You see, chief?"

"Yes, I see, Abdel . . . And then?"

"Here's where it gets interesting! Listen . . . I dug around the room for a while and pretty soon I stumbled on this big cardboard box in her wardrobe, like a shoe box, full of money, mainly fifty-euro bills and also some hundreds . . ."

"What? But . . . how much was in there?"

"I didn't count, chief, but I'd say there has to be at least five thousand."

"Five thousand!"

"Yeah . . . and that's not all. On the desk, there was a

planner marked with just the names of men—around three or four per week."

"Well, who'd have thought? The sly little thing . . ."

"And I haven't told you the strangest part, chief! At the bottom of the box, there was an envelope full of photos showing girls from behind."

"Girls from behind?"

"Yes, chief, girls from behind!"

"But what's she doing with those photos at her apartment?"

"No idea . . . Either she's the one who took them, or they're the American's."

Freddy got lost in his thoughts for a few seconds, before bringing his attention back to the conversation.

"Well, and after all that, do you have any idea where she might be?"

"Hold on, chief, I haven't finished. Just when I was about to leave, a girl came into the apartment. I surprised her and she was pretty scared. I introduced myself, and she told me that she lived there. I showed her the photo and I explained that we're looking for this person. She said the girl's name was Justine, that she was, in fact, her roommate, and she'd gone to Paris for a few days to visit her family . . ."

"Justine?"

"Yes, Justine, chief! Her real name! Natacha must be the name she gives to men . . ."

"Okay, I'm starting to understand . . . And then?"

"I showed her the box with the money and asked if she knew anything about it. The roommate immediately started crying, then she told me she didn't really know what her friend was up to, but that, yes, there were often men who came over, and the money might come from that, but she didn't know anything about it and had nothing to do with any of it."

"And what did you do then?"

"I told her not to contact Justine under any circumstances, otherwise she'd have to deal with us. I suggest we let her take her time coming back from France, and we arrest her right when she gets off the train. According to the roommate, Justine gets in tomorrow on the 7:45."

"Nicely done, Abdel! Prostitution, abuse of a handicapped person . . . Ah, yes, she's going to have quite a lot to explain to us, this pretty little Frenchy."

Freddy hung up before standing and taking a few steps toward the window, then looked down at the street. How many cases had he solved in his career? He no longer remembered exactly, but in nearly forty years in the profession, this was among the most efficiently handled ones, solved in less time than it took to type up the lousy police report.

The inspector's watch, a gift from his wife on their twentieth anniversary, read 4:55 when he headed back to the room where the American was still under surveillance. Freddy opened the door and gazed paternally down at the little man, who was busy counting the square tiles on the wall.

"I have some good news for you and some bad news. Which would you like to hear first?"

"I don't know," said the American, as if he'd been asked to choose between a vanilla or chocolate ice cream cone.

"In that case, let's start with the good news," said Freddy. "All suspicion of murder and kidnapping has been lifted. As soon as you've signed your deposition, you can go home and continue with your little life in peace."

"Really?" said the American, as if he'd heard that the dog he'd lost as a child had just been found.

"The bad news is, well, I'm afraid that your new girlfriend might be a whore. And between us—and I tell you this from my years of experience, without wanting to hurt you—I'd be shocked if that wasn't the case."

"A whore?"

"Yes, a whore," said Freddy.

"Really," said the American, as if he'd just been told there'd been a mistake, and the dog that had been found wasn't his after all.

PART III

Room to Maneuver

IN THE SHADOW
OF THE TOWER

BY ÉMILIE DE BÉCO

Reyers

S he had grown up in the shadow of the tower. Literally. At the upper end of rue Colonel Bourg, with all the appearance of a dormitory town for miners, the two major Belgian broadcasting organizations sat at the foot of the colossal structure: Vlaamse Radio-en Televisieomroep on one side, Télévision Radio Belge Francophone on the other. A concrete nail seventy meters tall, its head thirty-four meters in diameter, the tower, now timed to light up red like a whore-house after dark, was once just as austere as the programs it transmitted.

Schaerbeek was often described by those who loved it as the municipality that best represented the multifarious spirit of Brussels. Here, the broad avenues lined with old bourgeois houses, their window boxes filled with flowers, stood side by side with slums where the religious radicalism of the poor spread like weeds. When you mentioned that you lived in Schaerbeek, you had to say on which side.

To the west, a rotting tenement; to the east, a man-sion. Here, gobs of spit on the sidewalk; there, picturesque cobblestones.

As for Lydie's neighborhood, it was just plain ugly, much like most of the 1990s in Belgium, a time when the streets and the culture were brimming with corduroy, tassel loafers, athletic socks, and, of course, tinted glasses, which would soon become a rallying sign for the biggest local stars: pedophiles.

On August 15, 1996, the nation witnessed the liberation—practically in real time—of Sabine Dardenne (twelve, close-cropped hair, terrorized) and Laetitia Delhez (fourteen, shoulder-length hair, in tears) from a makeshift dungeon in a house in Marcinelle.

This was how Belgium came to know its public enemy number one: the predator Marc Dutroux, forty years old, mustached, greasy-haired, sporting his famous glasses.

First came fear, followed soon by anger. Then revenge. On Dutroux, certainly, but on all the others too: the perverted schoolteachers, the abusive vicars, the "borderline" camp counselors and lecherous sports coaches; and on all those not-quite-normal men, about whom one had always known, always felt, or suspected; that look of his, the way he spoke . . .

The people wanted to take over for the police, as well as for the judge and jury, to correct the authorities' mistakes by whatever means necessary, acting only as citizens whose hands are not tied by any professional code of ethics can.

Soon the press joined the wolf pack, publishing daily photos of presumed sex offenders along with details as to their whereabouts, doing its part to help the burgeoning executioners to carry out their work.

It was in this context that one day—it was a Wednesday afternoon—the five o'clock news team from the TRBF walked down three flights of stairs, across a hallway, and past the guardroom, tangling equipment cables in the revolving door, and made their way on foot—a rare occurrence—until they arrived at no. 33, rue Colonel Bourg. A yellow house, its roughcast walls flaking, its windows smudged with the wet noseprints of a dog. It was Lydie who opened the door. She hadn't looked through the peephole; she was expecting a visit from her best friend Véronique, whose parents allowed her to run about the neighborhood in spite of recent events and her being only six years old. It must be said that these people were living more or less in poverty.

Lydie would long remember the affable smile on the face of this very tall, very handsome man, wearing a tie with a Provençal pattern, a microphone in hand, all set to record, this man who had stroked her head and asked her if her papa was at home.

He was. Unemployed ever since the automobile factory had closed, he spent his days watching cartoons. With his daughter if she was at home, otherwise alone.

He dragged himself off the couch, his T-shirt covered in crumbs, his pants smudged with stains, his hair matted and sweaty, his face sallow with boredom and the alcohol that was eating away at his liver. This was how he appeared to all of Belgium on the five o'clock news: as a presumed sex offender, just one name on a list sent anonymously to the media; the only one to have the honor of a visit from the TRBF, simply because he lived nearby. Jean-Marc Peereman slammed the door as soon as the reason for the visit was announced. The journalist, Claverie, went on to comment on this reaction—a revealing one, to his mind—for a solid minute and a half.

At the end of Claverie's report, he reminded his viewers that the case in question had yet to be officially filed, but it was too late: Peereman looked the part and, in the public mind, immediately became a child rapist, a monster to be abhorred, who deserved to have his house stoned and shit left on his doorstep.

Jean-Marc Peereman was quickly, but perhaps too ambivalently, redeemed to the public. The actual criminal's name, as it turned out, was a near-homonym—Peeremans, with an *s*. A nineteen-second correction on the next morning's news, rattled off between soccer scores and a report on protesting dairy farmers. *Never look back, always ahead,* was the "law of the airwaves" that had been declared by the newsroom's editor-in-chief. With an air of seriousness, Claverie briefly presented the photo of Lydie's father, offering his apologies on behalf of the news staff. Then: "Moving on, the mad cow disease crisis: should we or shouldn't we buy meat at the supermarket?" For the viewers, however, there was no smoke without a fire, and they planned to hang the bastard. Out of distraction or laziness, the newspapers and radio broadcasters failed to relay the correction, leaving the public to believe that a case was still open. The harassment continued, reaching its height on the day when Peereman found his door vandalized with bold spray-painted letters announcing to the neighborhood: *Get fucked here.*

Six months later, Jean-Marc Peereman committed suicide. Hanged himself in the stairwell, leaving no note, one cold, gray morning.

Eighteen years later

Lydie had struggled to complete her studies. She'd repeated a year twice, taking seven to earn her degree in journalism from the Université libre de Bruxelles. That had given her plenty of time to explore the hereditary dimension of alcoholism: her fellow students nicknamed her Sterfput, "the drain." But perhaps for reasons other than her thirst for booze.

As her teaching assistant often gushed, Lydie was truly "made for television." She spoke well, she wrote well, she had "everything going for her," but never managed to remember the ownership structures and cross-interests of the Belgian and international media. This subject matter was not concrete enough, in her view. But Lydie was a hard worker. Watching her grow exhausted from studying into the small hours night after night, her instructors had tried to dissuade her from pursuing this path—*With journalism, you either have it in your blood or you don't,* they said. *You have the gift, the knack, the thing, or you don't.*

Lydie had always politely deflected their attempts to push her toward publicity or public relations. She would be a journalist or nothing at all. It was her guiding force, her calling.

She had found her path in life very early, as a little girl, and ever since the first grade she'd written the word *journalist* next to the phrase, *What I want to be when I grow up,* on the worksheets the students had to fill in each year.

But once she'd earned her diploma, she hadn't sent out a single résumé. She had waited. Patiently. A month went by, then two, three. It would eventually be time for the recruitment test given by the TRBF, an open exam the public broadcasting organization was obliged to hold at regular intervals.

In the meantime, she studied. She read the papers, listened to the radio, watched TV. She watched *him.* Daniel Claverie, still very handsome, his teeth so white, so personable, so kind. He no longer dirtied his hands with on-the-ground reporting; he hosted the evening news on the main public channel. The viewers adored him. He always came out on top in the yearly rankings of anchors preferred by Francophone Belgians. Among his qualities, according to the viewers: "his seriousness," "his empathy," "his calm strength," "his credibility."

Claverie was a gentleman who always took the time to

give autographs to those who recognized him in the line at Delhaize; he ran a 20k race to help raise money for cancer research, he donated blood and plasma, and he was publicly outraged over the deafening silence surrounding the plight of Somalian children facing famine once again. An all-around good guy, this Claverie.

Lydie had already spoken to him once, during a job visit organized by her university. He was the only person who had deigned to answer her questions when they checked out the editing room, explaining, among other things, what "that button, there" did. Lydie couldn't help but recognize that Daniel was a charming man, a model of the perfect son-in-law or older brother.

She couldn't wait to meet him again.

Five hundred hopefuls sat in the lecture hall at the Université libre de Bruxelles, filling in multiple-choice questions, one Sunday morning in December. At last, the recruitment exam for the TRBF. The test of general culture covered the last two centuries of Belgian history; it was wiser to leave an answer blank than to guess incorrectly. She had crammed. Knew the Red Devils and the Mad Killers of Brabant like the back of her hand, knew the ratio of Flemish speakers to Francophones in Brussels, could cite the federal state debt to the nearest euro, and remembered the exact name of the law regulating the private security service sector in Belgium.

Lydie was the last to exit the room. Nothing could be left to chance, and nothing was. She received her score a week later: 66 out of 100, an honorable performance. The ticket, in any case, to the second phase of recruitment: the jury.

Twelve journalists licensed by the organization bombarded

her with questions, assuming a professional track record she obviously didn't have, fresh out of school as she was.

"You run into King Albert II in the elevator, what do you do?"

"How far along is the RER project in Walloon Brabant?"

"Give me five ideas for news stories that come to mind when I say the word *slagheap* . . ."

She had tried her best to respond articulately, like a trained chimpanzee, though she was certain that these questions had nothing to do with the reality of the field—she held back the fire ready to flare from her nostrils.

Only the amiable Daniel Claverie had shown a hint of kindness. She had immediately felt, upon walking into the room, that she would be able to make an ally of him. In a smooth voice, he asked her, "Deep down, why do you wish to pursue this difficult profession, mademoiselle?"

Lydie didn't have to think for very long. "You might find me a bit sentimental, but I truly believe that only honest, thorough, impartial, high-quality reporting is capable of preventing—even repairing—injustice, in the broadest sense of the word."

Two or three hotshot reporters snickered, but her response had hit home with most of the jurors—she was accepted, congratulations.

The 7 and 25 tram lines stop just beneath the TRBF headquarters, at Diamant, one of the least-scintillating public transport stations in all of Brussels. Its walls are a dirty white and grayish yellow, its platforms lined with trash cans constantly overflowing with old chewing gum and apple cores. A perfect incubator for cynicism. Waiting ten minutes for the tram there is already depressing; to be stuck for an hour is close to torture.

Yet this was the misadventure that had befallen Luc Durant. The veteran cameraman, whose career had been as long as a day without beer and whose nose was blooming with broken capillaries, had had a particularly rough morning. It was a Sunday, a car-free day as mandated by the European institutions, whose representatives probably thought their initiative was amusing and original, even if they had never set foot in the Brussels metro—except, perhaps, to take part in roving gastronomic tours guided by master chefs.

Despite his protests—goddamn, it was Sunday after all—Luc Durant had been sent alone to the city center, to film an "on the scene" report, a series of mute images that were commented on air by the host of the morning news, an old buddy of Durant's who no longer bothered saying hello to him in the hallways. The station was swarming with loud families, and he had to be careful not to run into anyone with the heavy equipment he was carrying on his back.

When the headlights of the 7 glimmered into view, Durant felt the crowd pushing him forward. Shoving him. He couldn't see where the movement was coming from; his equipment made it too hard to turn around.

He cried out loudly in protest. "Hey, watch it!" They kept pushing him. Beneath the soles of his shoes, he felt the raised edge of the platform that was supposed to warn the blind.

He couldn't step back, couldn't move away; he was too weighed down by his bag, his camera, and his tripod. The tram was already hurtling down the track. He closed his eyes and saw himself crushed beneath its wheels.

And so he kneeled and removed his harness to crawl his way back through the crowd. His camera made a pathetic sound like a dead leaf crackling under a child's foot as it was demolished by 51.8 tons of steel.

* * *

Before she'd started working there, Lydie had always imagined TRBF headquarters as a beehive: swarming, buzzing, electric with constant activity. She soon realized, however, that the only one working on site day and night was the tower itself.

As for the long Soviet-style building perpendicular to the tower, it kept nine-to-five hours, after which only drafts blew through its complicated maze of gray corridors. Drafts and new hires: interchangeable young freelance journalists exploited at will, made to believe they were enormously lucky to be there and that their rivals' CVs were piling up in the department heads' drawers. A formidable school of depression, the TRBF began indoctrinating its students as soon as they came in the door.

Lydie, on the other hand, was drunk with happiness. She was realizing her life's dream. And so she took everything in stride: the blows, the humiliations, and above all the "filler" assignments, the street interviews and seasonal stories that none of her established colleagues found worthy of their commanding presence. In the newsroom, a journalist's importance was measured by his bedsores: the more respected he became, the less often he left his chair.

Lydie's work was clean, never flashy or overzealous: good material for the nightly news. She quickly became indispensable to the program, and spent plenty of time in the editing room, laughing with the technicians and fiddling with buttons.

Soon, she was lunching every day with the team at Max, a Sardinian restaurant in the neighborhood—not expensive, but not cheap either, which helped to keep the penniless interns away.

Daniel Claverie had made the place into an office of sorts, and Lydie into his protégé. He taught her the tricks of the trade, between mouthfuls of escalope Milanese and preening smiles at the police officers who walked by.

"You'll see, one day you'll take my place," he decreed. "Until then, do as I do. Smile at these gentlemen. It'll be your best employment insurance."

Clav, sensing in her an empathetic listener, soon began to tell her about his personal life: his wife had just left him for a plastic surgeon, dumb as a rock, without warning or any consideration for their children. In short, she'd proved to be "a superficial, egocentric slut." It was just the three of them now, Claverie and his little boys of two and seven, his nuggets, his darlings, his joys. "You can't really understand if you don't have kids of your own."

And so Lydie had invented for herself an ardent love of children, and was delighted when Claverie invited her to dinner at his place on boulevard Général Wahis. It was one of Jacques Brel's former homes, an enormous villa with the gabled roof and half-timbered facade typical of Alsace, Daniel's most beloved region. Tom and Steve adored the young woman right away, even cried when she decided to go home after having discreetly massaged their father's penis through his flannel trousers underneath the kitchen table.

"No, I can't—I want you, but you're my superior," was, in essence, Lydie's argument for not unzipping her boss's fly. Claverie had started to beg—"Come on, please, just show me your tits!"—only two months after the young woman had been hired. His pleas left Lydie's panties completely dry, but brought tears to her eyes—the emotion of nearing her goal, at last.

The news had quickly made its way to the coffee machine on the third floor. Pierre Romand, the former editor-in-chief of the morning news, was dead: he had thrown himself from his office window. Nothing shocking in itself; the poor guy had been slowly burning out since the late nineties ("overworked" had been a catchphrase at the time).

More unusual, however: Romand had been in a wheelchair due to a recent stroke, and his window was high up. Yet this did not raise any particular suspicions; a wheelchair-bound man had arms, after all.

He left his colleagues the memory of a good-natured man with an appetite for women and drink—*a bon vivant*, as they wrote on his funeral wreath, the type of remark he would have appreciated. He had covered the Gulf War in 1991; the story of a Kuwaiti mother whose son's eyes had been gouged out with a spoon by Iraqi soldiers had cemented his cynicism. Getting laughs out of his colleagues was his way of politely masking his private despair. Like a cardiac surgeon who works all night on hopeless cases but quips about breast implants in the morning.

That was Romand. He seemed hardened, and he was. But if you looked more closely, you saw the cracks in his exterior. For that matter, it had taken only a single anonymous letter posted to his mailbox to break him. A videotape, a few archives of the morning news from 1996—from two days in a row—and a snapshot from a police file, showing a man of an indeterminate age hanging in a stairwell, his chin covered with dried foam.

In the photo she texted, Tom was in tears, but it was Steve who had the sharp edge of the knife pressed against his carotid artery. *You're going to follow my instructions calmly*, was the message Lydie sent a few seconds later.

How did you get into my house, what kind of sick joke is this?

Where's the nanny? Daniel replied by text in a panic when Lydie wouldn't answer his calls.

If you tell anyone about this picture, I'll know, she texted back. *And I'll kill them. So do what I say.*

Jesus, what do I have to do? Please! You wouldn't hurt them!

We'll see about that. First, you're going to host the morning news as if everything were normal. If I see or sense anything unusual in your behavior or in your voice, or if I notice any strange activity in front of my house, I'll cut your sons' throats. Or I'll disembowel them. I'm not quite sure yet. I'll probably just go with my gut.

Are you fucking with me? You're completely insane! What's come over you? What did I do?

You'll figure it out soon enough. Don't send me any more messages, I'll decide when we talk. If you break this rule, I'll cut off one of their fingers. Then two, then three. Break a leg, Daniel. I'm watching you.

He walked on set, his armpits soaked in sweat, a panty liner stuck under each arm, his neck bulging against his yellow tie. Despite his promise to behave normally on the air, Daniel doubted he would be able to keep calm while his almost-mistress played knives on the necks of his children. The thought that she might have mutilated or killed their nanny did not disturb him: he barely knew the first name of the fat old Moroccan woman whose sour smell disgusted him a little.

On the other hand, that she should touch the flesh of his flesh drove him into a blind rage. He had, for that matter, worked all his life to protect the sanctity of childhood, and reserved a special hatred for abusers of all stripes.

He remembered very well the euphoria that had washed over him in the midst of the Dutroux affair, when he'd managed to expose the identity of a child molester to the public, who took care of finishing the job. He had felt useful then; he'd felt that his work, his very existence, was justified. This was why he had become a journalist: like Lydie, he had his heart set on repairing injustices. And what could be more unjust than the suffering of little ones?

Of course, at the time, he was only a measly freelance journalist—no one knew his name or asked him to sign rolls of toilet paper at the supermarket—but he had made a real impact on the world. He had acted heroically, within his means. For Belgium, the 1990s would always be marked by a seal of shame, and for Daniel Claverie, one of pride. Those years had allowed him to climb the rungs of the ladder toward his seat on the evening news, where he'd remained ever since. Only the blow jobs regularly offered him by a few zealous interns could make him feel any excitement about sitting his ass there every day.

At 7:28 p.m. he took his seat, eyes bulging, sweat flowing in rivers from his temples. At 7:29 he had a coughing fit. At 7:30 he opened the news segment as if nothing was wrong, fresh and dashing as always—the mark of a true professional. Only the most astute viewer would notice the vein pulsing slightly on his forehead.

At 7:57, after he'd delivered all the evening's topics and was about to close the segment, he saw more words appear on his teleprompter, in italics, words that were not his own. A long silence went over the air while he read them to himself.

You're going to read what follows on the air, without adding anything, without blinking, without raising an eyebrow. Your confession must seem as natural as possible. If I doubt your sincerity, you'll find your bathtub full of your sons' blood when you come home.

In his earpiece: "What the hell? Should I roll the credits? Daniel?"

Go ahead. Read this: Bisou.

Claverie let out a gasp but said nothing. He pushed his microphone away.

On his phone, a text: *This was a test to judge your docility. You failed. Prepare yourself for the worst. Don't say a word to anyone. See you tomorrow. Bisou.*

When he arrived home, no one was there.

The next morning, he blew his nose into his Tartan tie in the middle of the morning news, as Lydie had ordered him to do a few minutes before. Jokes began to spread over social media networks, poking fun at an anchor who seemed to be losing his sense of what was and wasn't in keeping with television etiquette.

The next day, he appeared without makeup—Lydie had forbade him from wearing any—and scratched his head intermittently when the order was given.

Daniel and Lydie continued to cross paths during the day and maintained the appearance of a cordial relationship. She was warmer than ever, obliging him to converse at length with her in public, and to give her news of his charming little boys. When would she see them again? Would he bring them to the office one day? They weren't feeling well? Couldn't have visitors at the moment? What a shame. She insisted that he wish them a prompt recovery on her behalf, even brought some candy for them one day and hoped that they were allowed to eat it.

In the following weeks, Claverie had to fit several words into his segment—this was something he often did to amuse his friends: a challenge well-known to those who speak on the radio or appear on TV.

For his friends, Daniel had said "goodness me," "butternut squash," and "Hula-Hoop." For Lydie, Daniel said "table," "carrot," and "bidet." Then Daniel said "Tom," "Steve," "dead," "dishonor," and "horror."

He was called into the office of the executive director, who was taken aback by his recent behavior—erratic, to say the least—on the air.

The chief recommended he take a week's vacation. Claverie attempted to decline, but he wasn't given a choice. He was at the point of breaking down, confessing that he had to continue working in order to save his sons' lives, but he managed to hold himself back, knowing that his tormentor would not pardon this error as easily as the first one. When he'd left, Lydie stuffed his mailbox with photos of decapitated children.

The apotheosis took place a week later, on the day he returned to host the news.

At the end of the segment, Claverie recited the words on the teleprompter: "Ladies and gentlemen, before I sign off, I have one last thing to add. I'm taking advantage of the national platform offered me here to make this confession, which has weighed on me for such a long time. I am attracted—sexually—to young children. Sometimes I touch them. And it gives me pleasure. Yet I don't believe that I'm a monster. You'll remember that I was, in the nineties, a sort of white knight of virtue. Well, it was during that time that I realized the truth about myself. This is a message to all the men, and even the women, who suffer . . ."

The credits went hurtling down the screen, too late. The director, mouth gaping, had been too shocked by what he was hearing to cut the star anchor's confession in time.

All over the city, in the backs of bars, in living rooms,

hospitals, and newsrooms, jaws dropped. Had they heard right? Were they hallucinating? The journalist had seemed strange recently—should they take his confession seriously? Telephones rang: *Are you watching the news? Did you hear Clav too? God, it's insane . . .* Some laughed nervously. Others sobbed (the elderly, mostly). The clip would soon be posted on Facebook, on Twitter. *I knew it,* people would type in the comments.

The news sites would repost the video, as well as the many commentators who attempted to analyze it, endlessly discussing topics which the TRBF would not comment on. Not right away, in any case. A few young women who'd kneeled under the TV star's desk in the vain hope of securing themselves a job would testify anonymously, bearing witness to his manipulative sexual behavior.

For the moment, Claverie choked on his own vomit as he walked toward the studio doors.

In the narrow cocoon of her apartment, Lydie conscientiously spoon-fed little Tom in front of the TV, while Steve, frowning in concentration, played with cars on a tablet. The young journalist was living her greatest night. The social media networks, like the blood in her veins, were buzzing.

The morning after Daniel Claverie's confession, and seven million YouTube views later, Lydie returned his children to him. On the phone, he had drily declined her invitation to meet her at Max; he was, as she might have guessed, in no condition to lunch, and besides, the police and his ex-wife were in his living room. He had agreed to delete all traces of their communication from his phone (she had done the same with the TRBF computer system), and to thank her, on his doorstep, for taking care of his little ones during this tormented night when he couldn't have been mentally present for them. Lydie, playing the remarkably professional babysitter, had alerted the police—despite her great respect for the father—of a few worrisome observations: Tom and Steve covering their faces with their hands whenever she raised her voice, signs of loss of bladder control in the oldest. Little things, here and there, all confirmed by Fatima, their devoted nanny. Perhaps none of it meant anything; after all, Daniel Claverie was a respectable man, she was certain. But she still felt it was her duty to have a word with the authorities. This was how she had been educated—to report all signs of possible wrongdoing, regardless of any personal bias. Daniel would understand her perfectly, attached as he was to the notion of moral integrity.

Before leaving for work, she assured her superior of his colleagues' respect for him and wished him courage for what he would have to confront. She gave him a sly, meaningful wink that horrified the TV star, causing him to gag on his bile once again.

Lydie was on remand when she heard the news.

Ever since her confession, she'd occupied a pleasant cell in Prison de Forest. There was plenty to read and write about, and her cellmates, though foul-smelling, were not so inhospitable as the American television shows would lead one to believe. She wasn't so bad off. Lydie had often complained that the Internet had altered her ability to concentrate and that she was unable to write her memoir, *In the Shadow of the Tower*, a project she had nurtured from girlhood (she would dedicate it to her mother who'd died in childbirth, the lucky fool); there were too many distractions. In prison, there was no Internet access, or very little, and that was a good thing.

And so she had been among the last to know. But deep down, she didn't care; she'd already had her revenge, and in the most delicious manner.

Of course, Daniel Claverie had returned to his job within a few weeks, his innocence proved by the police and by Lydie's confessions. But the public did its utmost to "finish the job," just as it had before. It had been, in a sense, reassuring to witness that in this world gone mad, where everything appears to change so quickly, certain human instincts remain intact.

The lovely half-timbered facade of his home was now obscured by hateful messages spray-painted a few days after the star's confession. The former public friend number one had been beaten up in broad daylight, in the street, by a group of parents outraged to see him walking free. The TRBF had reaffirmed their support, offering viewers the "true" version of events: the story of a rejected young woman, crazy with rage—crazy, period—willing to go to any lengths to destroy him. Lydie had found it amusing to see her face appear suddenly on the old plasma TV in the prison cafeteria. As Claverie had predicted, she'd taken his place on television—a good half of the screen, in any case. All of Prison de Forest had been impressed by her strategy, and showered her with praise.

She was still relishing her moment of fame when the host, a complete unknown, delivered the news.

It was at five o'clock that afternoon that they'd discovered Daniel Claverie, forty-six years old, hanging beneath the dome of the telecommunications tower, his corpse tossed about by the autumn wind, in full sight of the cars stuck in traffic on boulevard Auguste Reyers. The viaduct's demolition was underway, and at rush hour, when you entered the fray surrounding the boulevard, you never knew when you'd get out. In backseats, children wondered: Was it a statue?

Santa Claus? A robber? More than an hour passed before the emergency paramedics arrived and managed to climb the tower and cut him down. Clav hadn't left a note; he hadn't known what to write.

ECUADOR

BY ALFREDO NORIEGA

Ixelles

> *Translated from the Spanish by John Washington*
> *and Daniela Maria Ugaz*

> *Dedicated to the memory of Samira Adamu,*
> *killed on a plane by Belgian police*

> *There are toxic places. Everything speaks to us or against us.*
> —Henri Michaux

I t wasn't hard for me to go to Brussels; at least it wasn't
hard for me to leave Paris where I'd lived the past twenty-five
years dogged by bad luck, or, as they say in my country,
living from blunder to blunder, trapped in the inhuman drama
of existence—what can I say, there's probably no European
city as cruel as the French capital. Which is why landing in
Brussels was a relief. Our apartment was located in the district
of Ixelles. There are a total of nineteen, I think, or twenty dis-
tricts, I'm not sure, don't have a clue, and I have little desire
to check on Wikipedia just to avoid looking like an imbecile.
Ixelles, in my newcomer's eyes, was beautiful, cosmopolitan
enough for me to feel at ease, but not so much that I felt
ill at ease with the traditions of the Congolese or Moroccan
families or, on the flip side, the niceties of the Eurocrats; both
abound in Ixelles.

We lived in a house whose owner, an Italian who arrived in Belgium more than forty years earlier, had made his fortune with a roof renovation business. A man who exhaled hatred and tenacity, those basic ingredients of any entrepreneur. The proof of his success was his Porsche convertible, which slept in the garage. As we looked around at the house, he observed us with puppy-dog eyes; later, he'd ignore us, and what was more, I had the impression that he was set on making our lives impossible, but my wife, a Brit and a diplomat, had the sort of status that put a stop to his xenophobic impulses. A guy like me didn't give him a good feeling, especially since I'd spend all day at home. We liked that house because it was close to everything my wife wanted: her work, our son's school, and her best friends. To me it didn't matter if we lived there or anywhere else, as long as I was with her and the little one, and far from Paris. From our balcony we could see the European Parliament, and near the horizon the Belgian flag waved over the Royal Palace.

I seldom went out. Sometimes I'd go down to Flagey Square and sit at Café Belga, a place whose only defect was being too trendy and packed with a clientele made up mostly of women who were so attractive and so inaccessible they'd make me nervous, which is why I'd only go when I could no longer bear my confinement. I'd read on our balcony, no matter the weather, which was usually rainy, and from there I'd observe the life of the city—or better said, the life of the neighborhood—without ever making out enough details to get any real idea as to who lived in the surrounding buildings. I intuited that one guy was an official who worked at the European Commission, that a group of people were an ordinary family, over there were a pair of students, a single woman, a single man—in short, the boring miscellany of any city in this piece-of-shit world we live in.

Below was a vacant lot abutting an abandoned house. Most mornings there was a kid, twenty-some years old, who would tag or paint on the walls. Street art isn't my thing, I don't understand how Banksy can rouse so much commotion, and above and beyond anything else, I hate art installations, the boring egocentrism of artists today. When he'd finish, the kid would put away his paints with great care, he'd use some product to wash his hands, he'd change his shirt, and then he'd leave. While he worked I'd pull out the binoculars and, forgive the hyperbole, take great pleasure in watching his naïve strokes. I'm a creature of habit, or in any case, I'm repetitive; that's why, in part, I do what I do: because there are no surprises in life, and if somehow I'm still surprised then it's my fault and I'll have to deal with it alone. That's been the only way for me to distance myself from people and, though it seems contradictory, to get closer to their vacuity.

At three o'clock I'd pick up my son from school, only five minutes away from our house. For three hours we'd play, or watch TV, or I'd take him to the park, and sometimes when he'd close himself up in his childish world, I'd return to mine. My wife would get home at seven. Hearing her keys turn in the lock, my love for her would swell in my chest and remind me where I was standing and why. I'd have little to tell her, and yet, over dinner, I'd talk to her about my day, attempting to lend my trifles some meaning. She'd listen with the easy pleasure of someone whose days were spent confronting the giants of European politics, which is to say, spent in the limbo in which we've all chosen to live, approaching neither hell nor heaven. One day she'd be at a NATO event, another at a conference about youth unemployment; one week she'd be dealing with the Germans and the French who now threatened to abandon the Union. Deep down, human impotence seemed to dictate not only her fate, but the fate of us all.

One morning, after dropping my son off at school, I sat right down to my desk. I was hoping to see if the kid was around, but I had such a strong, almost violent urge to write that I was completely absorbed for three whole hours, as if I were a pilot flying through a storm (a bad analogy, I know— my apologies). When I finally got up I went to the balcony. The kid was there, but not alone; there were two cops thrashing him. Someone must have filed a complaint, I figured, one of those sons of bitches who proliferate in all parts of the world and don't have anything better to do with their time than mess with the lives of others. The bigger of the two cops pulled out his truncheon and whacked the kid with it, the other cop caught him with pepper spray right in the eyes. It seemed they were overdoing it, but I guessed that the Belgian police were just as bestial as all police, and that was that. The kid covered his face with his hands and fell back. They whacked him with the club again. When he tried to defend himself, the cops unleashed themselves on him without holding back. I screamed, but the wind covered my voice. None of my neighbors' heads popped out of their windows.

The kid collapsed. I went to look for my camera. When I got back, the cops had disappeared, leaving him sprawled on the ground. I left the apartment, running. I didn't know how to get into the vacant lot. A wall encircled the empty house in front of it. I went back up to my apartment to see if I could locate an entrance. I couldn't see the kid now, so I got my binoculars. There were no signs of him, or of the cops; just the first strokes of his painting on the wall. If he could get over the wall, I thought, I should be able to do the same.

Before heading back down I drank a glass of water since my throat was dry. I went and stood in front of the empty house; it was incredible how many abandoned structures there were, as if they were the city's scars, or its sad memories. All the front windows had been boarded up, the front door too. At first glance, it seemed impossible to enter. Maybe the way to get in, I thought, was from the other side of the block. I checked it out. In the building on the opposite side of the abandoned house there was an open iron gate leading into a large patio. I went in. It was a little public park, which, from my window, I had thought was the interior courtyard of the building. I climbed up the wall that separated the lot from the abandoned building, and, dropping down, found myself inside.

The site, in some way, seemed like it mirrored my own life: chaos, abandon, a delicious sort of anarchy, confinement. I peered up. From this angle, my balcony, with its wicker armchair, looked set like a perfect stage. You could even see a few of our pictures on the walls and a corner of my desk. The kid, then, must have known me just as well as I knew him. He probably waited for me before he started performing, probably saw me looking through my binoculars at his paintings. I went to the spot where he was beaten. There was a small bloodstain, two jars of paint, a broken bracelet. I grabbed the bracelet and put it in my pocket, then went home. I lay down on the couch and fell asleep.

I woke with a start, thinking I had slept past the time to pick up my boy at school, but no. I still had time to eat and take a shower.

The afternoon was a pleasant reminder that I still had a future and dreams ahead of me. My son was a little agitated, probably he'd had a bad day, a fight with a little friend, a scolding from his teacher, or maybe a stomachache. We watched TV and fell asleep together—a grave mistake, as he didn't end up going to bed that night until much later, trampling on my few moments of tranquility with my wife, when we could talk together, make love, or just hold each other on the balcony like a couple of teenagers.

By ten we were finally alone. My wife was scared about the latest news that the extreme right had won elections in France. In all of Europe, she told me, the xenophobic and Nazi parties were about to achieve historic results. They're hysterical, I said; the two words—Nazism and hysteria—had always been tied together for me, like conjoined twins sharing a single heart. We spent the night talking politics, wondering about our own destinies in this world without memory. We imagined ourselves on the beach in my country, eating fresh fish with fried plantains, building sand castles. I couldn't tell her what I'd seen happen to the kid in the vacant lot; it seemed like it would dampen her night.

Though being witness to something like that would usually have unsettled me, I slept soundly. I woke up before my son started crying for his milk and went out to the balcony wrapped in a blanket to watch the sunrise. To my surprise I saw that the new painting, only started the day before, had been completed. I felt an enormous relief; Brussels, so devoid of angels and so full of waving flags, once again seemed like a beacon of hope. My morning proceeded as usual. I went out to the balcony a few times with the hope of catching sight of the kid. But I never saw him. I examined his painting through my binoculars, and it seemed to have a rougher style than usual, without the subtleties I'd seen in his work before—maybe a by-product of his encounter with the cops, or of having been finished in the dark.

My wife was tired when she came home from work. I told her what had happened the day before as we watched, on

French TV, a sensationalist news story on the growing success of the extreme right.

You have to report it, she said to me.

But the kid came around, I explained, telling her about the finished painting. You shouldn't let them get away with these things, she responded, and then she gave me the address of Committee P, which is the force that polices Belgium's cops.

I fell asleep and had nightmares. I woke as early as I had the morning before, sat in the wicker chair, and again witnessed the day dawning before me. The painting was still there, without so much as a new brushstroke. On the way to school we walked past the police station of Ixelles, which is next to the Maison Communale, as they call the town hall in Brussels. I guessed that the cops I'd seen were based at this station. Two officers caught my eye, and they seemed harmless enough, consumed by their own apathy.

On my way back, I decided to go in. I walked up to the counter where a female officer was talking on the phone. When she hung up, I told her what I'd seen in the vacant lot. I spoke, I admit, hastily. Her eyes widened and, without saying a word, she motioned a coworker over. The coworker asked to see my ID.

I don't have it, I said.

What are *you* doing here? he asked.

Nothing, I snarled; I don't like it when strangers use the familiar pronoun *tu* with me.

The guy got rough, as if I'd somehow provoked him. He came around to my side of the counter. Take everything out of your pockets and put your hands up, he said.

Why? I haven't done anything wrong.

I'm not asking what you've done, do what I say.

Sir, I replied, maybe I haven't explained myself, but I'd like to report something.

The guy couldn't hold out any longer; he grabbed me and slammed me against the wall, pressing his forearm into my neck. A sharp pain stabbed into my side as the officer prodded my ribs with his truncheon.

You're going to calm down, he whispered in my ear, as if he were confessing something.

Yes, I said breathlessly.

He let go of me. I stood petrified. Regaining my breath. My name, where I lived, that I was the husband of a British diplomat—I told it all to him—and that my ID was back at my house, I was just on my way to drop my son off at school, which is why I didn't have anything on me.

Get out of here, the officer said, we don't want to see you around here again. He grabbed the collar of my shirt and pushed me into the street.

The sun, beaming brightly over the buildings, overwhelmed me. For a moment I lost my bearings. I started walking. A few yards ahead, as I reached a flower shop, the neighborhood became familiar once again. I spent the rest of the morning wandering the streets. Though I hate beer, I drank one at a bar whose name, under the circumstances, seemed rather ironic: le Sans Souci. I don't know why, but it reminded me of Quito's Capilla del Robo, with that colonial, baroque style that always manages to sadden me—I've never been able to distance myself from the horror and loss I see in those buildings. My city, I thought, buried by the Andes, trying to seem devout just so it could exist, exactly like I was doing now.

I went to fetch my little one. I avoided walking past the station. He, a creature of habit like me, didn't understand why we took a different route home. We'll get to know a new park, I told him. I took him to the park next to the vacant lot. We spent awhile there; he playing on the slide while I stood at the exact angle from which our apartment was visible. It started to drizzle and we went home. I didn't tell my wife what had happened, she had enough problems; dealing with technocrats and politicians was nearly as rough as dealing with armed, cocky men in uniforms.

The kid never came back. His painting was left intact; I studied it every day to see if it had changed, but nothing ever happened. One night, my wife confessed that she'd noticed me acting strangely; I seemed different, she clarified.

Come on, I said, I hate it when you interpret my moods, you know that.

She knew my moods usually had to do with my work more than anything else; how often I'd suffered for my pipe dreams, how many times I'd been left dumbfounded, tied up in a foolish knot. It's all part of my unwillingness to deal with reality, my way of watching it without daring to touch it. She said she was sorry.

That Sunday we went out to eat at an "ephemeral" Ecuadoran restaurant. I call it that because it only ever opened on the first Sunday of every month, out of a living room in the municipality of Schaerbeek, in a mostly Moroccan area. The owners decorated the entrance with tables full of pots and trays of the delicacies that any far-flung compatriot dreams of: steamed fava beans, empanadas, ceviche, mote, chochos, tostados, hornados, fritadas, and an extensive et cetera. My wife loved it; I'd say she craved Ecuadoran food more than me.

You're a very folksy gringa, I'd often say to get a rise from her.

You're an idiot Frenchified impostor, she'd shoot back. Though it isn't very British of her, she'd learned to defend herself tooth and nail against my dumb jokes.

We sat at a table next to another family: father, mother, their three children, the mother's sister, and the father's cousin. They chattered like any carefree family, as if in that space they could finally own their idiosyncrasies. And you, the woman asked, when did you move here?

I told them a little bit about our story, so different from their own that I seemed a foreigner in their eyes; for them, coming and settling down in Brussels had been a heroic act. Stories of immigrants. If I wanted to make someone cry, I'd tell such a story, but I exhaust my experience of the topic in two paragraphs. I listened to their stories with an ethnologist's arrogant air.

One story, however, was worthy of retelling: that of the restaurant owner they were friends with—a guy from Babahoyo, which is surely one of the ugliest cities in Ecuador, a sort of slum built in the middle of a tropical plain, where the eponymous river and the Caracol River meet. He came here alone, and after four years of radical struggle he was able to bring his family. Among them came his eldest son, a seventeen-year-old kid. One Sunday, playing basketball at a nearby park in Schaerbeek, a Moroccan boy, accusing him of cheating, stabbed and killed him. All hell broke loose. The police came, not only to get the killer, but to contain the anger of some thirty young Ecuadorans seeking revenge. These were two communities not used to interacting, living similar stories in Spain and in Belgium.

The police, of course, couldn't do anything; only deal blows or spray gas. The victim's father put a stop to the brawl himself. Someone gave him a megaphone and he was able to quiet everyone with a few phrases. Damn you! he screamed at the boys. My child's death must be respected! If you ever want to look me in the eye, then come to his burial with your hands clean!

At least that's what they told me he said. I raised my eyes at that short and stout man, sweating, busy with the dishes, who didn't look like the prototypical hero, just the opposite; in my eyes he had the look of the classic crafty Ecuadoran who has only one guiding principle: the dollar bill.

Anyway, the story didn't end there, it took another turn, having to do with the restaurant. After the burial, the parents of the killer came to visit. They found that they were similar—both were fighters, and both had that timeless, borderless ethic of ordinary people. The Ecuadoran lived with his family in a two-bedroom flat in a basement of Schaerbeek, a spruced-up rathole. I tried to imagine the broken-language encounter between the two sad families—one family from the desert, the other from the tropics—with gestures and mannerisms becoming more and more emphatic, exaggerated. They spent all evening sharing the grief of having lost their children, feeling the betrayal of fate, maybe also the betrayal of God, but this is all conjecture. By the end of the evening, the Moroccan man handed over a room to the Ecuadoran, with which he could do as he pleased. That's how this family climbed out of their hole, becoming a model of success for their countrymen; though what propelled their success was death.

Ideas would usually show up in my head without prior notice, just as my friends back in Quito used to appear at my place on Riofrío Street. Ideas coming without warning, stealing my sleep, my appetite, my solitary joys; sometimes I'd let them knock on the door and, hidden in the closet, I'd wait until they gave up and went away. Then I'd go to the window to watch them amble downhill, saddened, in search of someone else willing to open the door for them at this late hour. Those friends of mine in Quito would get so wrapped up in your business you'd find them bobbing in your soup, opining about your life with nearly as much gusto as your mother; they knew you better and loved you less, and would never shy away from offending. This is how ideas would come to me, how they would treat me; occasionally I could escape them, but if they persisted I would finally succumb.

I was on the balcony finishing a book by Erri De Luca about vengeance and justice, and it reminded me of the Lone Ranger. I decided to go down to the abandoned house. It was a sunny day. The weeds had started to take over, even climbing up the walls. I approached the house. From my angle I could see in through the barred windows; surprisingly, the interior seemed to be in good shape—a few minutes with a broom would make it inhabitable again. I was amazed that a group of squatters hadn't already moved in. It was a perfect place for those folks who hope to change the world by preaching age-old idealistic mantras. I sat against the door. The painting had already begun to lose its shine, from up close it looked frighteningly bad, almost worse than the little drawings my son would make. I stepped closer. The painting, I figured, was an allegory, however poorly done, of a meeting between a succubus and an incubus, and it was signed, *W.O.T.N.*, initials that, of course, meant nothing to me. The two paint cans were in the same place they had been on the day of the attack; the bloodstain, however, had disappeared.

I scanned the neighboring houses. From that vantage you could see a lot more clearly the comings and goings of the neighbors. The kid probably was, without any of us realizing it, a point of connection in our disparate lives. I went back inside, grabbed a book I had been wanting to read, the Prix Goncourt–winning *Trois jours chez ma mère* by François Weyergans, and went back to the empty lot. I read for two hours straight, glancing up whenever I saw movement in any of the houses or buildings in front of me. A young woman stood next to her bathroom window and blow-dried her hair; a little boy, sickly looking, pressed against his window glass in what looked like a pose of angelic nostalgia. On page 88 I found a description of how to shrink heads. I nearly jumped— I've written about shrinking heads before. I read it through three times. Lucky for me, Weyergans didn't have the Amazon in his bones, and his writing was rather lackluster. I took in a deep breath, but a second later I saw what a fake I was; mine had been a stupid invention as well, a mere fantasy. I got up and went back home. I spent the afternoon with my son, lulled by the routine of my paternal duties.

European elections rolled around, with extreme-right parties winning in both France and Great Britain, the German Nazi party even electing a member of parliament, and the Nazi party of Greece electing three. The press and the politicians were stunned.

Always the same circus, said my wife.

Damn history repeating itself, I said, only the Italians saved face. For once, I added.

We were like two winos in the twilight of life and alcoholism. We sat down to watch the news, holding hands, without the least desire for a glass, ready to tip into the abyss together. My wife went to work the next day with her head hung; the shifts in the new parliament had put her position at risk. Soon we'd have to pack up and set off—not to Paris, thank God, but probably to London, or, if she was up for it, and if I was too, to some African embassy. If we were looking to make it rich, we could have decided to go to Afghanistan or Iraq, but that wasn't us. We needed a place where I'd have the opportunity, but not the necessity, to shut myself indoors.

I went back down to the empty lot to finish the Weyergans novel. I felt really close to the main character, even if, as I was reading it, he was pretty much my opposite. Every once in a while I'd look around at the neighboring buildings: the same young woman was blow-drying her hair in front of her window, but instead of seeing the sick child, silhouettes flitted by like ghosts. It started to rain, but I didn't go back inside. Protected under the balcony of the abandoned house, I continued to read. I returned to our apartment at one in the afternoon, ate, and took a nap. Then I rushed out to get my son. As I walked past the police station, I recognized the officer who had jostled me in the doorway. There was a whole gaggle of policemen; I guessed it was shift change. They came smiling, joking, most of them speaking Flemish, all of them brandishing their arms, their batons, and handcuffs. Two of them were the guys who had attacked the boy that day while patrolling the neighborhood. Just because he'd tagged a wall in a vacant lot? At least that's how it seemed. If I had the gall I would have searched the city for W.O.T.N. because surely he had tagged other neighborhoods and was probably recognized in the circle of local graffiti artists, those urban tribes that seem identical across Tokyo, Santiago, and New York—to such an extent that they bored me before I ever got to know their work. But we weren't in a novel and my character had no desire to dive into that plot. Above all, I was not in a position to prove anything to anyone; those years were long gone. I had my plan, less literary than cinematic, and I was set on following it to the end; surely that's what motivated me the most.

For three weeks I went out every day and read in the vacant lot. I'd take a stool, an umbrella, a thermos of coffee, and some fruit or a sandwich. I reread *Le Chercheur d'or* by Le Clézio and *Un barrage contre le Pacifique* by Duras—the first two books I'd ever read in French. They excited me, not so much because of their stories, but because they brought me back to the late eighties and that stupid nostalgia for my country. Le Clézio as much as Duras pushed me toward fruitless searches and grandiose dreams; maybe I too had let myself be hypnotized by them.

The sick child wasn't only sick, but dying. Every day his features sharpened more, his gaze languishing. There, with his face on the other side of the window, was the perfect metaphor for injustice. Every morning the girl would reappear to dry her long brown hair. The silhouettes of the first few days gave way to faces, every once in a while stares, even smiles; so quickly does the unusual become part of the landscape, or at least an element of daily life. The initial surprises were forgotten; the vacant lot became my place. When I'd grow tired of sitting on the bench, I'd read as I walked or squatted next to a wall; the brush would give way to my steps, even the house seemed to come alive with my presence and absence; whenever I'd come or go something within her would move. I had the hope (in Spanish we say, literally, *I have the illusion: Tengo la ilusion*) of seeing W.O.T.N. reemerge. The British would never think of such a phrase, they'd think it was hysterical or even hypocritical. In French, the word *illusion* has a negative connotation, sort of like a lie, a mistake. I started a novel by Roth, the character was named Consuela Castillo, she was the daughter of exiled Cubans (they call them *worms* in Latin America), and I was surprised by the *a* at the end of Consuela;

because in Spanish the name ends in *o*: Consuelo; this detail disturbed my reading.

After three weeks, I decided to stay in for a few days, hoping to create a little suspense. I observed the vacant lot and the neighborhood from my balcony with affection, as if it were a part of me. Four people were killed in the Jewish Museum in Brussels. The Belgian police were petrified. It was the French who found the suspect, out of pure luck, in France. It was deemed an attack by a "lone wolf," as they call those young men who come back from the civil war in Syria with the hope that the world will become what they think it is. Helicopters flew over our house for a while, the traffic near the Parliament and the police station was total chaos. My wife would leave every morning and come back every night dejected. She spent a night with Obama. Well, not with him, but near him, and she participated in a meeting with the French, German, and British foreign ministries.

For me, this marked the time to return to the vacant lot. The house received me graciously, a beautiful light streaming in through latticed windows, illuminating the bald walls and the dusty wood floors. *How many dead have passed through here?* I wondered—as I have a habit of imagining horror instead of happiness. The first to appear was the boy, along with his mother; he no longer had hair and seemed stripped of all hope. He smiled and with his small fingers waved hello. The mother also smiled, and I felt relief in her expression, as if her gazing into the vacant lot was her only moment of quietude. The boy said something, his mother responded. I sat with my book on my lap; when I glanced up they were no longer at the window. I started to cry. The girl with the long brown hair appeared and she did as she always did; I was thankful to the repetition that gave the morning its consistency.

At one in the afternoon two officers showed up. They didn't enter by hopping over the fence and circling the park, but came right through the abandoned house. A man appeared for the first time at the window where the girl was drying her hair. These are the surprises of any type of writing, whether fiction or nonfiction, whether in the story line, the connecting narrative threads, or the hidden truths. I peered down at my book, my fingers could barely hold it up; the words hardened as if they'd transformed into warning signs, jumping from the page, changing shape.

I saw their black boots. One officer grabbed me by the arm and ordered me to stand, the other snatched my book: *Ecuador* by Michaux. He's a Belgian author, and I told this to the cop, who stared at its cover in disbelief. Be quiet, the other said, squeezing my arm. They arrested me inside the house. It was in that moment that I realized my script had failed me. I tried to free myself, but the two officers lifted me into the air and threw me halfway across the room. My clothes were covered in dust. They beat me to a pulp.

When I came to, I was lying on a rickety old bed in a locked cell. My left eye was swollen shut. My skin was covered in dried blood. I pulled off my clothes. I'd never seen my body with so many colorful bruises. I thought of my son crying at school. I called out; there was no response. Had somebody at the school gotten ahold of my wife? I tried to remember what info I'd given when we enrolled him: our address, my cell number, our names . . . but not my wife's number. What were they going to do when I didn't show? In France they'd call the police. But in Belgium? Surely they'd call the authorities, or maybe even try to reach my wife after not being able to get ahold of me, but she might be in one of those secret, behind-closed-doors meetings. I screamed again. Nothing. It was my fault my son was scared and crying. I'd let myself get carried away by my stupid ideas, and now I was going to have to face the repercussions of my own naïveté. Please, I yelled. Help me! A sepulchral silence (forgive the idiotic description) surrounded me. I was in a clandestine prison, in the Belgium of today, with a new king but the same dull fight between the "haves" (the Flemish) and those supposedly leeching off of them (the Wallonians).

Shit, I said to myself; these stupidities were still passing through my head instead of anything that could actually help me: the world is the same and will go on being the same *ad vitam æternam!* I should tell myself stories so as not to go insane, find inspiration in my friend Samuel Blixen who was locked in a hole for years during Uruguay's dictatorship. The horror of cliché took over in those first few hours in the cell. Yes, *my* cell—I should call it like it is, otherwise I'll lose my mind. Let me confess something personal: since I was twenty I've suffered from panic attacks and anxiety; it comes in waves, sometimes fiercely and sometimes it's bearable, but when an attack comes, without exception, it is tenacious, pushing me to the edge of something without body or weight, some nameless fear, an annihilation, pushing me up to the border but not over, this limbo that I've already mentioned, where I'm at risk of finding myself completely alone, without even a memory of my wife or child. In my cell there was an old bed, a hole to shit into, and a crude faucet above the hole. It was about thirty square feet and six feet high. The temperature was probably fifty-five degrees but humid, a perfect place to store wine or provoke attacks of rheumatism for somebody so disposed, as I was.

There was an outlet in the wall. It was the only thing that seemed to come from the outside world. Good God, how those two little slits could signify the entire world for someone like me: the television where my parents and I watched the blurry image of Armstrong walking on the moon. My radio in Paris, the French culture programs, *Là-bas si j'y suis*, of Daniel Mermet, FIP, and the melomania—banal as it was—that reminded me so much of myself. The enormous radio in my Grandpa Riofrío's house. The lamp on my work desk, rusted and beautiful. The lamp on the nightstand, which we would leave on as we made love because seeing is just as important as feeling. Charging my first cell phone. The rechargeable batteries we used in my son's toys, his small lamp with the cosmic shade. The blender and the toaster, neither of which we could live without. My electric razor and toothbrush. My wife's hair dryer. The ridiculous plugs of Great Britain, those of my own country, the plugs in the hotels I've passed through—so many. The dresser drawer where we store our chargers—probably, I kid you not, twenty or more—for our cameras, our phones, the innumerable other gadgets we use or we neglect to use, that we still have or that we lost years ago. Life could be reduced to that act of plugging and unplugging, charging and draining, turning on and turning off, these verb pairs that seem to contain some truth, and yet in the end are pretexts to avoid yourself, to deny your own stupid human condition.

The cuts and bruises healed, or at least improved. A doctor came, or someone who said he was a doctor, along with two guards. Doctor, I said when he approached me, they don't have the right to lock me up. I told him my wife's name, told him that she was a diplomat, and then begged him to contact her. He left without speaking a word. I thought of the Argentine priests giving extreme unction to political prisoners during the dictatorship. I thought of Gustavo Garzón, a classmate of mine in Ecuador, who was disappeared by the Ecuadoran police. I thought of the Restrepo brothers, assassinated by the Ecuadoran police, though we never found their bodies. The world is full of the disappeared, people we forget about too soon. How soon will they forget about me? Which of my friends will have the courage of the Restrepo family?

The guards came back. I thought they were going to torture me; I couldn't stop my imagination from running wild. After all this time spent incommunicado, my mind had started to blur the line between simple thoughts and sinister scenarios. Though violent, I told myself, the police are still sane. From when I first came to Brussels until the day I saw them beat W.O.T.N., cops in Belgium seemed more relaxed than anything, almost provincial.

Both guards stood in front of me. Your wife, one of them said, is disappointed in you.

What? I replied, thinking I had misunderstood.

She's figured out that you're just as disgusting as all the blacks.

I know, I said, our relationship was only ever about sex. Plus, I added, she likes Dylan Thomas and I like Alfredo Gangotena.

One of the guards tried to make sense of what I'd just said; the other smiled ironically. You're an idiot, he said, you'll see this is no joke. And then, with a theatrical gesture, he pulled a plastic bag out of his pocket, inside of which was a bracelet. He held it up to me. Recognize this?

No, I said.

Well, we found it in your house with, unfortunately for you, traces of blood.

Then I remembered picking up the bracelet that same day that W.O.T.N. disappeared. And? I spit out.

You're going to have to tell us who you killed.

I didn't kill anybody, but I did see you beating the hell out of that kid in the vacant lot.

They both laughed. We've come to an agreement with your wife and your lawyer, they told me, and then they left.

The next day they took me out of the cell and drove me to an airport. I was locked up with a group of men and women. My fellow detainees spoke Lingala, and at first they tried to talk to me in that language. They were from the equatorial region of the Congo. Both they and I were tired of being from a place whose name people always mixed up.

We're from the equator, we must be able to understand each other, no? they asked me.

That's true, I said, then asked what was happening to us.

Nothing, one of the women responded. Just life. Her black eyes drilled into me. I'd never given much consideration to my African roots; I'd always thought that my life was guided by words, by their sounds; I never wanted to be what people wanted me to be, I never wanted the circumstances they chose for me, and yet, unfortunately, I'd become the unwanted surprise, the intruder, the mistake.

The cops burst into the room, brimming with law, authority. The woman started kicking, screaming: My name is Semira Adamu and I am a free woman!

They took us to the same plane. I went in front, handcuffed but relieved that I would soon be far from this piece-of-shit city and near my son and wife. They made me sit down and asked me to keep calm. This sounded strange, incongruous even. Yes, okay, I replied. The woman, on the other hand, fought like a wild animal. The policemen surrounded her, and the intensity of her battle gradually subsided. Then there was silence. Suddenly the police got really nervous. One started to give her a cardiac massage, the other mouth-to-mouth.

I was petrified and not strong enough to stop them, by God, not strong enough because of that stupid Andean idiosyncrasy, because of the helicopters flying over our apartment, because of the dying child, because of W.O.T.N., because of my wife and son who were waiting for me in our new life, because of the fiction that distorts everything in the most inopportune moments.

Based on a true story

PAINT IT, BLACK

BY BOB VAN LAERHOVEN

Parc de Forest

This story was originally written in English

I

Tumultuous roaring. Very picturesque. Also very annoying. Peeping through the window. Peeping is an art form. Some houses farther, in the café at the corner of the rue de Bosnie, there is a top-of-lungs argument. The curtains—red-and-white checkered—in the windows of café El Principado have been closed. I'm familiar with that sign: hoo-ha between Muslims and genuine *kiekenfretters*, as the residents of Brussels are nicknamed. Lots of creative curses and threats. Someone storms out of El Principado, chased by a heated individual armed with a wooden bat. Police sirens. Oh well, night business as usual in this working-class district of Brussels, the metropolis of Manneken Pis and the European Union, in that order.

I return to my atelier. I've equipped the veranda of the old house I'm renting with sunlamps, normally used for growing plants in winter greenhouses. The lamps are there to focus, to get the color right, to blindfold my dreams until they become paintings. Already, the title of my new painting has descended upon me: *Les mangeurs des enfants*. First I had *Cannibals*, but no, not intricate enough. *Les mangeurs des enfants* is disturbingly elegant. Politicians, clergymen, and teachers around the table, dissecting spastic young children. *Child Eaters*.

Spectacles on nose, brush in hand, anticipation in breast. What comes creeping? A void between the image I have of the picture, and the brush. The moment of magic is gone due to the argument at the café. Thank you, Brussels lowlife, thank you, followers of Allah. The ringing telephone is a God-given excuse to stop painting.

But who could be ringing at two o'clock in the morning?

"I noticed a pattern in your work, Drees De Grijse." Serge Butoyara talks with a drawl, not a good sign. "You can't paint a picture without at least one naked woman." Fuck, here we go for another nighttime telephone marathon. Serge is on the warpath again, fueled by God knows how many lagers, and wondering what is more important: his hatred for all living beings or his self-hate.

"It so happens that I love naked women, Serge."

A weird sound, something between chuckling and hissing. "So I noticed."

"Is that the reason for your call?" Something in me is stirring. It's caution.

"Each time I wanted to run away from home, my father threatened that he would cut off my big toe."

"Why your big toe?" Humor him, he'll get to the point.

"Without your big toe you can no longer walk," Serge Butoyara clucks. "I already prepared myself for my new name: *Nak Gudwa*."

"Oh?" Politeness is a wonderful thing. It makes you blank.

"It means *eight toes*. Why don't you come over and have a beer? Or we can drive to Paris and order champagne."

"Where is Jeanine, Serge?"

"Or we can fly to Stockholm. Picture it, Drees: a coal-black man like me in a pure-white world. Symbolic, don't you think?" Serge begins humming some lyrics of the Stones's "Paint It, Black." Nice falsetto.

"I'll come over one of these days and paint you in a snowy landscape, okay? Where is Jeanine?"

"She's on her knees right before you, Drees, and she has your dick in her mouth. You're swelling, oh yes, you're swelling, and she sucks slowly, only she knows how to do it like that—and you're laughing at me, you bastard, you think I'm a miserable joke."

Time to put down the phone.

Serge has figured it out.

What happened between me and his wife.

Three nights later. Telephone ringing. Picking up.

Sniffing sounds.

"Serge?"

No answer. Humming. Then: ancestral African dialects, who knows what curse the damn Tutsi is reciting? I softly place the phone in its cradle.

Two minutes later: *ring ring*. Fuck off, Serge. But I know that I'll pick up again and be nice to him.

"Hello."

"A survival trip, Drees. The two of us. Now. A race to the finish. Parc de Forest . . ."

"And having my dick bitten off in the park by some mutts from those asshole dogfight organizers? I know better ways to get my kicks, Serge."

"I'm aware of that." He's being very polite. Not a good thing.

Silence. I'm a patient man.

"But you're out of touch as always," he goes on. "The cops

have cleaned up the place. Bye, nightly dogfights . . . Only peaceful greenery now."

"I'm not a nature freak. Besides, it's well past midnight. I need my beauty sleep."

"A survival trip in the park as warriors. You and me. If we survive, we'll split Jeanine."

"Oh? Which part do you get?"

"Don't try to be funny, Drees. You're not. Never have been."

"Fuck you, Serge, it's one thirty. I want to sleep."

"Coward. No-balls-man."

"Okay, I'll be at your den within half an hour, you simian."

I know I shouldn't go. Serge is a wreck. He sniffs too much ether. I can't instill a more subtle need in him, like cocaine for instance. Ether in this day and age . . . How full of self-loathing can you be?

With Jeanine away on a trip to Italy, maybe I can convince Serge that it was her fault.

His wife seduced me, oh how she seduced me.

A confident push on the bell button. Drizzling rain in the middle of the night. A survival trip in a godforsaken Brussels park? Knowing Serge, it'll be a booze run again. Oh well, let's hope he has forgotten everything about Jeanine and me. He can't keep his thoughts together for longer than ten minutes; his short-term memory is fucked. That's why Serge is not a famous painter like me but a forger who earns lots of money, ten times the amount that I do, fucking celebrated as I am.

I don't have to worry. Serge won't hurt the man who sells his brilliant forgeries to Mafia men who in turn hawk them to rich nitwits.

But more than anything else: I don't want Serge to think

that I'm afraid of him. The Tutsi thinks I'm a white shithead? I'll show him that Drees De Grijse is solid.

"Nagaibara, Drees!"

Oh Jesus, look at him standing in the doorway with his bells, his beads, a ring through his nose, his shield, his assegai. His long naked legs reflect the light of the street lanterns.

"And then they say I don't have all five together, you simian."

You should see his nostrils when he laughs royally, their delicate vibration.

In my car, I ask him, just to start some conversation: "Are you progressing with that forgery of the Greuze?"

That must be the source of his recent überfoolish behavior: the falsification of the Greuze is hellish work and demands tons of concentration and the lifestyle of a monk. Serge knows that. He must realize he's wasting time being mad because of Jeanine and me. When he's immersed in an all-demanding forgery, he knows that his wife has to freak out now and then. That's how Jeanine is; she has not been dealt with a generous amount of patience. She doesn't mean any serious harm.

"The Greuze is tougher than I thought, old chap." Now he sounds like some queer old Englishman. That means his condition is worse than I thought.

"Meijers is getting impatient."

"Meijers can drop dead and fuck his dead mother."

"Be careful with Meijers. He would follow your advice and then blow your brains out."

I'm the middleman between Meijers and Serge. Meijers makes tons of money on the forgeries. For my part, I try not to complain.

Serge's mouth sags. He smells of gin. "I'm not careful. I'd rather die than be fucking careful."

"Okay, okay." I shouldn't pique him too much.

What I saw of the Greuze forging is perfect. In the Renaissance, Serge would have been a master painter. Now he's a falsifier who has to watch his step. The art business is controlled by gangsters. They're very civilized and all that, so they hire big guns when you're a pain in the ass. Serge is always a pain in the ass, whether he's sober or drunk.

He once told me he killed his father when he was ten. I don't buy it. He has a big mouth and lots of delusions. It's been a few days since he told me he knew about Jeanine and me, and everyone is still alive.

So why should I be afraid?

While I park the car on l'avenue du Parc, Serge mumbles: "What would you do if you thought you had cancer?"

"Spend all my money on one gigantic party with naked black women in, yeah, spatterdashes, their bellies circled by beads in the most politically incorrect colors. We'd bathe in champagne and perform exquisite and lavish hanky-panky, then take the plane to Gauguin's grave where I would put a bullet in my head while my Negro goddesses chant some heavy gospel."

"I think I have cancer." Serge points at his crotch. "There. Ball cancer."

"In civilized countries they have ball doctors."

The whites of his eyes suddenly seem extremely bright in the light of the street lanterns that bestow a romantic touch upon Parc de Forest. In daytime, lovers walk the park lanes holding hands. People who hold hands can save the universe. Serge and I don't hold hands.

"Serge Butoyara in a hospital?" he says. "A warrior in a sickbed that you can adjust to sixteen positions?"

"Don't you think you exaggerate a little with that warrior pose?"

"I'm not exaggerating enough."

"Cancer, my ass. I bet it's just a nervous breakdown of your niggerish thingy due to stress."

"Oh? And how, pray, has my niggerish thingy become so nervous, Drees, my dear friend?"

"How should I know?"

Serge doesn't answer and stares past me at the trees, the strategically placed small sculptures in the park, the romantics, and so on. I've always considered trees to be sneaky bastards and at night they're even worse. Greenery is for animals. I like street scenes filled with Flemish lowlife and the smell of paint.

When he gets out of the car, Serge's plumage hooks behind the door.

"Did you think you're Shaka Zulu? And where did you get those feathers?"

"From the Senegalese Dance Theatre. They performed in Brussels yesterday. At the Ancienne Belgique. I told them I was looking for props for a painting."

"Wait a second."

I take a picture of him.

In black-and-white.

My lungs are about to burst. I try to keep my eyes steady on the feathers before me. I may be almost forty-nine but I have the heart of a thirteen-year-old, give or take a few years. Serge doesn't do a freaking thing all day except paint, munch fast food, and gulp down weird cocktails of his own making. But now it seems he has grown wings. His long, sinewy legs pump up and down with terrible efficiency.

"Serge! There! A rabbit! Spike it with your assegai!" My voice is croaking. Serge doesn't stop, doesn't even turn his head. I'm wheezing like an old cow. I get it: he wants to humiliate me. I have to come up with another trick to hide the fact that he's much younger than I am and that his breath takes him much farther than mine. I'll pretend that I'm tripping over something and—

I trip over a tree root; pain shoots through my left ankle. I cry out, with my nose engulfed in the rich smell of dung and leaves. I roll over and grasp my ankle with both hands. The pain fades slowly. I groan loudly again just to be sure that Serge gets the message. Yeah, I'm having a ball lying on the wet ground in the fine drizzle that sweeps over a very somber Parc de Forest at two thirty a.m. Loneliness, that's what I feel. Even the street lanterns of avenue de Forest behind that wall of trees seem a galaxy away.

Serge has stopped running but doesn't inspect my injury. The way he's standing, he is really looking down on me. His naked chest gleams as if it's oiled.

"Don't shine your flashlight in my eyes, damnit . . . Help me!"

Serge doesn't move a finger. The light from a street lantern some ten meters away polishes his assegai with an eerie glow.

"It's because of Jeanine, Drees, that I'm feeling this way."

"This way? What way?"

No answer. Suddenly, I'm not feeling so secure. Why didn't I turn my heels and go home the moment I saw him standing in full African regalia in his doorway?

"Don't start again, Serge. Better help me."

"I know how Jeanine is. When she closes the door of our house behind her, she is not the same as when she's with me. I understand that. I've learned that. If she has some booze in her delicious belly, she becomes another person. Eight times out of ten she comes back to our house unblemished,

238 // Brussels Noir

where I sit and wait. Maybe even nine times out of ten . . ."

"Serge, I think my ankle is broken. And don't be so melo-dramatic! Shaka Zulu gets paid to rant like a biblical prophet on TV."

"Those other times, those few other times, those very few other times . . . well, I don't know. Maybe there have been other such occasions. I don't want to know about them. They don't understand Jeanine, they don't know me. But you . . . you know both of us. And I am a very old-fashioned man: I value my honor."

I try to get up. I can handle this. I must be able to look him straight in the eye.

In spite of the biting pain, I crouch up on one knee. Softly, Serge pushes me back with the shaft of his spear.

I remember clearly how excited I was when Jeanine finally gave in a month ago. Probably she was weary of my endless cajoling. Or maybe I had made her curious bragging about my prowess in bed. Jeanine turned out to be far from a disappoint-ment. I flew on cloud nine when I left her in the drab hotel room we had rented to make it more sleazy. I was mighty flat-tered. But later that evening, I began worrying about Serge. Suddenly I strutted a lot less. This simpleton, this gifted artist, this goddamn Tutsi, was my friend. A friend who loved his wife definitively and was very possessive of her. Oh Jesus, I thought, no good can come from this. I telephoned Jeanine, told her precisely that. A hoarse chuckle, followed by a whis-per: "It wasn't worth it." I didn't ask what Jeanine meant by that and hung up.

"Surely your honor can wait till we get home—we're not in some kind of backward bush here. We're in Belgium, for God's sake."

"You could have asked me for money. I would've given you

money to visit the most exquisite Somalian hooker in Brussels. Your hairy white body pressing against a woman the color of old copper, with muscles like an antelope—wouldn't that have been a sight to behold?" He pushes the assegai against my belly button. "Hmm?"

"Oh yeah, a treat, definitely. You can't blame Jeanine, Serge. I was like a cockroach to her, blinded by the light . . . It was stronger than myself." I try to push the spear away. "Actually, I didn't really want it to happen." The spear doesn't yield a millimeter.

"But still you made it happen."

"Because Jeanine is the snake in paradise, you fool! You of all people should know that!"

"*Narobong geteng ino.*" The spear is traveling down my belly to my balls.

"Oh God, not this mumbo-jumbo again. This is not the moment for silly curses, Serge."

"The correct translation is: *Go fuck an ox.* I can even transform you into one."

"In that case, I prefer you slicing my throat, if you don't mind."

Fast as lightning he plants the spear between my legs, only a breath away from my testicles, into the ground. Ay, oh my, I can see raw passions marching over his face.

"I was just a fancy for her, Serge, but only you can truly handle her, you're the man . . . If only you could see that."

"That's not what this is all about."

"It's exactly what this is all about."

I struggle upright, lean against a beech tree. A flash of brown and silver. With great power the assegai is pushed into the tree, again with uncanny precision and this time only a whisper away from my head. We eyeball each other.

240 // Brussels Noir

"You're not going to off me, are you, Serge?" I try to stretch my leg, but the pain in my foot makes me somersault down on my ass again.

"You're under my spell now, fish belly. You'll never touch a woman again, and you can forget painting anything meaningful from now on."

"Never again?"

"Never again, Mr. Pale Dick."

"Okay. I'll never touch a woman again, and from now on I'm a lousy painter."

"You remain my best friend. But from now on you'll be a lousy painter."

We exchange crooked smiles.

Then Serge lifts me off the ground and carries me to the car. He decides to drive when it becomes clear that I can't use the clutch with my right foot.

The whole way back I'm sweating blood and water. At this hour there are almost no living souls on the road, but Serge has only once before in his life driven a car: when he let his white Belgian father bleed to death in the bush.

"Drees, light of my eyes! I'm in the Hilton bar. Meet me here, we have to talk."

"I'm very busy, Eliath."

"Oh, painting a masterpiece again? Why should you? So famous already! Must be no fun being workaholic Drees De Grijse. Come on, let's wine and dine at Comme Chez Soi."

"I'm having it here, *comme chez moi*, Eliath."

"Drees, be nice to me. I want to talk about Serge. That boy's in great trouble. He's a bigger hassle than the whole goddamn intifada. I'll have to set him straight, teach him the ropes."

"I'm on my way."

Cursing in Flemish the whole way in the car. Traffic jam in the city center. I crawl toward the boulevard Emile Jacqmain and the Hilton at the place Rogier. Oh well, the painting I was working on when that bastard Meijers called has every chance of becoming a failure anyway. *Les mangeurs des enfants* is eating me.

In the Hilton bar I only have to follow the din to find Eliath Meijers. With great cunning, he wears the disguise of a potbellied sugar daddy. In reality, he nearly chokes on his own venom. Meijers is the CEO of an import/export firm and has Lebanese—a Lebanese pretending to be a Jew—and Belgian citizenship, is registered in Liechtenstein but lives in the well-to-do village of Drogenbos near Brussels. He is married to a Dutch Valkyrie by the name of Birgit Waarsenbergs.

Underneath the mask of the jolly uncle who's fond of tasteless jokes, Meijers is the uncrowned king of the murky trade in very expensive and very fake paintings.

"Sit down, Drees." Blinking innocently at me, he taps the stool next to his well-filled ass.

I sit down close to him and put my right arm around his shoulder, pushing my thigh against his. "Come on, Meijers, don't be shy, give me a tongue dance."

Grinning, he leans over so I can kiss his Azzaro-sprinkled cheek. He would like to cuddle me, I'm sure, but we're not alone. Off to the side, one of his bodyguards is staring through his glass of tea at us. His face is consumed by the solipsism of Allah's righteousness.

Meijers glances at me, his eyes flickering mischief. "You've become fat."

"What, you don't have a mirror at home, Meijers?"

He has watched too many classic mob movies, ingested

too much Hollywood. He wants to be treated like a capo and I'm treating him like he's Dostoevsky's Idiot.

"A drink? Some food? They have delicious—"

"No, I don't want a drink or some food. Let me guess why you wanted to see me: you've decided you have way too much money and you want to bestow it on me as redemption for your many bloody sins."

He chuckles, but not too enthusiastically. There is something on his mind.

"If you want me to falsify a Mondrian for one of those über-rich, stiff-upper-lip bitches who can't see the difference between a toddler's drawing and an algebra exercise, then the answer is no."

Meijers pretends he's laughing so hard that he's nearly suffocating in his next gulp of coffee. He simply loves my charade and so he acts as if I'm his idol.

"You're still boxing, garçon? Oh, you've got those heavy, strong arms. Let me pinch them, come on, they can't be real."

"No English boxing, Meijers. Nippon kempo and Thai box."

"Could you beat a regular, sound boxer with all that fancy Eastern stuff, Drees? Can you prove it to old Meijers? I'll arrange something. No-holds-barred."

"That sounds to me like an old-fashioned street fight, Meijers. Good enough for me. But I'll bring my own assistant. Yours would drug my drink so that you could win the bets you'd surely organize."

Roaring laughter. Eyes toward the ceiling, exposing his throat.

We look each other in the eye. We're akin. We're not friends.

"Serge has threatened me." Meijers always changes the subject like that. And never, ever, even during the most delicate conversations, does he lower his voice. "He said he would show me the color of my intestines with his assegai, something like that, very poetic, that boy. Such a beautiful kid, totally different from you, Drees, you hairy ape . . . Serge is a . . . a reed, a gleaming black stallion, a—"

"Let me guess: Serge threatened you because you paid him a lot less than what you'd promised for the false Greuze."

Meijers leans toward me. Tiny beads of sweat on those bulldog cheeks. I don't like the man but he's never stood in my way. He loves money. I love money.

"You know him well, Drees. You think he's up to it? You should've seen him foaming at the corners of his mouth. A creature of the wild from top to bottom."

Before my mind's eye, with razor-sharp precision, I picture Serge in the Parc de Forest, his assegai pointed toward my balls.

No, Serge isn't up to it. I chuckle.

"Why the laughing?"

"He slaughtered his own father, Eliath."

His small eyes blink into mine.

"Serge is as mad as an armadillo with tropical fever rattling in his skull." I'm on a roll now, puffing steam. Oh hell, this is exhilarating. "I would be very careful if I were you. And afraid."

"Did he really kill his own father?"

"He told me the story, every detail of it."

"And you believe him?"

"Fucking A."

Eliath sighs, slurps the last drops of his coffee. He groans like a small child plagued by a nightmare.

"He has a pretty wife, Drees. And what I heard is that you—"

"Gossip. People project their dreams onto me, Eliath. Why? Because I am the Artist with a capital fucking A. I rob their souls and transcend—"

"Yeah, yeah. But Serge . . ."

"Oh, he'll get you sooner or later. The things he'll do with your puny circumcised dick, sweet Lord, I don't even want to think about . . ."

"Drees, you foul-mouthed barbarian, I'm so fond of your blabber." Meijers smiles. His eyes reflect the light, nothing else.

"How's your daughter doing?" If he can change subjects abruptly, so can I.

Gitte, Meijer's daughter, is a bouncy, black-haired teenager with Lolita eyes. She leads Meijers by the ring in his nose. Nasty rumors suggest that Gitte can't be his—the beauty and the beast, etc. Whatever. If you want to change the subject, just mention her name and he goes off like a firecracker.

"She's the light of my life, Drees. She's so *artistique*. Of course she must grow. She adores your paintings and she thinks you're real macho. But tell me more about Serge."

Ooh la la, so quickly with his feet on the ground again: Serge is for sure weighing heavy on his mind. Let's rev it up here . . .

Half an hour later I say goodbye. As a bonus, on top of the bloodcurdling stories I invented about Serge, I lick Meijers, grunting like a Labrador, over his mustache while bear-hugging him. His upper lip tastes of sour sweat and pomade.

The whole trip back to my house, although stuck for a long time in a traffic jam again, I'm grinning like a lunatic.

Three weeks later, someone—I don't recall his name, which is strange, it must have been a mutual friend and I don't do ether—told me that Serge's body had been found in a crack in a rock in the vicinity of the village of Beez, close to Namur, in the Ardennes. Suicide by hanging was the verdict.

Jeanine looked gorgeous at Serge's funeral, graced by the attendance of nearly the whole Tutsi clan of Brussels. A journalist and art critic, whose blood I could drink, told me a few days ago that rumor has it that a doctor sedated Jeanine so she could attend the funeral. According to him—frog's eyes and a Schiller collar—the drug made Jeanine look even more torpid and defenseless than usual, and thus even more sexy. He also wanted to communicate that Serge had squandered his huge talent—but I cut him short: "Serge Butoyara was a much better painter than I could ever be." I saw in his face that I had sold him a headline for his next article.

Eliath Meijers didn't attend the funeral but he did send an enormous garland, flashy as a parrot. The monstrous thing had to be carried by three men.

Listen carefully: I am 100 percent sure that it was suicide. Meijers had nothing to do with it.

Serge was that unstable type you find everywhere: unable to give his life shape and meaning.

If we painters can't give shape and meaning to mankind's measly existence, who can?

Moreover, not everything I told Meijers was a lie.

Serge really killed his father.

He confessed it to me.

A story like a nightmare, really.

"We were cruising through the jungle, Drees, my father and I. He was a freckled Flemish redhead. Imagine that. I never knew how he survived Rwanda's mighty sun. Freckles . . . in our sunbathing mountains.

"He used to beat my mother and me. We lived in Save, at his mission post in the mountains. Yeah, sure, Rwanda is the African equivalent of Switzerland and all that crap . . .

"I never knew what he was thinking or what kind of mood he was in. He hardly spoke to me, except when he hit me. On those occasions, he grunted the same expression over and over again, a Flemish curse I suppose. Oh, almost forgot: each morning he would snarl the day's chores at me. So much for conversation between father and son.

"I used to look at his reddish fringe of beard that kept rising and falling like a small ferocious animal when he was cursing at my mother and me.

"We rode into the valley of Save, had to stock up on supplies. My father drove the Land Rover hard, as usual. I don't remember much about the accident. At the moment of the crash, I was staring at the sky going misty behind the ridges and fantasizing about the mythical Rwandese hero Ryangombe, who my mother used to tell me stories about. That very morning she'd related the tale of how Ryangombe threw himself on the horns of a giant bull to save other people. I was wondering why Ryangombe had done such an utterly foolish thing. He had to know that he would be punctured, the moron. The tip of the Nubaru Mountain suddenly tilted. Something seemed to puncture me and I heard a thrilling cry, like that from a bird of prey, precisely the same cry that Ryangombe had uttered when he died.

"When I regained consciousness, the Land Rover was lying on its side next to me. My father's upper body stuck out of the window. My back hurt, but I seemed okay. I stumbled toward my father. Blood trickled down into his red beard, pooled upon his closely shaven skull. His eyes, however, were open.

"*Open the door, boy, help me.* So soft, his voice. I had never heard it before, that kind of tone. It scared me. As if a ghost in his head was talking to me after he had left his body.

"Now he looked at me. What he saw made him turn his eyes away.

"What I saw made me turn *my* eyes away.

"I sat down beside him and I watched the mist engulfing the faraway ridges, like bleached cotton on black river pebbles. The village of Save was close enough to go there by foot and ask for help. My father didn't mention the car door anymore. He remained silent. When I stole a glance at him, he was staring at a pebble on the ground.

"I stayed sitting there until dusk. I must have been there for about nine hours, but I didn't feel hungry or thirsty. When three farmers found us, there was no breath left in my father's breast.

"The farmers couldn't drive. I told them I could. Between the four of us we managed to get the car upright.

"We drove back to Save. I was immensely proud behind the steering wheel with the three farmers crowded together in the front seat and the body of my father bouncing up and down in the back. Faster and faster we went. It was the ride of my life. When we arrived, the farmers, myself, and my father's body were covered with gray dust.

"The farmers said I was crazy. I had driven so fast I could hear the wind whistling in my hair.

"And I told them that from now on, my name was Serge Butoyara, my mother's name."

You dream of me while I'm crouching on your chest like the simian you said I was, Drees.

Shed my leading role in your nightmare. Wake up and move that bleached old man's body.

Don't lie snoring contently in your bed with your mouth wide open.

Your closed eyes don't fool me.

You're awake and still you can feel me, can't you?

You have killed me just as I killed my father.

Get up.

Don't you hear the telephone ringing?

You've had many calls over these last few days.

Breathing calls.

Your phone is ringing in the middle of the night.

Any moment now, you'll open your eyes, you'll bolt upright, grab the phone.

You'll hear the breathing.

Maybe Meijers has decided that you've become a liability.

That you know too much about Serge and him.

Maybe a woman whose heart and soul you wounded is planning revenge on you.

There . . . there you go, Drees . . .

Only the sound of breathing and the thumping of your heart.

II

You want to understand my artistic vision of life?

Okay, take a peek at my last painting. Took me months, an Eiffel Tower of Campari bottles—yes, I drink Campari, dickhead—and buckets of sweat.

After that canvas, I haven't had a single brush in my hand.

And I finished it a year ago, go figure.

I'm sure Serge managed to implant the horrid image in this fine piece of art in my brain. *From now on you'll be a lousy painter.*

Revenge from the grave.

I exhibited the painting in the Memorias gallery in de

Wolstraat. It was a group exhibition, so I thought I could risk it.

"Has the Renowned Artist Drees de Grijse Gone Mad?" was one of the headlines of a critique in a "quality newspaper."

For sure drunk and stoned and deep in Alzheimer's, that slimeball.

My artistic thesis for this painting is as follows: life is one of those giant eels crawling in a muddy seabed with a maw bigger than its tail.

So I went ahead and painted one of these fuckers. What's the big deal? Pic-fucking-asso would've gotten away with it.

Okay, my background—nothing but mud and slime—is a bit monotonous on the canvas.

But the eel . . . man! The eel's head looks more like a suction cleaner, actually. Sucks everything into the shit deep under the muddy water.

When life wiggles its tail, you hope something out of the ordinary will happen: you fall in love, you betray your best friend, you fuck his wife, you endure painter's block.

You do those things and the result is a shitload of problems. Your best friend ends up dead, followed by night-calls—*pant pant, wheeze wheeze*—mystery, suspicion, fear.

And a thumping heart.

And then—nothing.

No more calls. No more mystery. People do normal things again. The woman named Jeanine, a dangerous sphinx in my opinion, moved to Amsterdam to become the lover of the proprietor of a goddamn weed shop.

As if that woman isn't already high enough from herself.

So you forget what happened. So easy to settle again, squander your days, waiting for your earthly demise—in the meantime wining, dining, fornicating.

But not painting. The famous Drees de Grijse has retired, hey-ho.

Only, just when I—by pure luck—had sold my exceedingly *mauvais* eel painting to one of those blasé MEPs wasting the European taxpayer's money—he considers my eel avant-garde!—precisely then, life immediately grabs my throat again.

Brussels may be an unkempt and filthy city with way too much traffic coursing through it, and with an architecture that has no spirit to offer except greed and contempt, but the pearl-gray light of a September evening can turn some of its corners into a cozy fantasy.

I'm sitting on the terrace of Marché aux puces on place Jeu de Balle with a half-empty bottle of Campari, celebrating the sale of my horror painting, simultaneously wrestling, however, with a linguistic problem. There was a time when *puces* meant *hookers,* wasn't there? Or does it only mean *flies?* The Campari and the candy colors of some of the nineteenth-century houses surrounding the plaza, bordered with sycamores, don't do much to enlighten me. Hookers—definitely.

"Drees! Drees de Grijse! Of all people . . . Coincidence doesn't exist."

I look up.

What a coincidence.

Gitte Meijers. Little Gitte. Daughter of Eliath Meijers and Birgit Waarsenbergs. The light of Eliath's eyes. And he had such tiny piglet peepers, the scumbag.

Gitte Meijers. Her eyebrows so wide, her upper eyelids painted black, her face geisha-white, her lips dark as sea anemones, stars on her cheeks, mandalas on her arms.

She's—what—eighteen, nineteen now? In spite of her extravagant makeup, she has that dark look of her father. How long ago kaput, that hog Meijers? Two, three years? Time flies and all that jazz. Some devilish cancer. Pancreas? In any case, it went lightning-fast. Great reception after the funeral. Lots of expensive booze. Blond Birgit looked extremely fuckable in her black outfit. I told her so and she agreed.

Her daughter wears a bodysuit with fucking beach sandals, the outfit a maze of white and gray circles. She moves en vogue, yeah.

"Do you like my color palette, Drees?" She points to her face.

"*Bellissima.*"

"Going to a dance party." She comes closer, almost leans over my shoulder. "Did you know that I have reproductions of all your paintings in my room?"

"Kneel before them every evening and say your prayers; they'll bring you luck."

She laughs. She's young, she doesn't sense that I'm tense. Gitte. Gitte Meijers.

"Want to come along? I was waiting for my friend, but he's more than an hour late." A shrug of her slender shoulders. "These days he's more obsessed with dealing than with me." Her face brightens. "There will be a top-class deejay at the rave."

With some decorum, I grope in my leather jacket and put on my dark glasses. She giggles. Years ago, I wrote a threatening letter to her father, stating that I knew he was a murderer. I didn't send it. Instead I buried the letter in the small village of Beez, close to Namur, in the Ardennes. In a certain crack in a rock. There, I asked Serge's spiteful spirit to take revenge on Meijers, sooner or later. I was apeshit drunk, so I forgot my vow; however, nature in the form of Meijers's cancerous pancreas did the rest.

Much obliged, nature.

Hours later. Gitte isn't going to no party. She sits on the terrace with me, listening breathlessly to my ramblings about one of my forefathers who was of Spanish descent, and a nobleman to boot. Sadly enough, that *capitano* couldn't resist raping girls. "*Querida, querida!*" he howled during his vile acts, whereupon, his beastly lust quenched, he strangled those poor lasses.

She giggles. The filly giggles.

I'm wearing my leather jacket, my floppy hat, and my dark glasses. A little chill in the September air; I see her sitting hunched over. When will she grow tired of the bullshit I'm feeding her? I resort to silence.

She clears her throat. "Drees, you know . . . I'm also into painting. I would be very flattered if you would . . . " Oh God. So that explains her patience with my oafish tales. Look at that: poignant hesitation, fluttering eyes, the works. "Would you care to see them and give me some pointers?"

"Where's your studio?"

"I don't have a studio yet . . . but I paint every day!"

Every day. Christ Jesus.

She owns an MG. Fiery red.

"Did you drink much?"

"Only a Campari or two." Let's see how observant she is. The bottle stood between us on the table. Empty.

"Care to drive?"

"My pleasure."

When I'm drunk, I remain lucid. I take risks though. They make my tummy tingle.

I'm fucking Stirling Moss, that's who I am. Gitte shrieks in delight in the MG's small, leather-clad cabin while I skid along the road. Her pert butt quivers along with the hard suspension of the small sports car.

"I got stuff in my apartment. Want some?"

Hadn't expected anything else.

"*Dux femina facti.*"

"What did you say?" She puts her left hand on my knee. Just a tiny moment, but the hand was there.

"Latin wisdom. Look it up. What kind of stuff you got?"

"Cocaine. Gift from my boyfriend. Market's best."

I push down on the accelerator.

Her student apartment in a stately nineteenth-century town house, built in French neo-Renaissance style, on rue des Moines, is a bit petit bourgeois, in spite of the old radio casing, now serving as a planter, and the oversized xylophone in a corner. In another: a balloon with a lipstick heart on it, tied to a broom.

"Conceptual art?"

She shrugs and then rummages through a drawer of the fairly unclean small kitchen. "Just a joke. It was meant for my boyfriend, but he left it here."

"Being disrespected is manna for the artist's soul."

She looks up swiftly, as if frightened by something. That curtain of coal-black hair reminds me of Eliath.

"Where are your paintings?"

"Later. I don't have them here."

"I thought that Eliath's daughter would be housed in a place a bit more luxurious."

This time she doesn't look up. "My mother owns the house and rents the other apartments. I wanted to live here."

"Between the riffraff."

Smiling. "Yes, between the riffraff."

"What are you looking for?"

"Attributes." What a strange word for that kind of girl.

In the farthest corner, there is a small bookcase.

Metamorphoses Book 2.

"You read that?"

"Hmm?"

"You read Ovid?"

"Why not? My father loved him."

Jesus, the pitiless Eliath Meijers was fond of Ovid. So it's true: mankind is inscrutability incarnated.

She reappears in the living room with an old-fashioned snuffbox. "It's about changes."

"So I gathered."

"I would like to change."

"Change isn't like putting on another dress."

She opens the box and lays out two generous lines on the coffee table. "You believe in life after death?" she asks, seemingly nonchalant.

I must cut this shit off, snort my free line, and get the hell out of here.

"You believe in life before death?"

That look again, as if frightened by something. She doesn't answer, bows her head to the first line. Her mascara is a bit smeared, as if she was crying in the kitchen. I follow her example, our heads nearly touching above the small table.

"Oh, wow . . . Gitte, I'm on fire. I see your father burn in hell. I stand next to Eliath and, man, he's burning real good."

She offers me a smile that should be knowing and conquest-minded, but fails miserably.

I've heard my own voice telling her everything about Serge

and my suspicion that her father killed the raving Tutsi. Gitte rolls her eyes. Red-cheeked and huge pupils—this baby chick is getting off on her father's sins, if you ask me. Her head pulsates. Oh wow, am I really that high? Like a Boeing 727?

"Interesting." She yawns. "But I liked your *capitano* story better."

"Oh?"

"*Querida! Querida!*" she crows.

I get the message.

"Where are your paintings?"

"In my mother's house."

"She still lives in that mansion in Drogenbos?"

"Yeah."

Silence.

"So, let's go."

"Now? It's half past one."

"Art knows no time."

"Maman will be asleep."

I get up. I want to know if the daughter of Eliath Meijers has it in her. "No problem. She'll be glad to see me."

"Did you date her after my father died?"

"Of course I did. And we called it *fucking.* Come on, let's go."

She rises slowly. Suddenly, I pity her and that makes me even more vicious.

"Hurry up, your friends' panties will get wet when you tell them what fun you had with the notorious Drees de Grijse."

She shakes her head, a bit compassionately, it seems. "They only get wet for pop stars."

We're at the door when she says: "Just a minute." Leaving me standing by the front door, disappearing into the kitchen again. Coming out with another snuffbox, this time a blazing red one with a bright yellow star on it. "Before we go, a special treat. It isn't every day that a humble young woman like me receives a visit from the great Drees de Grijse."

Is that irony? Derision, even? Payback for my remark about her mother?

Her eyes are bright and shiny. "A special blend, concocted by my friend. Real designer stuff." She beckons me over to the coffee table.

A minute later I'm snorting like a delighted horse.

When we descend the stairs, it dawns on me that she hasn't tried the designer stuff herself.

It's warm in the MG's cabin. Outside, a capricious wind blows.

She drives fast and recklessly.

"I haven't painted in over a year now," I say.

She doesn't react.

"I've filled 168 canvasses. I'm fifty. Why should I go on?"

"Because you can't do anything else."

She hunts the night with her red car and I ponder what she said. It can't be that simple, can it?

At our right skulks the Anderlecht Canal. She takes the rue de Biestebroeck, speeds toward the Quai de Biestebroeck.

Maybe she has a mind as deep as the canal, maybe she's . . . What's this? I have the sudden feeling—the certitude—that Serge is coming for me with a vengeance.

I start to sweat. Is my head lolling on my neck? Am I losing control over my muscles?

Do I hear her laugh softly?

What has she given me?

I see it. The Land Rover. At the opposite side of the quai. No lights on. A dark vehicle of doom. It's charging toward us.

The flaming ghost of Serge Butoyara at the wheel, and I know he can't drive.

Look at Serge laughing; this ghost of flames and fury is having wicked fun.

I grab the MG's steering wheel and turn it sharply to the right. The lightweight sports car veers off the road, crashes against one of the iron poles lining the quai of Biestebroeck, and screeches when it starts spinning like a carnival ride.

Then there is the feeling of zero gravity.

A deafening splash.

A spine-jolting shock.

Double vision.

It's worse.

Double me.

I'm floating above the canal; I see white moonlight bobbing on the water.

I'm also in the sinking car. Getting very dark in here. What a breathtaking sight, this fluid darkness. The girl beside me screaming, her head bloody against the steering wheel. Water gushes through the leather canopy of the convertible. My other me, floating like an angel above the water, signals that I must turn down the window. I obey. The canal water stinks. The door opens. Where is Gitte? Too dark to see.

I feel a jolt like an electric current when I'm reunited as one.

I'm a strong man, a good swimmer. My head surfaces—and who is fluttering above? Goddamn Serge. His smile is as cold as the whole fucking North Pole and South Pole combined. I cough. The high cranes at the other side of the canal resemble the martians in that black-and-white movie of the H.G. Wells story. Cold, it's so cold in the water. I swim toward the gently sloping shore where the concrete quay ends. Ever so slow. But fucking Serge is screaming that I will live, that I have to suffer some more before I perish. That godforsaken black ghost hits the nail on the head. Where's the fucker now? Vanished already, like always when the going gets tough.

Feeling mud under my feet. Stagger up the slope. Wind tugging at my wet clothes.

Turning around. Facing the dark water, the martians, the pale concrete quay.

"Gitte!"

No Gitte rising out of the waves. No floating head that I can rescue and kiss passionately.

Only wind and waves.

And my brains bursting apart, suffering the power of one hell of a designer drug.

I'm in survival mode.

Yeah.

I'm only body.

The body thinks: *Dry clothes, warmth, house, shelter.*

The body thinks: *Nobody will know that Gitte Meijers had a passenger. The water will have cleaned my presence from the car.*

The body has instinct.

The body feels wallet in leather jacket.

It's grosso modo twenty minutes walking to the rue Pierre Marchant and then through the deserted streets of Anderlecht to the boulevard Sylvain Dupuis. This quest will harden the body, while the brisk breeze stiffens the clothes.

On the boulevard, hail one of these Taxis Bleus. Get your story ready: *Man, what a party! Jumped rat-assed drunk with all my clothes on into the swimming pool. Freezing, man, I tell you, my balls almost fell off, but I was the star of the evening. So sorry for the smell—the pool hadn't been cleaned for two months.*

The body dreams of the warm softness of a soapy bath.

The body thinks: *Birgit will cry a river when she hears about her daughter.*

Tja.

The body thinks: *Why am I so fucking alone?*

You dream of me while I'm crouching on your dick, Drees.

You gasp, but you don't feel a thing.

Shed my leading role in your nightmare. Wake up and move that old man's body.

Don't lie there snoring in your bed with your mouth wide open.

Your closed eyes don't fool me.

You're awake and you can still feel my presence, can't you?

You have killed me to take revenge on my father.

Get up.

Do your thing.

Grab the phone.

Dial the number.

When a woman picks up, start breathing through your nose.

The woman, a grieving mother, shouts at you, wants to know who you are.

You want to tell her what you did.

You can't.

You breathe.

She slams down the phone.

Your finger creeps toward the redial button . . .

There . . . there you go, Drees . . .

Only the sound of breathing and the thumping of your heart . . .

THE BEEKEEPER

BY JEAN-LUC CORNETTE

Woluwe-Saint-Lambert

A fter three days of constant rain, the Semois finally returned to its banks. The flood hadn't spared the campsite. Dank puddles spread across the paths and underneath the trailers. The smell of frost and wet grass hung in the air. The guy sat, as he did on the same day every month, in the small living room area of Melchior's mobile home. His presence didn't bother the cats napping on the edges of the furniture. In summer the guy liked to wear Hawaiian shirts. "Nice shirt," said Melchior, just to make small talk. The guy refused a Nescafé. Melchior made himself one and wondered if the guy might be afraid of leaving remnants of his DNA. After asking the few customary questions, the guy left an envelope on the plywood table and slipped away. His car tires squealed on the humid gravel of the visitor parking lot.

It would soon be two years since Melchior had moved into the Saint-Roch campsite in Florenville. Before that, he'd lived in Brussels. A gardener at the Château de Laeken—the prince's gardener.

Melchior thought back over the past six decades, to the days when his name had been Joseph. He recalled his most cherished moments, watching *Visa pour le monde* on TV with his dad. It was a game show in which the contestants competed to win a trip around the world. Every Sunday, the host, Georges Désir, asked complicated questions pertaining to a specific country. Radio Télévision Belge had designed a set resembling the interior of a Boeing 747. Joseph and Léon, his dad, shared a passion for faraway countries, exotic landscapes, and primitive regions. Mexico fascinated Joseph. In front of the TV set, he transformed into a young Zorro riding across the scorching desert on the back of his loyal Tornado. Later, when his hormones kicked in, he pictured himself with a Robin Hood mustache. His dad was passionate about Asia: rice planters in tunics and pointed hats in the highlands of Vietnam, white-faced Japanese geishas in silk kimonos, and Indian dancers in gold-threaded saris—these were the visions reflected in his glasses. It was thrilling to observe those flashes of joy in his otherwise aloof functionary's gaze. But Léon had never seen the splendors of the world. He'd never even left Brussels. Not once had he brought his family to the coast or to the Ardennes. He was born in Woluwe-Saint-Lambert, had gone to school in Woluwe-Saint-Lambert, had married the amiable Maryvonne Van Goidsenhoven of Woluwe-Saint-Lambert, and everything was pointing to the fact that he would croak from a heart attack on a sidewalk in Woluwe-Saint-Lambert.

Maryvonne, a seamstress, worked in her living room, tailoring the dresses that chic ladies bought at the department store l'Innovation, on rue Neuve. Léon Brotchi issued passports at the city hall. The families that stood in line at his counter never failed to divulge, with a blissfulness approaching arrogance, which paradise on the other side of the world they were headed to for vacation. And then the day came when *Visa pour le monde* aired an episode on China. The Mosuo tribe, indigenous to the Yunnan Province, was only briefly mentioned. But from that moment on, Léon was forever changed. The light in his eyes would never again go out. His brows stiffened into disconcerting horizontal lines as his thoughts guided him, little by little, toward an irrevocable decision. He submitted a request for a passport. A good employee, honest and respectful of his fellow citizens, he did not move his application to the front of the queue. He waited. And the whole time, he said nothing to anyone.

Three weeks later, on May 22, 1967, the same day that l'Innovation went up in flames and nearly four hundred people died, Léon left for a region where men have no responsibilities. In Moso society, women are dominant; they pass their surnames on to their children. Men are lovers, progenitors, or uncles—never fathers.

Joseph stopped watching *Visa pour le monde* and began to grow cacti on his windowsill. It took a year for the young man to understand that his father had chosen to be reborn in the form of a benevolent penis offered to all those who wished to receive its blessing. He'd converted himself into a sexual object unburdened by the demands of family life; he'd permanently freed himself of the bonds of paternity.

To assuage his grief, Joseph began growing cannabis between his cacti. The first little seed he planted marked the beginning of the forty-five-year countdown, joint by joint, to his flight from reality. His exile to a mobile home on a bank of the Semois was already quietly preparing itself.

Maryvonne compensated for the loss of her husband's love with a disproportionate affection for feral cats. Several old ladies fed strays on the outskirts of the old Etterbeek cemetery, near their apartment on avenue Edouard Speeckaert. Abandoned the year before in favor of a new, modern cemetery in Wezembeek-Oppem, its grounds were rapidly transforming into a jungle and a shelter for these vagabond felines. Maryvonne kidnapped one, a Siamese, and had it neutered. A growing need for tenderness pushed her to continue these abductions. She finally stopped once she had seventeen at the house. "One for each year spent with the other Chinese," she joked.

A decade of buying kitty litter and Whiskas flew by. Joseph had dropped out of university, worked in a few bistros, and continued to cultivate his balcony garden. His fine mustache and long hair gave the young man something of the air of a bourgeois bohemian. Maryvonne lost more and more of her clients. A new dressmaker opened up shop in the Tomberg district, between the city hall and the old cemetery. Sainte-Rose, the seamstress, was a tall, proud Martiniquaise with luxuriant black hair that fell down to her hips. Her long, curved eyelashes quivered in the breeze like the feathers of a crow, and her dark eyes betrayed no emotion. In this bourgeois neighborhood, her bronze skin intrigued men and fascinated women. The ordinary racism trolling the avenues of the capital muttered a thousand insults behind her back. Fearing that this siren of the islands would turn their husbands' heads, the neighborhood vipers hissed all the more fiercely.

A single woman with a three-year-old girl aroused all kinds of suspicions. People spoke of voodoo, of dolls stabbed with sewing pins, of decapitated chickens, and all manner of black magic. Those were the days when Moroccans had not yet dared to leave the most working-class neighborhoods of Brussels. Apart from Sainte-Rose and Moana, her little girl, foreigners in Woluwe always remained foreigners. If you were born in Woluwe-Saint-Lambert, you lived there and you died there, before you were taken to be buried in Wezembeek-Oppem. A similar practice was expected on the part of immigrants: let them live and die in their own neighborhoods! But the weeks went by and turned to months, and no one ever saw

Sainte-Rose with a man. From sunrise to sunset, she dedicated herself solely to her work and to her daughter's education. The rumors slowly died out and, repelled by the lingering odor of cat urine that seeped into the fibers of their skirts, the ladies of Woluwe-Saint-Lambert started going to the new boutique in Tomberg to have them tailored by a Creole princess.

Around the same time, Georges Désir stepped down as host of *Visa for the World*. He became a founding member of the FDF, a new political party that vowed to defend the rights of Brussels's citizens. He was elected mayor of Woluwe-Saint-Lambert. If Léon hadn't fled the city in order to scatter his seed among a few Moso women, he might have had the chance to work under his favorite TV host. Life can sometimes be so cheeky.

Joseph launched his small-time narcotics business. The balcony on avenue Speeckaert was soon abandoned in favor of a much larger crop spread over various green spaces in the municipality. The first plot was staked in the old cemetery. Five hundred meters from there, behind the city museum in Roodebeek Park, he cultivated a few more plants. The harvesting and selling usually took place after sunset, since Joseph was determined to devote his days to a legal professional activity. He answered an ad for a position as a gardener. At the first interview, he talked about his passion for cacti and neglected to mention the one for cannabis. He was taken on at the Château de Laeken. Joseph joined a team that cared for the tropical plants in the palace greenhouses. The twenty-six-hectare estate also had to be mowed, raked, and watered regularly. Gradually distancing himself from the steamy atmosphere of the greenhouses, Joseph focused more and more on the maintenance of the gardens. The immense lawns and ponds were bordered by woods rarely visited by the sovereign.

And so began the cultivation of cannabis on the royal estate.

The king was a shy man who didn't laugh much. And the only respect in which the queen was at all imaginative was in her curly permed hairdo and collection of ridiculous hats. At sunset, they walked their dogs along the paths of the estate, greeted the gardeners, and returned to the palace.

In 1993, near the end of July, the king, fragile of heart, collapsed in Spain between a card game on the terrace and a poolside glass of rosé. His reign had lasted forty-two years. For weeks, a flood of tears swept all across Belgium. The mourning of the Belgian people was accompanied by a rise in the consumption of cannabis. Joseph Brotchi made good money and bought salmon croquettes for his mother's cats. Sixteen years in the service of the king's lawns, botanical gardens, and shrubbery came to an end.

In the evenings, Joseph went back to his mother's house. With no more clients, she spent her days petting her cats and anesthetizing herself in front of the Bavarian adventures of Inspector Derrick. After supper, Joseph went back to the old cemetery or to Roodebeek Park and sold his most recent harvest. The home he shared with his mother and her foul-smelling menagerie was not a propitious environment for a burgeoning relationship. Joseph adjusted to the situation and started having flings with a few of his customers. He discovered that he had a strong liking for torn fishnet stockings and darkly made-up eyes. He brought a few of these silly birds into his bedroom and stroked their feathers, oily with the tar of disillusionment. They would lose themselves in a cumulonimbus cloud of cannabis smoke and sink into the royal gardener's arms. These brief romances suited Joseph. Maryvonne insisted on mending the ripped jeans of these young women, who were horrified by such an absurd proposition. His poor mother didn't understand that times had changed and it was more elegant to wear a torn-up garment than a repaired one.

The new king, the younger brother of the deceased, did not move into the estate. The monarch and his royal spouse remained in their belvedere. Their son, the prince, took possession of the castle, and it became the nest where his princess hatched four little ones. At the end of the day, the prince would go for a walk alone in the park while the princess looked after the kids. He liked to fly his helicopter and practice landing on the vast lawn that sloped toward the pond. Joseph observed him from a distance. He sensed the profound sadness of this young man who'd been conditioned for so many years to become the chief of state. No faux pas would ever be allowed him, no word spoken louder than another. Joseph was sure of it: this prince needed to shout, to run, to turn somersaults on the lawn, to have a few grand adventures. But alas, heredity had locked him into the role of figurehead. The prince was exhausted from awaiting his hour.

The old Etterbeek cemetery was converted into the magnificent Meudon Park, with a fountain and a playground for children. The hemp gardens were flattened beneath the tracks of bulldozers. Joseph had to concentrate his horticultural activities on Roodebeek Park and the royal estate. In July, the pistils of the Mary Jane flowers darkened, indicating that harvest time had arrived. One day, the prince came upon Joseph filling large trash bags with the harvested buds. The gardener didn't try to cover up his business. He confessed everything in detail: the parks of Woluwe, his mother, the cats, his father in China. The prince followed suit: his wife, their children, his rebellious brother, his father the king, a half-sister he'd only just met, the training for his future title, and the agony of not knowing when it would begin. They told each other all their woes, passing three joints back and forth, and Joseph taught the prince how to roll. The sun had set behind the Atomium long before they finally went their separate ways.

They saw one another often after that. They would talk for long hours in front of the pond. The prince helped Joseph with his harvest. And in no time, he could roll a joint with as much skill as any Belgian.

The prince led commercial delegations abroad. He was never at ease in front of a microphone, a crowd, or a camera. His words escaped him. His hands became moist, his legs went wobbly, and his complexion paled to gray. Some thought he was dumb, or even retarded; the people, often cruel, refused to accept that their prince might simply be timid. He was heir to the crown and could scarcely string together three sentences. The most awful slander spread through the streets of the kingdom. When it made its way back to the palace via the pernicuous press, the prince was horrified. Fortunately, Joseph was always nearby with his excellent hydroponic weed to help His Royal Highness relax. His wife, the princess, was blossoming in her role as a mother. The people were impatient to see her crowned queen. The prince's father was aging gracefully, not showing a hint of impatience to give up the scepter. What would it take for him to abdicate the throne? Would the prince have to wait to be as old as a pope before he became king? For his fiftieth birthday, Joseph gave him a cake with fifty joints stuck into it like candles. They laughed and did somersaults in the grass, and the prince fell into the pond.

Joseph had hardly noticed the years go by. His hair had begun to fall out along with the autumn leaves, and his mustache was turning gray, but otherwise, life outdoors and the products of organic farming had kept him in good shape.

One afternoon, after having swallowed a ham sandwich with a little Devos & Lemmens mayonnaise, Maryvonne nodded off while watching Inspector Derrick—who was following an apple-green Volkswagen filled with young heroin addicts and prostitutes—and did not wake up. Joseph found her with the remote control in hand. Three cats were asleep on her cold knees. Another was finishing off the pot of mayonnaise that Maryvonne had forgotten to close. Joseph cried and cleaned up cat vomit for forty-eight hours. He buried his mother in the Wezembeek-Oppem cemetery, as local Woluwe custom dictated. He continued to feed the cats and clean their litter boxes.

That year, George Désir, after thirty years of service to the city of Brussels, was no longer represented on the voting ballot, and Woluwe-Saint-Lambert elected a new mayor.

Joseph was heading toward his sixtieth birthday. Often, in the evening, after having filled the cats' bowls, he went to meet his friend Fat Dan for a drink. With the arrival of the Congolese to the neighborhood, then the Polish, and the rise of cell phones, drug dealing had become a less artisanal business. The local Mafias sold everything and anything. Chemical products had poisoned the weed and made smokers sick. Joseph began to fear his customers. Scores were settled with fists or knives. Joseph Brotchi no longer understood young people; they no longer interested him. Not even the girls. Fuck-buddies—often floozy, slightly rundown forty-somethings—had taken the place of his former girlfriends. The good old days of punkettes with torn jeans and darkened eyelids had faded into vague memories. Joseph frequented single mothers, divorced, abandoned. He was the second wind, the hint of spontaneity in the routine lives of these weary women.

After he found a young mafioso laid out stiff beneath some

bushes one night, Joseph decided to leave the profession. He kept only his crops in the royal estate.

A bar named the Tap had opened its doors in Meudon Square. The terrace was near the entrance to the park that Joseph no longer frequented. Fat Dan, who operated the photocopy machines in the Tour des Finances, spent his evenings grafted to the zinc of the bar. Together, they drank Ramée blondes and talked about getting laid. They had a knack for transforming the monotony of their daily lives into radiant legend.

Sometimes, walking home from the metro station, Joseph passed in front of the Sainte-Rose boutique. The Martiniquaise panther had returned to her island, and her daughter Moana had taken over the shop. The girl, whom the residents of the neighborhood had seen arrive at three years old, was now over thirty. Even more beautiful than her mother, the caramel-skinned young woman didn't have to endure racist remarks or abject rumors. Moana was adored by Saint-Lambertians, especially the men. Her two improbably long legs disappeared under tiny skirts, suggesting a Creole paradise that troubled Joseph. Her little nipples in their too-tight T-shirts pierced the gardener's heart. Moana was still a young woman, while Joseph had long ago become a *monsieur*. Joseph was quite aware of this and behaved with Moana as no more than an older friend, a little seduced, perhaps, but well-behaved. And yet, he would have killed for a chance to taste the cane sugar of her sex. He would have chopped all his mother's cats into tiny pieces if it would mean he could spend one night under her gentle caresses of the South Seas. But Joseph Brotchi was a sensible guy. He went home to collapse on his couch covered with cat hair, to suck on a joint and forget about how quickly life was passing him by.

* * *

Joseph's cell phone vibrated. He grabbed it and read the text: *Meet at the pond in 5 min.* Joseph turned off his phone, leaned his rake against the trunk of a beech tree, and started walking down to the pond. The prince, in a white shirt and jeans, appeared a few seconds later.

"I'm leaving Monday. Economic mission in Brazil."

"Lucky you!"

"Yeah, well . . . you know, I really don't like giving these speeches. I'll have to do it in Portuguese. I have to rehearse and rehearse, like an actor. If you knew how it's stressing me out . . . Anyway, come on, let's roll a nice fat one."

Joseph took out a baggie of Black Widow grown on the estate, as well as a packet of tobacco, from the pocket of his green work overalls.

"Roll it yourself, Highness. You're better at it than I am."

The prince fashioned a little L joint with a dexterity that would have astonished his slanderers. "Can't stay long. The wife's waiting for me to start supper."

The prince lit the tip of the cone and took a long puff that whirled deep in his bronchial tubes. Then suddenly, with a quickness that Joseph didn't know the man possessed, he grabbed all the evidence—the bag, the pouch of tobacco, and the lighter—and dropped it into the gardener's hands. Like a dog who senses a storm coming, the prince had detected the presence of his Chief of Protocol. He'd had just enough time to stick the joint into Joseph's mouth.

"Your Highness, the princess sent me to inform you that the meal—" The Chief of Protocol went silent. His eyeballs doubled in size. Joseph thought they were going to spring from their sockets and roll down the lawn all the way to the pond.

"Your Highness, the gardener . . . the gardener is smoking."

"Yes?"

"He's smoking . . . drugs!"

The prince, who'd just spoken of honing his acting skills during meetings abroad, did his best to appear convincingly innocent. "Oh, my, are you sure?" He turned to face Joseph. "My Chief of Protocol tells me you're smoking narcotics, Monsieur Brotchi . . ."

Joseph was dismissed from his post as royal gardener, and in order to avoid a scandal, he was given a healthy severance payment. He remained friends with the prince and they called each other often.

The Tap became Joseph's second home. He went there every night. Fat Dan gave detailed reports of his peregrinations in the many-storied Tour des Finances. He was basically an easygoing guy, but if there were two things he didn't mess around with, it was photocopy machines and their maintenance. What would become of the ministries if the photocopy machines disappeared? It was quite simple: the country would come to a halt. It would be the collapse of the entire system. One night, Joseph ventured to compare the filling of toner cartridges with the upkeep of the royal grounds. The layer of fat surrounding Dan's heart was pierced straight through by the dagger of his friend's assumption. How could Joseph suggest that the maintenance of photocopiers, the true guardians of the country's stability, was of no more importance than the mowing of a lawn enjoyed by a single, useless family that would surely end up being decapitated one day? Joseph didn't like to hear people speak ill of the prince. The man was his friend, after all, and he understood like no one else the pain of being so well-born and so unfortunate all at once.

With eyes closed and elbows raised, the rim of the glass

between his lips, foam seeping into his mustache and nostrils, Joseph sipped his Ramée. He appreciated how the bitterness of beer could momentarily sap the bitterness out of life. His phone vibrated in his right pocket.

"Oh shit!" he slurred. "It's him! His Highness . . . I'm going out . . ."

Joseph stepped outside to the pedestrian crosswalk. As he circled the roundabout, he listened to the prince and responded thoughtfully. Once he'd made three complete circles, he went back into the bar and sat down on the stool beside Fat Dan.

"I can't believe the prince just calls you up like that! On your GSM! And at the Tap!"

"He didn't know I was at the Tap. And that's sort of the point of GSM."

"Well, fine, okay. But what did he want, His Majesty?"

"Nothing. He's just a little depressed . . . He's fifty-two years old and he feels useless. All his life, he's been preparing to become the king, but his father doesn't seem to want to let go of the crown. What he told me is that if his father gave him a date, even far in the future, he'd be able to relax. But for now, he doesn't know, so he's spending his whole life waiting. I told him to go roll a big fat spliff; that'll calm him down. I gave him one three days ago."

"Yeah, well . . . if I were him, I'd take full advantage of being on vacation year-round. I'd go to the Costa del Sol . . ."

Joseph watched the foam dissolve in his glass. He tried to think of a solution. "Well . . . could we hire a psychic?"

"You believe in that?"

"I dunno . . . some of them say stuff that turns out exactly right."

"And do you know any?"

"No . . ."

Joseph kept thinking. The prince was counting on him. His neurons were swimming in gray matter when Moana's pointy breasts appeared in his mind's eye. The mysteries of the Belgian cerebral mechanism are impenetrable, though often predictable. "We could ask Moana."

"Moana? She's a psychic?"

"No, I don't think so. But she's Martiniquaise, or something like that. Apparently her mother was into voodoo stuff, black magic. We'll have to ask her about it . . ."

Exhausted after a long day of tailoring the neighborhood grandmothers' pants, eardrums ringing with the sound of sewing machine bells, Moana collapsed on her sofa. Her cell phone vibrated. She answered, and twenty minutes later she was sitting on a barstool at the Tap.

Fat Dan was dripping with sweat. The photocopy machine operator knew what he was worth on the glamour market: his rating was very low, near absolute zero. When he found himself in the proximity of a woman he considered inaccessible, his sweat glands went into overdrive. The well-mannered young seamstress acted as if everything was normal. After a few sips of Ramée had brought his body temperature back to normal, Fat Dan could finally speak without stuttering.

"Moana, we were wondering if your mother practiced voodoo and if she'd taught you a thing or two. Like, telling the future, you know . . ."

"Voodoo? My mother was a seamstress, not a witch! What on earth are you talking about?"

"You can't help us, then?"

"Um, probably not . . . but what do you want to find out?"

"The future. It's for a buddy of mine . . . He's going to start a new job, but he doesn't know when. He'd like to know—"

"Ah, okay! Maybe if we have a table-turning séance . . . I've heard that can work and it isn't too hard . . ."

"Isn't that how you talk to dead people?"

"Yeah, but dead people—they know lots of things that we don't. Things about the future. When you're alive, you live at the same time as everyone else, in the present moment. But when you're dead, you're dead for eternity . . . time is no longer important. The present loses all its meaning. And so they develop this incredible knowledge about the future."

Moana's theory seemed solid. The boys were pensive.

Suddenly, Fat Dan jumped to his feet. "Of course! The table! In Roodebeek Park! The museum! There's a table there that turns!"

Joseph placed a friendly hand on Fat Dan's shoulder to try to calm him down. "Catch your breath, Dan! Take a sip of beer and explain it clearly to us. Because if it's simply a table we need, you know everyone has one."

"Okay, okay, I'll explain. The museum, back in the day, in the ninth century or so, was a house. A house that people lived in. This filthy-rich carpenter named Devos—like the mayonnaise Devos & Lemmens—had it built. He moved in there with his wife. Woluwe was still in the countryside back then. At one point, they had an addition built onto the house and soon after, *poof!* His wife died."

"How?"

"That, I don't know. But she died. Of old age, maybe. Anyway, Monsieur Devos was sad over it. But not for too long. He fell in love with a young chick, a singer, and he remarried!"

"And the table? When does that come in?"

"Here, now! The singer, she liked talking with the dead. People did that stuff a lot back then. It was before the Internet, you know?" Fat Dan laughed at his own remark, letting out a few snorts. "She decided to build a rotunda."

"A rotunda?"

"Yeah, a rotunda. She moved a table out there and had séances with her snobby friends."

"And did the dead teach her anything interesting?"

"Oh, yes. Of course. But we don't know what. That's all secret."

"And the table is still there?"

"I think so. Anyway, the rotunda is. When Monsieur Devos died, the singer lived there all alone for a few years. Then she donated the property to the municipality of Woluwe, under the condition that the house would become a museum and the park would be opened to the public. Now there are donkeys, goats, rabbits, and birds of every color . . ."

"And guinea pigs too!"

"Yes, Joseph, that's true. I forgot about the guinea pigs."

Dan wasn't sweating at all anymore. He had captivated his audience. Joseph and Moana were astonished by their friend's knowledge of history. Who could have imagined that such a well of information was tucked away at the back of that fat head? Dan himself, absorbed in his story, had forgotten that the most beautiful woman in Woluwe was sitting beside him, her bare thighs next to his greasy jeans.

"You think we could ask to use the rotunda and the table?"

"No way, don't even think about it!" said Joseph. "These guys are civil servants. My father was a civil servant for a long time. I know them, they're nothing like photocopy machine operators or royal gardeners. They have rules to follow, opening and closing hours to enforce, permits to check, and they're very serious about it all. Forget it! It's an awful idea, the rotunda."

"We can go at night!"

"It's closed at night."

"Sure, but we'll open it. We'll force the door a little, and voilà! No one'll even notice."

"Are you out of your mind?"

"Oh, come on, I'm telling you this for your friend's sake. If you want to help him find out what the future has in store for him, I'm just saying, there's only one solution: the rotunda!"

Moana was in favor of the plan too, perhaps even the most enthusiastic. She was crazy about talking to the dead.

At five o'clock the next day, Joseph waited, black sunglasses on, for Dan and Moana at the entrance to the park. The cages that housed the rabbits, guinea pigs, and various species of parrot lined the left side of the path between the chaussée de Roodebeek and the museum. Fat Dan was completely defenseless in the presence of so many adorable two- and four-legged creatures. He stood frozen, his fingers grasping the wire mesh. He started making sharp little cries, attempting to imitate the birds' songs. Then, at the end of the path, where the aviaries were replaced by pens, the large white goats drew him in. And when he saw the donkey, he looked like he was going to melt. Joseph pulled him along by the elbow.

An elderly woman walking with her grandchildren called out to Moana: "Mademoiselle Sainte-Rose!"

Many of Moana's clients assumed that Sainte-Rose was her mother's last name and that it had been passed down to her by matrilineal tradition. Moana never corrected them. In reality, her surname, Adelphonse, had been passed down from her father, a snorkelling instructor in the Trois-Îlets whom she'd never met. Her mother had indignantly kept her own name, Sainte-Rose Monlouis-Bonheur.

"Mademoiselle Sainte-Rose, can I come by Thursday afternoon?"

"Of course, Madame Verstraeten. Your dress will be ready."

Wide rings of sweat soaked through Dan's T-shirt; he trembled all over and his breathing grew heavy. He approached Joseph and whispered into his ear: "Oh shit, we've been sighted!"

"Calm down, for God's sake. It's only a client of Moana's. We have every right to visit the animals."

Relieved, Dan turned back toward the donkey. Madame Verstraeten began chasing Dylan and Océane, her hyperactive grandchildren, and Moana came over to Joseph.

"Here's the rotunda . . . The windows are barred . . . the door's here, to the right. It looks like we can get in through there."

"I don't know, it seems pretty heavy. Dan? . . . Where'd that idiot run off to?"

Joseph's eyes scanned the row of pens and finally landed on Dan, who was kneeling behind the dovecote, collecting dandelions. "Help! Over here!"

"Me?"

"Yes, you!"

"Why don't you call me by my name? My name is Dan. At least I'd know it's me you're talking to."

"I know your name, moron. Why don't you shout your address at me too? You're so discreet."

"Oh shit, sorry, I forgot . . . Do I have time to feed the donkey some dandelions?"

"Drop your dandelions and haul your ass over here!" Joseph raised his hand to his forehead in disbelief. "Take a look at that door. You think you can break into it without a tank?"

Dan ran his hand over the perimeter of the door as tenderly as if it were the neck of a donkey or a pony. Then he kneeled to examine the lock.

"Discreet! Be discreet, please."

"Yeah, yeah . . ."

Fat Dan declared that with a crowbar and some biceps, the door would give in fifteen seconds. They'd have to be sure that no one was around, however, since the wooden frame could make a cracking sound as loud as a gunshot.

That same night, Joseph explained to the prince that he was expected the following Tuesday at eleven thirty on the dot, at 314, chaussée de Roodebeek. He advised him to come in an ordinary vehicle. Not one of his brother's Ferraris. And above all, not in a helicopter. The keyword was *incognito*.

Tuesday came quickly, but the last few hours crawled by at a snail's pace. In the time it took for them to drink two Ramées at the Tap, night had gathered the living to its dark breast. Joseph leaned over and grabbed his faux Nike bag at the foot of the barstool. His eyes slid over the curves of Moana's long legs. Her camouflage-patterned skirt, though very short, added a hint of elegance to their nocturnal expedition.

"What's in the bag?"

"Just what we need. You know, the blunt instrument that'll get done what we have to get done."

"The *what* instrument?"

Aside from words that pertained to the proper use of photocopy machines, Dan had difficulty with overly technical vocabulary.

Joseph, Moana, and Dan walked across Meudon Square, at the center of which a small palm tree was doing its best to grow far away from its family.

"Moana, you've got everything ready?"

"Don't worry, I looked on the Internet, watched some videos on YouTube. It's not that complicated. If you let me lead the way, we'll be communicating with spirits in no time."

"My blood's running cold! Can't I stay outside while you do your macabre stuff?"

"Better ask this now . . . Moana, will it work with just three people?"

"Yes, and even with just two."

They walked along avenue Heydenberg, brushing past the facades like nervous vampires, and headed down avenue Speeckaert. The chaussée de Roodebeek was shrouded in a darkness that the streetlights couldn't penetrate.

"Stop! Let's stake out here, by the wall."

The three apprentice criminals hid out behind the cars and bushes around the parking lot, on the corner of the chaussée de Roodebeek and rue de la Charrette.

A small orange truck pulled into the parking lot. On its side, azure-blue writing spelled out the words *Zeebroek Dry Cleaners*. Beneath the lettering was a golden lion against a black shield with the royal crown resting on top—the coat of arms used by suppliers to the Court. An individual dressed all in white, wearing a bizarre floppy hat, his face hidden by a black net, stepped out of the vehicle. He moved as clumsily as a poorly inflated Michelin tire. Closing the car door, he noticed the three accomplices lying in wait behind a Ford Fiesta from the previous century.

"Joseph, it's me!"

"Your Highness!"

"Himself, but incognito."

Amused and intrigued, Moana stood still, her arms stiff by her sides, her hands pulling at the hem of her miniskirt. Fat

Dan, his mouth frozen half-open, did not seem to understand what was taking place before his eyes.

"Good evening. It's me . . . the friend of my old gardener here . . . But anyway, let's be careful. We can't let anyone find out about this."

Moana asked what she should call him.

"Better not to use my first name, or my title. You can call me 'the beekeeper.' I like that, the beekeeper. And it goes with my outfit."

Then Fat Dan finally understood the provenance of this creature in a baggy jumpsuit with a black screen over his face.

They didn't kowtow; the confidentiality of their mission obliged them to throw etiquette to the wind. To maximize efficiency and reduce risks, Joseph took charge of assigning code names. He agreed on Beekeeper for the prince. Dan became Photocop, and Moana, Thimble. He dubbed himself Spliff.

While the residents of Saint-Lambert slept, tossing and turning in their pastel Swedish quilts, the four creatures of the night braved the darkness of Roodebeek Park. The chickens were asleep in their feathered nests and the long-haired rabbits snoozed like dormice. Dan stopped three times to try to get a better look at them.

"Come on, Photocop! We're not here for that."

Not the slightest sound disturbed the park. Joseph thought back to the moments when he'd collected the buds of cannabis in the moonlight. He suddenly had a terrible longing for a joint. But then he heard Dan calling the donkey.

"Little one! It's me, your friend Dan!"

"Aw, shut up, Photocop! You want us to get caught? Leave the poor creature alone, he has the right to some sleep."

"But I—"

"You nothing! Come open the door for us, then you'll stand guard. It'll take us ten minutes at most."

They skirted the shrubs that surrounded the dovecote and made their way toward the green door. The museum looked asleep too, with all its windows closed. Joseph opened his bag, took out the crowbar, and handed it to Fat Dan.

"You don't have the key?"

"No. But don't worry, Beekeeper, Photocop is an expert. At least that's what he told us."

"I told you fifteen seconds, and it'll be fifteen seconds, Your Highness the Beekeeper."

"You'll be careful about it now, hmmm?"

"Yeah, yeah."

Dan pushed with all his weight against the handle of the instrument. Strange veins appeared on his neck and forehead. The effort wrested a little grunt from him, which quickly rose into a deafening "Aaaaaaaaaaaaaaaarrrrrrrhhh!" The frame buckled at last, the lock exploded into pieces, and the door swung open. Dan, drenched in the sweat of a conqueror, let his muscles relax back to their original gelatinous state. But that didn't keep him from lifting the crowbar above his head and yelling one last, "Banzai!" Like an echo, the sound of the donkey's braying reached them.

"Shut up, Photocop! Shut up, for Christ's sake!"

"Okay, okay . . . Well, fifteen seconds, yes or no?"

"Yes, Photocop, good work. Bravo. Now can you keep guard? Silently?"

"Of course! I'll wait over behind the dovecote. Now go make the table turn. But be careful, okay? Don't wake up too many evil spirits."

"We'll be fine. Isn't that right, Thimble?"

"Yep, Spliff, no problemo!"

Joseph pulled a flashlight from his backpack, turned it on, and plunged into the cultural abyss of the Woluwe-Saint-Lambert Museum. Moana and the prince followed him.

"I'll send you a check for the door."

"We haven't used checks for years, Your Beekeeper."

"Well, I'll be damned, you've taught me something, Thimble."

Fat Dan looked to the right, then to the left, then to the right again. His gaze swirled. He stepped forward, stopped, stepped forward, stopped again, held his breath. He listened to the rustling of the leaves. He walked back over to the pen of the donkey, who'd been woken by the sound of the exploding door.

"Hello there. You remember me, little donkey?"

The animal saw in Dan a friend of animals. The latter pulled up a few handfuls of grass and reached between the bars of the pen. With equine grace, the donkey puckered its downy lips toward the measly twigs. Suddenly, the animal turned bright blue. Dan was mesmerized, but the donkey went back to normal. Then he was lit up again. He flickered. The entire pen flashed electric blue every few seconds. Dan turned around.

A police car was coming up the path. It drove past Dan and stopped in front of the museum. Two cops got out, side-stepping the dovecote. The beefier of the two, with the handsome, thick mustache typical of Brussels policemen, turned on a flashlight. The beam crisscrossed with the pulsing blue light, swept over the facade of the museum, and lingered on the debris of the broken door. The cop made a sign to his partner, who walked back to the car and announced over the loudspeaker: *"Woluwe-Saint-Lambert police! Come out with your hands up!"*

Dan had followed the the cops the whole time without their noticing. He approached them now, crowbar in hand. Joseph, Moana, and the prince—decked out as if he were going to collect honey—came out of the building.

"Set down the flashlight and the bag and put your hands on your head!"

The policemen, no doubt unaccustomed to dealing with such extreme criminality, were nervous. They kept their guns pointed at the suspects.

"Anyone else inside the museum?"

"No, Monsieur Policeman."

The cop shot the crowbar right out of his hands, then aimed at the others.

An irrepressible fury took hold of Fat Dan. "Don't shoot at my friends, you bastard! They're not criminals!"

The cop shot again. The sound of the bullet whistled in Dan's ears. A terrible howl tore across the night: "Hiiiiiiiiiiiiiiiiiiiiiiiiiiiihaaaaaaaaaaaaaaaaaaa!" The donkey's cry stiffened at the back of its throat as it fell on its side, dead. The ground trembled.

A ghostly silence fell over the museum esplanade. Dan, completely disoriented, let go of the crowbar and began to choke back sobs. Tears soon flowed down his cheeks.

"My d-donkey," he stammered. "They killed my little donkey, the bastards . . ."

"Go join the others, you. Next time, I won't miss."

The four accomplices lined up with their backs against the facade.

"You, the beekeeper, take off your hood!" ordered the mustached cop.

"Ha! Would you look at that, he looks just like the prince!" exclaimed his colleague. "The spitting image."

* * *

Joseph was placed in the care of the State Security Service witness protection program, which assigned him an absurd new identity: Melchior Magritte. They moved him and his cats into a white-plastic mobile home on a bank of the Semois, banning him from returning to Brussels or making contact with his family and former connections. Once a month, the guy in the Hawaiian shirt came by to check on him and left an envelope containing 1,600 euros. Melchior never learned what had become of his friends. When he got lost in his memories, he would see Fat Dan crying over the dead donkey. And he liked to fall asleep thinking of Moana's smile, but visions of Thimble's pert little breasts and too-short skirts plunged him into a Caribbean agony.

The Tuesday of the break-in, a spirit had spoken through the young woman's feverish mouth. The voice had announced that the prince's coronation would take place on July 21, 2013—National Independence Day.

A year had passed since His Highness the Beekeeper had become the King of Belgium. Melchior wondered if he still harvested cannabis on his estate and if, sometimes, at nightfall, he sat on the bench facing the pond and smoked a joint, remembering all the good years with his friend Joseph the gardener . . .

ABOUT THE CONTRIBUTORS

BARBARA ABEL, born in 1969, is an aficionado of theater and literature. At twenty-three years old, she wrote her first play, *L'esquimau qui jardinait*. In 2002, her first novel, *L'instinct maternel*, won the Prix Cognac. She was selected by the jury of the Prix du Roman d'Aventure for *Un bel âge pour mourir*, adapted for television in 2008. Her works, which have been translated into several languages, include *Duelle* (2005), *La Mort en écho* (2006), *Illustre inconnu* (2007), *Le Bonheur sur ordonnance* (2009), *La Brûlure du chocolat* (2010), *Derrière la haine* (2012), and *Après la fin* (2013). Since 2009 she has been a columnist for *Cinquante degrés nord*, a daily cultural magazine distributed by Arte Belgium.

KATIE SHIREEN ASSEF is a writer and translator living in Oakland, California. Her prose and translations have appeared in journals such as *Joyland*, *Asymptote*, *M-Dash*, *PANK*, and *Weird Fiction Review*. She is currently translating the novellas of French writer Valérie Mréjen, to be published by Phoneme Media in 2017.

AYERDHAL (1959–2015), awarded the Prix Cyrano for lifetime achievement in 2011, played with literary genres with a mastery that earned him numerous awards. After having renewed Francophone science fiction in the 1990s, he did the same for the thriller genre with, notably, *Transparences* (2004, Grand Prix de l'Imaginaire) and *Rainbow Warriors* (2013, Prix Bob Morane). He passed away in October 2015.

ÉMILIE DE BÉCO lives in Brussels and loves its joyful, organized chaos; she revels in the spectacle of trash cans spilling over its sidewalks. No doubt about it, she's Belgian. Emilie doesn't like fries or chocolate, however, and has no accent, which makes her completely exploitable internationally.

PAUL COLIZE is a Belgian novelist and short story writer. He was born in Brussels and lives in Waterloo. His novels *Back Up* (2012) and *Un long moment de silence* (2013) were published by la Manufacture de Livres and reissued by Folio Policier. They were both finalists for the Prix Rossel and garnered awards in France (the Prix Saint-Maur for

286 // Brussels Noir

Back Up, the Prix Landerneau 2013, the Prix Boulevard de l'Imaginaire 2013, the Prix Polars Pourpres 2013, and the Prix Cezam IDF 2014 for *Un long moment de silence*). His book *Concerto pour 4 mains* won the Plume de Cristal 2016 award.

JEAN-LUC CORNETTE was born in 1966. He is a Brussels native and lives in Woluwe-Saint-Lambert. A comic book author, his most recent works are *Frida Kahlo,* illustrated by Flore Blathazar (Delcourt), and a novel for children, *Le Pianiste, la sirène et le chevalier* (Ker).

PATRICK DELPERDANGE has published nearly forty works of fiction since 1985, including literary novels, mysteries, children's books, and comic books. Recipient of the Prix Simenon for *Monk* and the Prix Rossel for *Chants des gorges,* his most recent novel, *Si tous les dieux nous abandonnent,* was published by Serie Noire in 2016.

SARA DOKE is a translator, journalist, digital editor, event planner, host, and short story writer. Her texts play with the boundaries between reality and fiction and between the genres of fantasy, science fiction, and classic literature. Two collections of her short fiction are forthcoming.

MICHEL DUFRANNE was born in Brussels in 1970. He is a workaholic who is always pursuing different career paths, such as headhunter, university professor, editor of science fiction and comics, and publishing consultant. Currently he is a comics writer, and a book reviewer for a Belgian TV and radio show that focuses on thrillers and crime fiction novels.

KENAN GÖRGÜN, a graduate of the university of the street, was a market gardener, night watchman, and rock festival roadie before starting his career as a writer. Author of a dozen works of fiction and nonfiction, he is also a screenwriter and director.

EDGAR KOSMA, born in Namur in 1979, has lived and worked in Brussels since 1998. He has published two novels, *Éternels instants* (Renaissance du livre, 2010) and *Comment le chat de mon ex est devenu mon ex-chat* (ONLIT Éditions, 2015). He also writes the comic book series *Le Belge,* published by Delcourt.

KATIA LANERO ZAMORA was born in 1985 in Liège. After pursuing a degree in Romance languages and literatures and a master's in book publishing at the Université de Liège, she wrote *Chroniques des Hémisphères*, a young adult trilogy published by Impressions Nouvelles.

NADINE MONFILS has written nearly sixty books (literary novels, erotic fiction, mysteries), plays produced in Brussels and in Paris, and wrote and directed *Madame Edouard*, a film with a prestigious cast (Michel Blanc, Didier Bourdon, Josiane Balasko, Dominique Lavanant, Annie Cordy, Rufus, Andréa Ferréol, Bouli Lanners) and music composed by Benabar.

ALFREDO NORIEGA is an Ecuadorian writer who splits his time between Brussels and Paris. He has written several novels in Spanish, most recently *Tan sólo morir*, which was translated into French and published by Ombres Noires (2013).

DANIELA MARIA UGAZ is the cotranslator, along with John Washington, of *The Beast* by Óscar Martínez and *The Story of Vicente* by Sandra Rodríguez Nieto, from Spanish into English. She currently resides in Tucson, Arizona, where she works as a legal assistant for unaccompanied minors migrating from Central America.

BOB VAN LAERHOVEN is a Flemish writer who has published more than thirty books in the Netherlands and in Flanders. His novels have been translated into French and English. *The Vengeance of Baudelaire* received the Prix Hercule Poirot 2007 for best crime novel of the year and the USA Best Book Award 2014 in the mystery/suspense category. When he's not writing, Van Laerhoven looks after his princesses: four horses.

JOHN WASHINGTON is a freelance journalist, novelist, and translator. Find more about his work at www.jblackburnwashington.com.